OBSIDIAN

OTHER WORKS BY THOMAS KING

FICTION

Medicine River
Green Grass, Running Water
One Good Story, That One
Truth and Bright Water
A Short History of Indians in Canada
The Back of the Turtle

DREADFULWATER MYSTERIES

DreadfulWater
The Red Power Murders
Cold Skies
A Matter of Malice

NON-FICTION

The Truth About Stories: A Native Narrative
The Inconvenient Indian: A Curious Account of
Native People in North America

POETRY

77 Fragments of a Familiar Ruin

CHILDREN'S ILLUSTRATED BOOKS

A Coyote Columbus Story, illustrated by William Kent Monkman
Coyote Sings to the Moon, illustrated by Johnny Wales
Coyote's New Suit, illustrated by Johnny Wales
A Coyote Solstice Tale, illustrated by Gary Clement
Coyote Tales, illustrated by Byron Eggenschwiler

OBSIDIAN

A DreadfulWater Mystery

THOMAS KING

HarperCollins*Publishers*Ltd

Published by HarperCollins Publishers Ltd

First edition

HarperCollins books may be purchased for educational, business or
sales promotional use through our Special Markets Department.

HarperCollins Publishers Ltd
Bay Adelaide Centre, East Tower
22 Adelaide Street West, 41st Floor
Toronto, Ontario, Canada
M5H 4E3

www.harpercollins.ca

Library and Archives Canada Cataloguing in Publication
Title: Obsidian : a DreadfulWater mystery / Thomas King.
Names: King, Thomas, 1943- author.
Identifiers: Canadiana (print) 20190222360 | Canadiana (ebook) 20190222379
| ISBN 9781443455206 | (softcover) | ISBN 9781443457088 (hardcover) |
ISBN 9781443455213 (ebook)
Classification: LCC PS8571.I5298 O25 2020 | DDC C813/.54—dc23

ISBN 978-1-4434-5520-6 (trade paperback)
ISBN 978-1-4434-5708-8 (hardcover)

Printed and bound in the United States

LSC/H 9 8 7 6 5 4 3 2 1

For the Cretan across the street who drinks my espresso

ONE

Thumps DreadfulWater stood by the car and watched the Ironstone glisten under the night sky. In the distance, Chinook was an orange glow on the horizon. Years ago, he had stopped at the same turnout and looked out across the same panorama.

That time, he had been escaping. Running away.

This time, he was coming home.

Whatever that meant.

IT HAD BEEN over a month since the drive from Chinook out to Eureka on the Northern California coast. Three days on the road. A stop in Boise the first night. A second stop just outside Grants Pass. He had pulled into Crescent City just before noon on the third day and stopped for lunch at a funky café called Gordi Bros, a yellow building just off the main road that specialized in Mexican fast food.

He had ordered a pork chile-verde burrito along with a bottle of MexiCoke, a variation of Coca-Cola made and bottled in Mexico that used cane sugar instead of fructose. The café was busy, but there was a small table in a dark corner. He ate his lunch in silence while a table of men in tan and green uniforms drank beer and swapped stories about the inmates at Pelican Bay.

Thumps was familiar with the place from his days as a deputy sheriff, had always thought it ironic that the state had built a supermax prison along a tourist corridor, two miles off the coast, in the middle of a forest. He had seen an aerial view of the facility. No matter how you turned it, Pelican Bay was an ugly thing, a dull, grey scar, a hard-edged clear-cut that resembled the head of an axe.

At one point there had been legislative talk about making prisons pay their own way, and some bright light in Sacramento had come up with the idea of a "Pelican Bay Supermax Tour," where families on vacation could stop off and take a guided trek around the facility.

All aboard the Crime and Punishment Trolley. See dangerous inmates in their cages. Killers, rapists, and thieves.

Oh my.

Mental illness, addiction, and poverty.

The penal system's version of a *Jurassic Park* ride.

* * *

THUMPS HAD LINGERED in Gordi's, the Maslow file on the table next to his plate.

Nina Maslow.

Reality television.

Malice Aforethought.

Nina Maslow and Sydney Pearl had come to Chinook to do an episode on the death of Trudy Samuels, a local woman from a wealthy family. Samuels's death had originally been ruled a "misadventure." Maslow, with ratings in mind, wanted to prove it had been murder.

It hadn't. Trudy's death had been a tragic accident, but Maslow hadn't been fazed by this setback. As it turned out, she had already started work on another, more exciting, episode.

The Obsidian Murders.

Thumps picked up the folder. He didn't need to read Maslow's notes. He knew the case by heart.

Six years ago, ten bodies were found on a cluster of beaches along the Northern California coast, the work of a serial killer who appeared and disappeared without a trace.

Two of the victims had been Anna Tripp and her daughter, Callie. At the time, Thumps had been a deputy sheriff with the Humboldt County Sheriff's Department, had been away at a law enforcement forensics conference, had returned to find his lover and her child dead.

Maslow had known of Thumps's involvement in the case, of his relationship with Anna Tripp, and she had come to

Chinook not only to look into the death of Trudy Samuels but to try to convince him to be a part of the show she was planning to do on the Obsidian Murders.

FROM CRESCENT CITY, there was only one way south. Highway 101 was an old motorway, built in the days when roads followed slopes and contours, before highway construction simply flattened mountains and cut straight lines through the land. Instead of zipping along, the road took its sweet time, winding through stands of giant redwoods, running out along salt lagoons, and floating past long, narrow beaches that fronted the open ocean.

Just south of Trinidad, Thumps had turned off the highway onto a frontage road that ended in a small parking lot banked against sand dunes and seagrass.

Clam Beach.

This was where it had started. On this unremarkable stretch of shore and sky, fixed between Little River and Patrick Creek.

The Obsidian Murders. That's what the press had called the killings, each victim found with a small piece of black obsidian in their mouth.

Thumps got out of the car, intending to visit the spot in the dusty green and yellow grass where Anna Tripp and her daughter, Callie, had been found.

At least that had been the plan.

Instead, he stood in the lot, watching the fog come ashore, listening to the seagulls argue with the wind. And then he got back in his car and drove into Eureka.

RON PEAT'S HOUSE was within walking distance of Old Town. It was a two-storey shiplap Victorian that Ron had bought cheap when these white elephants were being given away to anyone foolish enough to buy them, before interest in such architectural extravagances had come around again.

Eureka was known for its ornate turn-of-the-century manses—the Clark House, the Pink Lady, the Carson Mansion—and while Ron's house was the same age, the similarities stopped there. His was one of the poorer relations, a plain-Jane Victorian with none of the gingerbread flourishes that celebrated the conspicuous excesses of that era.

Most people would have left well enough alone. Ron wasn't one of them, and all of his free time outside the Humboldt County Sheriff's Office had been spent fabricating wood rosettes, dentils, spindles, and patterned appliqués that he painstakingly added to the porch and the gables and the window surrounds.

Unfortunately, Ron's woodworking skills had not been a match for his enthusiasm, and the house had slowly taken on some of the more disturbing aspects of Frankenstein's monster, a creature made up of mismatched parts. Even a six-colour paint job had failed to hide the errors in shape and scale.

Still, Thumps had admired Ron's determination, had even helped him put up a pair of oversized and oddly ornamented wood brackets above the corner windows.

THE WOMAN WHO answered the door was young, the baby in her arms only a few months old.

"Hi," Thumps said. "I'm looking for Ron Peat."

"Mr. Peat?"

"Ron and I used to work together," Thumps told her. "Humboldt County Sheriff's Office."

"You're a cop?"

"Not anymore. But I used to be. Deputy sheriff. Serve and protect."

The woman warmed a bit. "He was putting fish-scale siding on the upper gable."

Even before Thumps asked the question, he knew the answer.

"They think the ladder twisted," said the woman. "I'm really sorry."

Ron had done all the renovations himself. Every Saturday morning, you would find him camped out at Pierson's hardware at the south end of town, sorting through tile and lighting fixtures, through kitchen sinks and toilets, walking the aisles, looking at saws and drills and sanders, in case there was a tool he didn't have.

"This house was his project." Thumps couldn't think of anything else to say. "Did you know, he did all the work himself."

The woman had shifted the baby to a hip. "My husband's going to fix it."

Thumps was halfway to his car when the woman called out. "What did you say your name was?"

"DreadfulWater. Thumps DreadfulWater."

"There's a bunch of stuff in the basement that my husband keeps promising to take to the dump. I remember. Some of the boxes have your name on them."

FIRST LIGHT HAD found the horizon. Thumps checked his watch. It would take him the better part of an hour to drive across the belly of the valley and reach Chinook. By then Al's would be open. He could slip into the café, sit down on his favourite stool, and pretend that he had never left. Or he could go home, crawl into bed, and hide out for a few days before he had to deal with Archie and the sheriff, with Al and Beth. And Claire. Especially Claire. People who would want to know what had happened, what had been resolved.

Thumps wasn't sure what he would say, wasn't sure what he would be able to tell them, what he would want them to understand.

In the end, the trip to the coast hadn't gone as he had expected. It had answered some of the questions that he had carried with him all these years. Not that the answers were going to bring him any peace. Some clarity perhaps. That was all. A measure of clarity.

But now there were new, more troubling questions.

Where did he go from here? That was the question he had asked himself on the drive back. What did he do now?

Of course, there was no rush, no reason he couldn't just stand by the car and wait for the dawn to find the river and fill the land. Sometimes doing nothing was the appropriate response to uncertainty.

Sometimes, doing nothing was the answer.

TWO

Thumps parked the car across the street from the café. He had read somewhere that when you travel, time stands still. And that when you return, it starts up again. As though you never left. An interesting idea, but it didn't seem to apply to Chinook. A month ago, the main street had been draped in "Chinook Summer Roundup" banners, the store windows painted with bucking broncos and stampeding cattle herds. Now the light standards were promoting a car show at the fairgrounds—"Cole's Classic Cars and Auction."

And the Chamber of Commerce's "Howdy" program was nowhere to be seen. Thumps guessed that the business community had discovered what most of the merchants had known from the start, that the city's campaign of bunkhouse hospitality and western jargon wouldn't be a big hit with tourists, that dressing up like Hollywood cowboys wasn't going to jump-start the local economy.

Al's, however, looked exactly the same. The turtle shell that Preston Wagamese had superglued next to the front door, with the word "Food" painted on it, was still there. The Fjord Bakery was still on one side. Sam's Laundromat was still on the other.

Wutty Youngbeaver, Jimmy Monroe, and Russell Plunkett were hunkered down on their usual stools at the counter across from the grill, watching the steam rise off mounds of hash browns. Stas Black Weasel and Chintak Rawat were sitting next to each other, locked in an animated conversation. Sheriff Duke Hockney was sitting at the end of the counter. The seventh stool from the end, the stool that Thumps considered his, was fully occupied by Cooley Small Elk.

Thumps stood in the doorway and wondered if this had been the best of ideas. He wasn't really hungry. Maybe he should have gone home and put off the official return for another day.

Wutty was the first to notice him.

"Shit!"

Both Jimmy and Russell turned at the same time.

"Shit!"

Wutty held up two fingers. "I was this frickin' close."

"Well, well, well," said Al. "Look who's back."

"Yes, yes, hello," said Stas. "You are here just on time. 1955 Mercedes 300 SLR or 1936 BMW 328?"

"In time," corrected Chintak. "I am thinking that the 1956 Jaguar XK140 is an excellent choice."

"You just get into town?" asked Wutty. "Maybe you've been back and didn't tell anyone."

Cooley slid off the stool. "Here," he said. "You look like you need this more than me."

"That's it, isn't it?" said Wutty. "You got home two days ago and you've been lying low."

The place looked like Al's, and Thumps recognized everyone, understood every word. But he felt as though he had wandered into an asylum from another dimension.

"So now you must choose most beautiful car," said Stas.

"Sit down," said Al. "I'll get you some breakfast."

Thumps could feel all eyes on him. "What's going on?"

"The pool," said the sheriff. "Lot of money riding on you."

"Pool?"

"On when you'd come back."

"There's a pool on when I was going to come back?"

"Twenty bucks a try," said Duke. "I had Tuesday last week and next Saturday before noon. Put another twenty on WNR."

"WNR?"

"Will Not Return." Al set a cup down in front of Thumps. "Lot of people put money on that one."

Thumps was pretty sure that this wasn't the homecoming he had expected. "People thought I wasn't coming back?"

"I did not make such a bet," said Chintak. "I anticipated that your medical conditions would necessitate a return."

"And Russians should not bet," said Stas. "Very unlucky. Long history of fracking wrong horse."

"Backing," said Cooley, "but you're married to a Blackfeet woman, and that's good luck."

Stas brightened. "Yes, this is true. Okay. Is too late for bet?"

Al had a notebook out and was flipping pages. "Looks like the winner is Moses Blood."

"Is there any money for being close?" said Wutty.

Al shook her head. "Winner take all."

The sheriff patted Thumps on the shoulder. "However, you get a free breakfast."

"Me?"

"That's right," said Al. "Figure if you did come back, the least I could do is throw in a breakfast."

"That's because you got ten percent for holding the money," shouted Wutty. "People who were close should get a free cup of coffee."

"Should have some sort of celebration," said Jimmy Monroe. "You know, the Return of the Native."

"Al should pick up the breakfast tab for everyone who was in the café when Thumps arrived," said Russell Plunkett. "That's fair."

Thumps closed his eyes, put his head in his hands, and let the argument flow over him. It had been a long drive, and now that he was sitting somewhere other than behind a wheel, he could feel his body begin a slow collapse.

"You okay?" Hockney actually sounded concerned. "Blood sugars low?"

That was, Thumps realized, a good question. He hadn't checked them this morning, and he hadn't eaten, so they probably were low. The testing kit was in his bag. Thumps fished it out and set it on the counter just as Al came along with his breakfast.

"You plan to bleed all over my counter?"

"Just need to check my blood sugars."

Al looked at Hockney. "You just going to stand there? Aren't there laws against bleeding in a restaurant?"

"None that I can think of," said the sheriff.

"You scare any customers away," said Al, "and we're going to have words."

Thumps flinched as the lancet stabbed his finger. Maybe in a couple more years he would get used to the sting.

"Just that little drop?" Al leaned in for a better look. "It's not all that impressive."

"Did you really take ten percent of the pool?"

"You're getting a free breakfast," said Al. "Leave it at that."

"I've got to get back to the office." Hockney pushed off the stool. "Stop by after you get settled. Got something to talk to you about."

Thumps spooned the salsa onto the plate next to the eggs.

Duke hitched his pants. "Macy says men would be healthier if we talked to one another."

"Is that what you do?"

"Hell no," said the sheriff. "I hold stuff inside and let it eat away at me."

BY THE TIME Thumps made his way to the hash browns, Stas had gone back to his garage and Chintak had left to open the pharmacy. Cooley had taken off earlier to tell Moses the good news. Wutty and Jimmy and Russell had argued some more with Al about a new concept they had come up with on the spot that they called "rightful compensation" before they gave up the ghost and piled into Wutty's truck.

Al appeared with the coffee pot. "You look like shit."

Thumps forced a smile.

"Something happened," said Al. "Didn't it? On the coast. Something you didn't expect."

Thumps sipped at the coffee. It was black and hot.

"Course you don't have to talk to me about it," said Al. "You can always talk to the sheriff. Or you can talk to Archie."

"Don't need to talk to anyone."

"But just because we're glad to see you doesn't mean we're going to let you crawl into a hole and rot."

"I'm thinking about selling the house."

Al ran her towel across the counter. "Claire's back. She and

Angie Black Weasel were in the other day. They had a fine time in New Zealand. Hot springs, beaches. Said the Maori were real friendly. Angie took a bunch of pictures."

"Great."

"Claire asked about you. I guess you forgot to tell her you were going to the coast."

Thumps finished off the last bit of toast and wiped his mouth.

"Selling your house is probably a bad idea," said Al. "When my sister got a divorce, she went out right away and got involved with a married guy. It's always better to wait until the dust clears before you make any big decisions."

"I should get going."

"Where?"

Thumps shrugged.

Al threw the dish towel over one shoulder and wiped her hands on the apron. "Yeah," she said. "Something happened. Something you really didn't expect. Something you didn't expect at all."

THREE

It took four trips to carry everything into the house. Thumps parked the camera pack and the tripod at the top of the basement stairs and took the suitcase to the bedroom. He set the banker boxes on the table next to the pile of mail that his next-door neighbour had collected for him while he was gone. Virgil "Dixie" Kane had taken the time to organize everything into three piles, bills, letters, and a small mountain of junk mail for which several perfectly good trees had been butchered.

Thumps took his time walking the rooms, hoping to find some memory of home. But there was none, no sense that he belonged here. The house felt old and tired. Worn out. Maybe that would change. A week. A month. And things would return to normal.

Whatever normal was.

And now what?

There was the question he had been dreading. Where to go from here? What to do next? He could unpack, and that certainly seemed to be the logical answer. Or he could go shopping and stock the kitchen. Or he could go to bed. His mother would have made a cup of tea while she considered the options.

Instead, he sat down at the kitchen table and opened the file that Nina Maslow had put together on the Obsidian Murders. He had read it any number of times. Now he would read it again. There was nothing definitive. One page was filled with questions about the order of the deaths, the weather, tidal cycles. Another page was dedicated to the motels in Eureka and in the neighbouring towns of Arcata, McKinleyville, and Fortuna. A third listed the public events and conferences that overlapped with the killings.

Most intriguing of all was the entry Maslow had set in block letters at the top of the last page.

Raymond Oakes, Deer Ridge.

She had circled the entry and drawn a star next to it in the margin. That was it. Thumps had done a quick Google search for Raymond Oakes and turned up a former hockey player, a wildlife photographer, a family physician, and a musician born in Bangkok but living in London.

Deer Ridge was a golf course in Brentwood and a resort near Newbury, both in California, a housing development in the southeastern quadrant of Calgary, Alberta, and a hiking trail near Granite Creek in Wyoming.

It was a thread that led nowhere.

Nor did a Raymond Oakes appear in any of the boxes that Ron had left for him. So far as Thumps could tell, Peat had copied everything to do with the case. Incident reports, photographs, DNA, the notes of the investigating team, the FBI's profile, and the statements of the people of interest who had been brought in for questioning.

So who was this man that Maslow had marked in a way that suggested he was important? And if he was important, why didn't he show up in the original police investigation?

THAT FIRST WEEKEND in Eureka, Thumps had gone online to see if there was anyone left from when he had been a deputy. Turnover in law enforcement tended to be high, and Humboldt County was no exception. There were three names he recognized but only one person he knew.

Leon Ranger.

The following Monday, Thumps had gone to the sheriff's office.

"Deputy Sheriff Ranger?"

The dark-haired woman behind the desk looked to be in her late twenties. "S. Tupper" on the gold name tag. Her uniform was pressed to a hard edge.

"What is this in regard to?"

"I'm a friend." Thumps began to run the possibilities. Sunny,

Smiley, Sympathy. He had known a girl named Sympathy in high school.

"Your name?"

"DreadfulWater," said Thumps. "Thumps DreadfulWater."

S. Tupper's face softened for a moment. "You used to work here."

"Another life."

"Are those doughnuts?"

Thumps held up the box. "They are."

"From the Donut Mill?"

Thumps opened the box. "Help yourself."

S. Tupper selected a chocolate raised. "Just to make sure we're talking about the same Officer Ranger, could you describe him for me?"

"Yeah," said Thumps. "Leon Ranger. Black guy with a big mouth. Tries to write trashy romance novels in his spare time. He's got a silver dollar he calls Flora, after his mother, that he flips whenever he makes decisions."

Officer Tupper tried to hold the smile in check. "Courthouse next door," she said. "In the basement."

"Basement?"

Officer Tupper took another bite of the doughnut. "Last summer, he arrested the mayor's son on a possession charge."

"Let me guess," said Thumps. "He offered to flip the kid for the citation?"

"Flora came up tails. Mayor's son was convicted and got

probation." S. Tupper handed Thumps a visitor's badge and helped herself to another doughnut. "Officer Ranger got the basement."

THE BASEMENT OF the courthouse was home to the property and evidence lockup as well as the department archives. Leon Ranger was sitting behind an old metal desk.

"Son of a bitch." Leon had leaped to his feet as soon as he saw Thumps. "Is that Officer Crappy Water?"

"Hey, Leon."

"Where the hell have you been, Tonto?" Leon grabbed Thumps by the shoulders and shook him. "I figured someone had shot your ass and turned you into a lamp."

"Not yet."

Leon cleared out a spot on the desk and pulled up a chair. "Those sure as blazes better be Donut Mill doughnuts."

"They are."

"I'm cutting back, you know." Leon patted his belly. "They got these new jerk-off regulations on weight limits."

"You don't have to eat any."

Leon took a silver dollar out of his pocket. "Call it," he said.

Thumps had played this game before. "Tails."

Leon caught the coin on his wrist and slapped his hand over it. "Damn," he said, peeking under the hand. "I lose."

"Tragic," said Thumps.

Leon nodded and lifted the lid of the box. "Crullers. You remembered."

The two men spent the better part of the next hour filling in the blanks.

"Got tired of apartment living, so I bought a small RV. Roadtrek Agile. They make them in Canada. Nineteen feet, Mercedes Sprinter chassis, diesel. Sweet ride."

"What happened to Barbara?"

"Didn't want to live in an RV."

Leon had photos of the van parked on the edge of a bluff near Astoria, Oregon, overlooking the ocean.

"You heard about Ron?"

"Fell off a ladder."

Leon shook his head. "Damn fool. Thought he was one of those repair guys on television."

"How's the writing going?"

"Four books done," said Leon. "Halfway through the fifth."

"Any published yet?"

"There's no rush," said Leon. "When I retire, the plan is to travel around and hit a bunch of writers' conferences."

Thumps shook his head. "Can't see you retired."

"Guy who took Ron's place is an asshole. I got my twenty in. Can walk out the door tomorrow, if I feel like it." Leon laid the silver dollar on the table. "So, Tonto," he said, "you still a cop?"

"Fine art photographer."

"No shit," said Leon. "I'm thinking about doing that. Not

fine art. Travel stuff. Drive around the country, take shots, do some magazine work."

"Why not."

"Hey, you could help me. Show me how to shoot."

"Sure."

"All right," said Leon, "let's can the small talk. What the hell has precipitated your return to this sorry backwater? As if I didn't know."

"I could use your help."

Leon tossed the silver dollar into the air. "Call it."

"Heads."

Leon peeked under his hand. "You're one lucky son of a bitch."

LEON SET UP a small table in the basement at the back of the evidence locker, and for the next two weeks, Thumps worked his way back through the boxes Ron had left for him. Along with Maslow's notes.

"Ron always figured you'd come back at some point," Leon told him. "I helped him put all this shit together for when you took up the case again."

"He couldn't have known that was going to happen."

"He was betting you wouldn't let it lie. So, who's this Nina Maslow?"

"Television producer," Thumps told him. "Ran a reality show called *Malice Aforethought*. Each episode was a cold case."

"And you got this Raymond Oakes character from her?"

"His name was in her notes."

"And you can't ask her?"

"She was murdered."

"So you have no idea who this Oakes character is."

"That's about it."

Working with Ranger in the courthouse basement allowed Thumps access to law-enforcement databases. There had been nothing in the California state database for a Raymond Oakes and nothing in the national database.

"We're still not talking to one another," Leon told him. "Local, state, FBI, CIA, NSA, ATF, and all the rest of the alphabet children. With all the bitching about national security and the need to share data, we still continue to play parochial games with information."

"I'm not even sure what I'm looking for."

"What was that name again?"

"Raymond Oakes."

"No, the other name."

Thumps double-checked Maslow's notes. "Deer Ridge."

"Shit," Leon said. "I must be getting old. Maybe it's time for me to hang it up and hit the road."

"You got something?"

"Oregon," Leon said. "Let's try Oregon."

* * *

THUMPS PUT THE KETTLE on and waited for the water to boil. So Claire was home. The last time they had talked, she had been in the process of adopting two little girls. Thumps remembered a breakfast. Or was it lunch? And a conversation about his involvement with Claire and the soon-to-be-formed family. He hadn't seen it coming, had been blindsided, had not handled it all that well, and the matter had been left unsettled. Then the adoption had fallen through, and Claire had gone off to New Zealand with Angie Black Weasel, and Thumps had gone to the coast. Now that they were both back, Thumps wondered if Claire would want to pick up the conversation again or if she would be content to let it die.

The kettle began its staggering whistle. Thumps found a bag of fennel tea and dropped it into the boiling water.

The smart thing to do would be to call her. Claire would already know that he was back in town. Any delay would be an answer in and of itself. Thumps tried to imagine how he would start.

"Hi. How was New Zealand? Glad you're back. Just calling to see how you are. How about this weather."

No good way in. No good way in at all.

Thumps waited as the phone rang and was surprised by the sudden sense of relief he felt when it rang through to Claire's answering machine.

"Hi, it's me," he said. "Just got back. Hope you're well. Give me a call when you have a chance."

Smooth, succinct, stupid.

Thumps set the phone to one side at a safe distance and went back to Maslow's file.

RANGER HAD FOUND Oakes on the first pass through the Oregon State Criminal Database.

Raymond Oakes. White male. Forty-one. Six feet. One hundred and eighty pounds. Brown hair. Blue eyes.

"I should have caught it right away," Leon said. "Deer Ridge Correctional. Just east of Madras. Used to be a minimum/medium security facility. They changed it over to minimum a few years back."

"Robbery/homicide?" Thumps scrolled down the screen. "Oakes got life. What's he doing in a minimum-security prison?"

"Overcrowding. Bureaucratic incompetence. Our penal system in action." Leon scrolled down the screen. "Okay, here's why. Our boy caught himself a technicality. The bastard got out on appeal."

Thumps felt his body tense. "Look at the release date."

"Shit." Leon took off his glasses and rubbed his eyes. "It gets worse," he said. "Check out the next of kin."

THUMPS WENT TO the living room and sat down in the easy chair. He was hungry but he had no interest in eating. He was tired but wasn't sure he could sleep. He knew about jet lag. Maybe there was car lag as well. Or maybe depression came in all sorts of shapes and sizes.

Tomorrow, he'd call Leon to see if the results had come back from the lab. Tonight, he'd drink his tea and pretend that in the morning, he'd know what to do with the rest of his life.

FOUR

When Thumps woke the next morning, he was still in the chair. Someone had thrown a blanket over him, and someone was in the kitchen cooking. Bacon by the smell of it. And coffee. Logic suggested that the blanket, the bacon, and the coffee were the work of the same someone.

Cooley Small Elk was looming over the stove. The large cast-iron fry pan that Thumps had inherited from his mother was filled with strips of crackling fat. Moses Blood was sitting at the kitchen table, enjoying a cup of coffee.

"Welcome home," said Moses. "I figured you might need a diversion."

"A diversion?"

"Something to take your mind off your worries." Moses raised the cup to his lips. "I always find that breakfast is a good diversion."

"You like bacon?" said Cooley.

Thumps rubbed his face.

"Quick, grandson," said Moses, "get your uncle a cup of coffee."

"We got eggs too, and some bread and butter," said Cooley. "Moses said you wouldn't have much in the way of food, so we stopped on the way in and got some groceries."

"Great."

Cooley made a face. "Moses thought you might like yogurt, and I said I didn't think Cherokees ate the stuff."

"It looks healthy," said Moses, "until you read the nutritional information."

"The smell is the clue," said Cooley.

"Some of those mini-cartons you see kids bring to school in their lunch have twelve grams of sugar." Moses shook his head. "That's three teaspoons."

Cooley held up the spatula. "You want your eggs scrambled or fried?"

"Scrambled is fine."

"Once you put those three teaspoons of sugar into that little cup," said Moses, "there isn't much room for the yogurt."

"Multi-grain bread okay?"

"Sure."

"Good," said Cooley. "Moses didn't think that white was a good idea."

"Six grams of sugar per slice," said Moses. "I guess that's why it's white."

Moses Blood didn't come to town all that often. Mostly he stayed on the reservation, on a piece of bottomland that fronted the river. But when Moses did come in, it was always for a reason. Thumps wondered if the reason for this visit was him.

Cooley set the bacon to drain as he whipped the eggs in a bowl. "Tell Thumps about the car show."

"That's right," said Moses. "There's a big car show in town at the fairgrounds. Old stuff that people like to collect."

"There's going to be an auction," said Cooley. "We're going to buy Moses a car."

Thumps couldn't remember if Moses had ever owned a car.

"Cole's Classics," said Cooley. "Travelling show. Old cars. Collectibles from the '40s and '50s. Show goes around to smaller areas than outfits like Barrett-Jackson. And people can bring in their own cars for an appraisal. Sort of like the *Antiques Roadshow*."

"I'm thinking about a 1956 Chevrolet two-door Bel Air," said Moses. "Blue and turquoise. Though I could be persuaded by a 1955 Ford F100."

"The F100 is a pickup."

"Yes," said Moses. "The eternal struggle between form and function."

"You know how to drive?"

Moses shook his head. "Nope," he said, "but I'm willing to learn."

"You know you're going to have to get a licence," said Thumps. "And insurance. There may even be an issue with your age."

Moses looked surprised. "What's wrong with my age?"

No one knew how old Moses was, and, so far as Thumps could tell, that included Moses. Old wasn't a word that defined the man. Moses was simply an elder, a respected member of a community that valued wisdom over birthdays.

"Well, sometimes the insurance companies don't want to insure people over a certain age."

Cooley brought the food to the table on two large platters. There was enough to feed eight people. Or two people plus Cooley Small Elk.

"Moses isn't going to need a licence or insurance."

"He will if he wants to drive a car."

Cooley helped himself to half the bacon. "He's okay so long as he stays on his own land."

"I can drive along the river," said Moses. "Maybe a convertible, so I can feel the wind in my hair."

"In the old days," said Cooley, "we had horses. Now we got cars."

"They're not the same," said Moses, "but it's important to be flexible."

"Moses was worried about you." Cooley took the last piece of toast. "He wanted to make sure you were okay."

Moses dug in his pocket and came up with a fold of money. "Almost forgot," he said. "This is your share."

"The pool," said Cooley.

"Fifty-fifty," said Moses.

"That's your money." Thumps tried sticking his fork in the eggs. Maybe if he pretended to eat, he'd find he was hungry.

"Sure," said Moses, "but it was a team effort."

"If you didn't come home when you did," said Cooley, "Moses would have lost. And I wouldn't have gotten a new rifle."

"It's solid logic," said Moses. "When you think about it."

"Rifle?"

"Bolt-action Remington 700," said Cooley. "I'm taking Stas and Big Fish elk hunting."

"You know," said Moses, "I've never seen the ocean."

"It's beautiful," said Thumps. "Another world."

"Maybe if I like that driving," said Moses, "I'll get that licence and that insurance, and I'll drive to the ocean."

Thumps smiled. "If you do, can I go with you?"

"See the USA," said Cooley. "In your Chevrolet."

Moses broke a piece of bacon in half and set the larger half on Thumps's plate. "Did you find any answers in that ocean?"

"Some." Thumps put his fork to one side. "Along with more questions."

"Sometimes questions are as good as answers." Moses helped himself to the coffee. "And sometimes they're not."

Sometimes, Thumps thought to himself, the trick was knowing which questions to ask and which ones to avoid.

"Tell me about Claire."

Both Cooley and Moses stopped eating.

"For instance, Stanley's father," said Thumps. "Who is he?"

Cooley dumped the rest of the bacon onto his plate. "Claire's never told you?"

"Where is he?" Thumps paused and considered the next question. "Is he alive?"

Moses closed his eyes and sat back in the chair. "You should probably talk to Claire. That way you get it right the first time."

"Is it a secret?"

Moses shrugged. "Don't think so. But with women, you never know."

"I can't just ask her."

"That's true," said Cooley. "It's hard to sneak up on something like that without being seen."

"You should just ask her," said Moses. "Asking shows you care."

"And if she doesn't want to tell me?"

"That's the trouble with life, all right," said Moses. "Sometimes, when you ask questions, you don't get the answers you want."

FIVE

The car show was at the Chinook fairgrounds. Thumps hadn't wanted to come, but Cooley and Moses had insisted.

"Good to get out," said Moses. "Sunshine is supposed to make you cheery."

"I'm cheery."

"You still got that badge Duke gave you?" asked Cooley. "Sometimes it's hard to tell the healthy cars from the sad ones. People selling their cars tend to forget the problems."

"You want me to flash a badge at them?"

"Most people want to be honest," said Moses.

"But a little encouragement never hurts," said Cooley.

Freddy Salgado was manning the ticket booth. "Hey, Mr. DreadfulWater," he said. "You're back."

"I'm back."

"So, that's two adults and a senior?"

Thumps frowned. "You have to pay to get into a car show?"

"It's just to help cover expenses," said Freddy. "And where else are you going to get to see all these great cars. You guys in the market?"

"Moses is thinking about a 1956 Chevrolet Bel Air," said Cooley.

"Fine car," said Freddy. "My dad really liked that year."

"A convertible," said Moses. "So I can feel the wind in my hair."

"So, that'll be $12.50."

"Quick," said Cooley, "show him your badge."

THE FIELD IN FRONT of the grandstands was littered with cars. Mostly they were well organized in neat rows, but as the rows ran out, the edges turned ragged. The ground itself was broken and churned up as though a cattle drive had come through on its way to a railhead.

"Chinook summer roundup," said Cooley, kicking at a chunk of grass and mud. "You missed it."

Cole's Classic Cars were in a roped-off section by itself. Chevrolet, Ford, Mercury, Plymouth. There was a 1956 Studebaker Golden Hawk and a 1957 Pontiac Star Chief. There was even a 1958 Ford Edsel Citation convertible.

"I read that the Edsel failed," said Cooley, "because people thought the front grille looked like a vagina."

"You'd think that would be a plus," said Moses.

Cole had two 1956 Chevrolet Bel Airs. One was a hardtop, white and turquoise. The other was a convertible, red and white.

"I like the blue and white," said Moses, "but the red and white is also nice."

"Look at this." Cooley raised the hood on the convertible. "It's got the Power Pack V8 265 with a dual-quad carb."

"You know your cars." The woman who came around the side of the car was tall and thick with a mass of red hair that ran off in all directions. Someone you would never lose in a crowd. "In '57 you could get a 283 with fuel injection, but I've always liked the lines of the '56."

"It's a nice car," said Cooley.

"Anderson Cole," said the woman, and she held out a hand.

Cole was dressed in jeans and a black and gold "Cole's Cars" T-shirt. There was nothing threatening about her appearance, but her voice reminded Thumps of Roxanne Heavy Runner.

"You know," said Cooley, "you sound just like my auntie."

"Yes," said Moses. "My heart is already picking up speed."

"The normal-looking hombre is George Gorka," said Cole. "George is my road manager."

Gorka was dressed in slacks, a Cole's T-shirt, and a sports jacket that was at least one size too big. There was a bulge on the left side under the arm.

"I know," said Cole, "you were expecting a guy."

"Fooled me," said Cooley.

"My dad started the business. I turned it into a travelling show. We go to places the big auctions don't. I bring in about thirty to forty cars, mostly late '40s and '50s. The rest of what you see comes in from other collectors and dealers. And there's always individuals who show up with a car they want to sell."

"Can you test drive the car?" asked Cooley. "Before you buy it?"

"No test drives," said Gorka.

"If we gave test drives, all we'd do is wear rubber and burn gas." Cole slid in behind the wheel of the car and started the engine. "Frankly, test drives are overrated. You can tell a lot just by listening."

Moses patted Thumps on the shoulder. "Now, that's good advice."

"But, you know, I feel like taking this one for a spin." Cole adjusted the rear-view mirror. "Maybe you'd like to come along."

"You bet," said Cooley, and he quickly slid into the passenger's seat.

"Some of the cars have a reserve. Some of them don't," said Cole. "But if your bid is the winning one, I'll throw in T-shirts for all of you."

Cooley opened and closed the glovebox. "You got a triple X?"

"George," said Cole, "we got triple X?"

"You're wearing one."

"Damn," said Cole. "I do have to cut back on the pasta."

THUMPS WATCHED COLE and Cooley and the Chevy head for the exit. He had to admit that the '56 was a handsome car. He could see why Moses liked that model.

"The specialty cars and some of the high-end collectibles are in the animal barn." Gorka kept his hands at his side, like a gunfighter in an old western. "You guys should take a look at the '67 Mustang."

"Yes," said Moses. "Those Mustangs were certainly popular."

"Wait until you see the paint job on this one."

"Steve McQueen drove a Mustang," said Moses. "In that movie *Bullitt*."

"That was a '68 GT fastback." Gorka looked over his shoulder. "I better get back to the cars. Don't forget to check out the barn."

THUMPS FOLLOWED MOSES as he toured the cars. The idea that the old man could drive a car on his property without a licence was true, but only in a limited way. Yes, he could tour the riverbank in both directions, and he could drive out across the flat to the foot of the coulees, but what was he going to do when he ran out of gas? Or when the car needed an oil change? Or new tires?

Or a tune-up? Once he left the protection of the river bottom and the reservation, he would need a licence and insurance.

"Victor Brandt," Moses said as they walked. "Mohawk guy out of Six Nations. He came through one summer. Stayed a couple of weeks. When he left, Claire went with him."

Thumps kept pace.

"Love at first sight," said Moses. "Happens all the time when you're eighteen."

"Claire was eighteen?"

"No." Moses slowed as he came to a cluster of vintage pick-ups. "Victor was eighteen. Claire had just turned fifteen."

Moses stopped at a 1959 Dodge. There was a sheet taped to the driver's side window with all the specifications typed out neatly in large letters.

"What do you think?" Moses walked around the truck. "Fleetside or stepside?"

"What?"

"Cooley likes the fleetside 'cause you can lay a sheet of ply-wood flat," said Moses. "Cyrus Old Person over in Browning swears by his stepside 'cause he can get to the hay bales easier."

"What about Claire?"

"Couple of years later, she came home with Stanley."

"And?"

"We were all happy to see her," said Moses. "And that Stanley, he was one cute baby."

There was a 1955 Chevrolet and a 1951 GMC, as well as a 1958 Studebaker. Of the three, Thumps liked the pale blue and white two-tone Studebaker half-ton. It had soft edges with gentle lines. It looked like a truck that would be sympathetic and listen to you when you were down.

"A pickup would be the practical choice," said Moses.

"What about Victor?"

"I could load firewood in the back and drive right up to my front door."

"Claire's never mentioned him."

Moses rested against the Studebaker and let the sun warm his face. "But if I got a convertible, we could drive it to the coast, and you could show me the ocean."

Stas Black Weasel came tramping across the field. "Hello, hello, old car lovers," he shouted. "I am here to save you from myself."

"Yourself," said Thumps. "Save you from yourself."

People who didn't know Stas reasoned that, because of his last name, he must be Blackfeet. In fact, the man was Russian through and through. From Kazan. He had come to North America to see the Rockies and met Angela Black Weasel, who was working as an interpretive guide in Glacier National Park.

"You are thinking of ancient car, yes?"

"Collectible," said Thumps.

"I'm leaning toward a pickup," said Moses.

"Mercedes-Benz make pickup trucks," said Stas. "Very good quality."

"Mercedes makes a pickup?"

"Sure," said Stas. "BMW also. But not in North America."

Thumps tried to imagine Moses behind the wheel of a Mercedes pickup. "They must be expensive."

"Yes, yes," said Stas. "When you buy, you must sign agreement not to put firewood in the back."

"What?"

"Also cannot drive into woods and get mud on tires."

"That's a joke, right?"

BEFORE STAS MARRIED ANGIE, his last name had been Fukin.

"Good name in Russia," he would say, "but not so good in English."

Stas was a master mechanic, had worked for Mercedes-Benz in Stuttgart, and after he and Angie settled in Chinook, he opened Blackfoot Autohaus. Stas's specialty was high-end European and Asian vehicles, but his passion was hunting and fishing, and whether or not the garage was open depended on the season. Blackfoot Autohaus had posted hours that Stas didn't necessarily keep and a phone in the office that he seldom answered.

"Elk do not have office hours," Stas liked to joke. "Fish do not take calls."

If you wanted an appointment, you drove to the garage and hoped that Stas was there and that you didn't find a sign on the bay door that said, "Closed for Moose."

Stas ran a hand along the Studebaker's flank. "Old cars are very beautiful. Interesting designs. Works of art."

"Ho," said Moses.

"Not so good as cars."

"Ho," said Moses.

"So, you look at old cars," said Stas. "Enjoy, enjoy. Then you come see me. I find you good car, good truck. Something safe. Something dependable."

Some people found Stas a bit abrupt and opinionated, but Thumps liked the big Russian.

Stas took a folded sheet of paper out of his pocket. "Also," he said, "I have a list of questions you must answer."

Thumps wasn't sure if Stas was talking to him or to Moses. "Me?"

"Yes," said Stas. "But before I begin, there is a . . . disclaimer. This is correct?"

"Yes," said Thumps, "'disclaimer' is correct."

"So, these are not my questions. These are women's questions."

"Ho," said Moses.

Thumps could feel his mouth go dry. "Women?"

"Angie," said Stas, counting on his fingers, "Delia Fox, Crystal Bull . . ."

"Stas . . ."

"Brenda Many Bears, Mercy Smith, and Angie's older sister, Thelma . . ."

Moses leaned in. "Are some of the questions about Thumps and Claire?"

Stas looked at the sheet. "Yes," he said. "Several."

"And do the women want to know what happened on the coast?"

"Yes," said Stas, "they do."

"And why Thumps came back?" Moses turned to Thumps. "Boy, it must feel good to know how much people care about you."

Stas held out the sheet of paper as though it were a piece of hazardous waste. "So, this is for you."

Thumps put his hands up. "I don't want it."

"If you're lucky," said Moses, "when the women stop by to talk, they'll bring food."

COOLEY WAS BEHIND the wheel now, and he looked good as he drove the Chevrolet across the field. He was sitting up ramrod straight, and if he had had a top hat, he could have been a latter-day Geronimo in his Cadillac. Only the car in the famous photograph wasn't a Cadillac. It was a Locomobile, probably from 1904.

The shot had been staged at the Miller Brothers 101 Ranch, and in the photograph, the Ponca, Edward Le Clair Sr., sits next to Geronimo in full feather headdress, while two other

Indians lounge in the back seat. One of the men is wearing a fur cap. The other sports a single feather. Geronimo is the only one in a black top hat.

Thumps knew the photograph well, had looked at it any number of times, and he'd always wondered where Geronimo had gotten the top hat.

And what in the world had possessed him to wear it.

"Mr. Small Elk is a natural." Anderson Cole patted her hair into place and touched the corners of her eyes where the mascara had started to slip. "I think this car has his name on it."

Cooley rolled his shoulders. "No power steering, so you got to be firm with the wheel."

"When you drive a car like this," said Cole, "people stop and look."

"Don't know that there will be that many people at my place," said Moses, "but curb appeal is certainly a strong selling point."

Cooley took his cellphone out of his pocket. "Ms. Cole has invited us to a party."

"That's right," said Anderson. "Pre-auction party. Tomorrow night. Going to be right here with the cars. We got a tent in case it rains. Hot dogs, burgers, beer, soft drinks. Even some live music."

"Hot dogs and beer is excellent." Stas held out the sheet of paper. "But you must take this or Angie will put me in cat house."

"Dog house." Cooley raised an eyebrow. "What is it?"

Moses rocked on his heels. "The women made up a list of questions for Thumps."

"Is my auntie involved?" asked Cooley.

"Roxanne Heavy Runner?" said Stas. "Yes, she is leader of questions."

"You might consider leaving town again. Just to be safe." Cooley handed the phone to Thumps. "But in the meantime, maybe you could take a picture of Moses and me with the car."

SIX

It was well after three before Moses and Cooley dropped Thumps off in front of Chinook Pharmacy. The show had proved to be more fun than Thumps would have imagined. Not for the cars. They were interesting, but after one circuit of the show, he was ready to go.

It was Moses.

The old man had wandered up and down the rows, stopping every so often at a car he recognized. And for each car he stopped at, there was a story.

"Delbert Night had one of these. One winter, he tried to drive it across the Ironstone. The ice was thick enough, but he couldn't get up the bank because he couldn't get any traction. So Delbert decided to try it from a running start. He was probably doing forty or fifty when he hit the bank and buried the truck. He had to walk home. The next morning, a chinook

45

came through and melted the ice enough so that the back end of the truck broke through the ice. That night, everything froze up again and the truck wound up sitting in the river until the spring thaw."

Moses found a 1948 Dodge sedan with a heavy visor over the front windshield.

"Edna Gladstone's dad bought her one of these when she graduated from nursing school. Edna took us all out for a drive on the lease road. She was real nervous with her new car, so she drove extra slow. Frank Bad Bull began teasing her about how slow she was going, saying that he could walk faster than she was driving. Finally, Frank jumped out and began walking circles around the car. At one point, he put his shoulder against the trunk and began pushing, which was when Edna hit the accelerator and left Frank to walk home by himself."

Moses was particularly pleased to find a 1957 Ford Thunderbird.

"This is just like the car Dwayne Sachs and Howard Goodstriker took down to Mexico. They stopped in Ensenada to do some deep-sea fishing and the car ended up in the ocean. If you ask Dwayne, he'll tell you that someone stole the car and drove it off the pier. If you ask Howard, he'll tell you that Dwayne had been drinking and thought the pier was the main road."

Thumps looked around to see if there were any 1982 Volvos in the show. The Honda Element that Sydney Pearl had given him was a fine car, but he still felt bad about having deserted an old friend.

NORMALLY, CHINTAK RAWAT would be behind the counter, dressed in a bright white lab coat that had been starched and polished to a shine. Today, he was dressed in a black polo shirt with red and white trim and a Jaguar badge on the left breast.

Jaguar. E-Type.

And he had a Jaguar cap on his head.

"Ah, Mr. DreadfulWater," Chintak sang out, "did Mr. Moses find the car of his desires?"

"Maybe he should get a Jaguar."

"That would be imprudent." Chintak touched the bill of his cap. "While the Jaguar is the epitome of styling and grace, to own one is to invite frustration and garage expenses."

"Speaking of expenses"—Thumps took the insulin kit out of his bag—"I'm going to need to refill my prescription."

"And it will be my pleasure to assist you in this matter," said Chintak. "However, you must first speak with Dr. Beth."

"What?"

"I believe she wishes to monitor your condition."

"I have to see her before I can get the prescription filled?"

"This is correct."

"I don't want to see her."

"No one wishes to visit a doctor," said Chintak. "Inevitably, there are tests that involve machines and injections and blood. Most distressing to be sure."

"I feel fine."

"Most encouraging," said Chintak. "Dr. Beth will be delighted to hear of this."

"I really have to see her?"

"And while you are there," said Chintak, "perhaps she can help you with the questions you have been requested to answer."

"What?"

"Chief Heavy Runner was in the other day," said Chintak. "She and several other women were talking. Your name was mentioned."

"She's not a chief."

"Most certainly," said Chintak. "But neither is she a woman with whom I wish to argue."

"Did Roxanne actually show you the questions?"

Chintak reached under the counter and came up with a sheet of paper. "She left a copy in case I saw you before anyone else."

"Anyone else?"

"Yes," said Chintak. "I believe she left a copy with Mr. Archie and with Sheriff Duke as well."

"Great."

"It is not just the women, of course," said Chintak. "All of your friends are curious as to your intentions with Chief Merchant and what transpired on the coast."

Maybe, Thumps thought, he should rent a hall for an evening

and do a PowerPoint presentation complete with visuals and music. *My Private Life and the Obsidian Murders*. Coming soon to a Rotary Club near you.

"And Chief Heavy Runner suggested that I encourage you to purchase candy and flowers. These are, I believe, intended for Chief Merchant."

"Suggested?"

"Yes," said Chintak. "Perhaps 'suggested' is of insignificant import."

"If you see Roxanne," said Thumps, "you might tell her to mind her own business."

Chintak paled. "We are friends, are we not?"

"We are."

"Friends should not suggest such dangerous enterprises."

"Roxanne is all bark."

"Ah," said Chintak, "then the stories of gratuitous violence are not true?"

THUMPS HAD READ somewhere that you should never put something off, that if you open a bill, for example, you should pay it immediately rather than throw it in a pile to be dealt with later. The article went on to talk about returning phone calls and doing other jobs as they presented themselves. Thumps could see where this was good advice, but he also knew that most people tended to do the easy and the pleasurable tasks first and to leave the difficult and distasteful to the very last.

Himself included.

Still, here was a chance to put theory into action. He did need the prescription. The old Land Titles building was at hand, just down the block. He didn't have any pressing engagements. With luck, he could slip in, convince Beth Mooney to take the hold off his prescription without him having to brave any medical experimentation, come back to the pharmacy, pick up the supplies, and disappear into his house before anyone else could run him down.

The old Land Titles building was a two-storey affair with a basement. Beth Mooney had installed an intercom at the front door with a three-button keypad. The top button rang the second floor, where Beth had her living quarters. The middle button rang the main floor, where she had her medical office. The bottom button got you the county morgue, where autopsies were performed and bodies were stored.

Thumps was trying to decide where to start when there was a sharp clicking sound and the front door swung open.

"So, you're back," said a voice.

The remote-control door was new. So was the camera mounted just above the brick lintel.

"Beth?"

"Second floor," said the voice.

The second floor of the old Land Titles building was Thumps's favourite floor. It had comfortable chairs and a sofa.

There would be tea and cookies. And it was as far away from the basement as you could get.

Beth Mooney was waiting for him on the landing.

"Took you long enough."

"I just got back into town."

"Your doctor should have been your first stop." Beth led the way into the apartment. "Remember the blood work we did just before you left?"

The last time Thumps had been in the apartment, the walls had been painted a soft yellow. Now they were a medium coffee. Beth had never been one for home decor and accessories, but now there were two old movie posters in frames, *Moon over Miami* and *The Invisible Woman*.

"Place looks nice."

"Don't change the subject. You want tea?"

Thumps wasn't going to ask what had prompted the paint job or the vintage posters, and he wasn't going to ask about the blood work.

"Aren't you curious?"

"Nope."

"You know, you give men a bad name."

Thumps could think of only one reason for the apartment facelift. "You and Ora Mae back together?"

"The results are troubling." Beth put the kettle on. "I want to redo the blood work."

"What?"

"Tomorrow. Nine thirty," said Beth. "And I want to send you to a specialist in Helena."

Thumps felt his body go cold.

"You're anemic," said Beth. "And I don't know why."

"What if I work out more?"

"It could be nothing."

"I could reduce my ice cream."

Beth's head snapped around. "You're eating ice cream?"

"What's with the door and the camera?"

Beth poured the water into the pot and brought it to the table. "Let's stay on subject."

Thumps didn't notice the sheet of paper until he had settled himself in the chair.

"That's for you," said Beth. "Roxanne dropped it off."

"Did everyone in town get a copy?"

"So your red blood cell count is down." Beth paused and sipped her tea. "Some anemia is hereditary. Sometimes it's caused by poor diet. Other causes are ulcers, overuse of aspirin, menstruation."

Thumps waited.

"Then there's things such as sickle cell anemia, kidney disease, diabetes."

"And I'm diabetic."

"Yes," said Beth, "you are. But I'm not sure that the diabetes is the cause. That's why I want you to see the specialist."

"How about I improve my diet and see if that helps?"

"How about you listen to your doctor?"

"Helena is a long drive."

"Says the man who just drove to the California coast and back."

Thumps could see he was losing the argument. The smart move would be to agree to the specialist and then decide whether or not to go.

"Okay."

Beth adjusted her glasses. "Is that an 'Okay, I'm going to listen to you and see the specialist,' or is that an 'Okay, I just want to get out of here'?"

"Will this involve more blood tests?"

"You'll probably have to have a CAT scan, maybe an MRI."

Thumps took a deep breath and let it out slowly. "So, why did you fix the place up?"

Beth pushed the list across the table. "So, what are you going to do about these questions?"

SEVEN

Duke Hockney was standing next to the old percolator.

"Your lucky day." The sheriff patted the pot as though it were the family dog. "Just made fresh."

"Yippee."

"That was last month," said Duke. "Mayor cancelled the 'Howdy' program. So, we can talk normal again."

"Yahoo."

"Roxanne Heavy Runner?" said Hockney.

"Okay," said Thumps quickly. "Truce."

"New coffee roaster in town." Duke handed Thumps a cup. "This is a dark Ethiopian."

How much had changed in a month? Beth and her high-end security system and new paint job. And now the sheriff talking about coffee varieties, when Duke had always prided himself on buying the cheapest beans and boiling them into submission.

"You even know where Ethiopia is?"

The coffee in the cup looked normal. Thumps rocked the cup to see if the coffee would move. It did. Having seen the sheriff's coffee in the past, this was a good sign.

"Try it," said the sheriff, "before you go all sarcastic on me."

Thumps took a sniff. "Just came from Beth's."

The sheriff carried his cup back to his desk and sat down. "The security system."

"Pretty sophisticated."

"There was a break-in," said Duke. "Couple weeks back."

"They take anything?"

"Beth says no, but she's still looking."

"Drugs?"

Duke shook his head. "Nothing of note on the premises."

"They wouldn't have known that."

"The break-in wasn't some smash and grab," said the sheriff. "It was smooth, very professional."

"But they took nothing."

"How's the coffee?"

The coffee was good. Thumps took another sip to be sure. Normally, what came out of the old percolator looked and tasted like roofing tar.

"Hard to believe you made this."

Duke shuffled around in his chair. "You ever think of getting back into law enforcement?"

"No."

"Can't be a photographer all your life."

"Yes, I can."

"And photography's not what it used to be. Everything's digital now. Where's the joy in that?"

"I still use film."

"Damn it, DreadfulWater," said Hockney. "I'm serious."

"I don't want to be a deputy."

Duke nodded his agreement. "You'd make a lousy deputy. But you just might make a respectable sheriff."

"Sheriff?"

Duke turned to the window. "I've got prostate cancer."

"What?"

Duke held up a hand. "And don't go getting all sympathetic on me. They say they caught it early."

"Shit."

"I go to Helena at the end of the month. They'll cut it out or they'll zap it with their X-ray gun, and I'll probably be okay."

"Hell, Duke, I'm sorry."

"There you go getting all sympathetic." Hockney pushed his cup off to one side. "It's going to be fine. But it got me thinking about life, and what I want to do with the rest of what's left."

"That sounds serious."

"It's Macy," said Duke. "She's always wanted to travel."

"You hate travel."

"True enough," said Duke. "But I love that woman, and over the years, she has put up with a lot, so I figure fair's fair."

Duke opened the desk drawer, took out a folder, and slid it to Thumps. "Been working on the job announcement. Tell me what you think."

The announcement was a single page. Thumps could see right away where all this was headed.

"Preference will be given to Native American applicants?"

"This is Indian country," said Duke. "Need someone who understands both worlds."

"No one is going to hire me."

Duke cleared his throat. "Already talked to several council members."

"Duke . . ."

"Drink your coffee and shut up." The sheriff lumbered over to the percolator and filled his cup. "All I'm asking is that you think about it. You got the skills and the experience. You know the town and you know the reservation."

Thumps stared at Duke.

"Course you could say yes, and save me the time and effort of convincing you." Hockney tried to look vulnerable. "In case I don't have as much time left as I think."

Thumps felt like laughing. He'd hardly been back a day, and he had already been dragged off to a classic car show, served with a list of personal questions, and offered a job he didn't want. And he hadn't even spoken to Archie Kousoulas yet. God knows what the little Greek had for him.

"What do you know about women?"

"Jesus," said Duke. "Is that a trick question?"

"If Macy had been married before she met you, would you expect her to tell you?"

"This got something to do with Anna Tripp and that serial killer case?"

So this was how it felt to get hit in the head with a stick. "How do you know about Anna Tripp?"

Duke gave up trying to look vulnerable and had a go at looking friendly. "Known since you arrived in Chinook."

"What?"

"Hell, DreadfulWater," said the sheriff. "Scruffy drifter lands in my town out of the blue in a beat-to-shit Volvo, claiming to be a former cop, and you don't think I'm going to check it out?"

"Scruffy drifter?"

"Didn't say anything because I figured it was your business."

Thumps took a deep breath and tried to slow everything down.

"I take it Tripp had a husband you didn't know about."

Anna hadn't talked much about Callie's father. Except to say he was dead. If she had ever mentioned his name, Thumps hadn't remembered it.

"Is that what you found out on the coast?"

Thumps remembered the sheet on Raymond Oakes that Ranger had received from Deer Ridge, remembered the name in the "next of kin" box.

Anna Tripp.

"Guy named Raymond Oakes," said Thumps. "Anna told me he was dead."

"But he wasn't?"

"He was in prison," said Thumps. "Oregon. Life sentence."

Hockney pushed back in the chair. "He escaped?"

"No," said Thumps. "There was a problem with the conviction. He got out."

"Just before the killings started?"

"A friend of mine at the Humboldt County Sheriff's Office may call," said Thumps. "Leon Ranger. I gave him your number."

Duke nodded. "Anything I can do?"

"No."

"You think this Oakes character is the serial killer?"

"Don't know."

"But you think he killed Tripp and her daughter."

"Don't know that either." Thumps could feel the tension in his face. "What I do know is that she lied to me. Why wouldn't she tell me about Oakes?"

"Embarrassed, maybe?" Duke rolled his chair around the side of the desk so he was knee to knee with Thumps. "But that's not what's eating you, is it?"

"Nothing's eating me," said Thumps. "I'm just curious."

"You're thinking that if you had known about this guy, you could have protected the people you loved. If you had known about Oakes, Tripp and her daughter would still be alive."

"She didn't trust me."

Duke sighed. "She was probably afraid if you found out she had been married to a murderer, she would have lost you."

"That wouldn't have happened."

"She didn't know that."

Thumps finished the coffee and set the cup on the edge of the desk. "So, what does that say about me?"

"No profit in going there," said Duke. "This Oakes character on parole?"

"No," said Thumps. "Oakes was released clean."

"So, he could be anywhere."

"He could."

"And you're going to try to find him." Duke rolled the chair back to his monitor. "We talking vengeance here?"

"Justice."

"Justice is good," said Duke. "Problem is, sometimes people have trouble keeping the two of them straight."

"I know the difference."

"Knowing it now," said the sheriff, "isn't the same thing as remembering it when it counts."

EIGHT

Duke was right. Photography had changed. Much of the film stock Thumps had used over the years had been discontinued. The same with the paper. He had considered moving over to digital, had gone so far as to price out a digital set-up and had come away shaking his head. It was not just the expense of a new camera and lens.

New computer.

New printer.

New computer programs.

And there was the learning curve. Digital would take him back to a new beginning where much of what he already knew would be obsolete. Light and shadow, framing, depth of field would all transfer to the digital world, but nothing much else would.

Maybe he shouldn't be so hasty in dismissing the chance for a career change. Being a cop had a certain analog simplicity to it.

Find the bad guy.

Arrest the bad guy.

Put the bad guy in jail.

The walk along Main Street to the Aegean gave Thumps time to sort through a selection of excuses. He had been gone for over a month, and Archie was going to want to know why Thumps hadn't bothered to call. Why he hadn't bothered to write.

The little Greek had a particularly bizarre idea of community, saw it as a vibrant collective where all members participated in the lives of one another.

On a daily basis.

Thumps understood community as an assortment of disparate and solitary individuals who only came together when they felt like it, or when a momentary crisis that demanded a group response appeared on the horizon.

There were large trucks in front of Budd's. The last time Thumps had been inside the old department store, it had been the production office for a reality television show.

Malice Aforethought.

Now it looked as though a major renovation was afoot. The windows were covered with paper, so you couldn't see in.

But the front door was open.

Choices, choices, choices. The bookstore with Archie waiting to lecture him on communal responsibility, or a leisurely tour of a construction site.

Budd's was being gutted, the old building taken down to the studs. The dust hung in the air like a dense fog. Thumps could taste the accumulation of all the years Budd's had been in business.

"About time."

A dusty figure appeared out of the gloom. Even in a hard hat and a dust mask, Archimedes Kousoulas was impossible to mistake.

"Archie?"

"Not even a postcard?" Archie slapped at his coveralls. "'Having a good time, wish you were here'?"

"A postcard?"

"Come on," said Archie, "we have to get you a hard hat and a mask."

Thumps could think of any number of places he wouldn't have expected to find Archie. A construction site was near the top. Then he remembered.

"You bought the building."

"Best investment I ever made," said Archie. "You know any-thing about drywall?"

The main floor was divided off with plastic sheets that had been hung from the ceiling like curtains. Archie pushed his way into the back area. Here the air was somewhat cleaner, and Thumps could breathe without feeling as though he had been caught out in a sandstorm. There was a large saw and a long table piled high with boxes of joint compound. Twelve-foot sheets of drywall were stacked on the floor, and a series of work lights had been set up to illuminate the space. At the far end of the room was a compressor that was making its annoying *rak-rak-rak* racket.

"Come on." Archie picked his way through the work area to the rear door. "Let's go outside. So we don't have to shout."

Budd's backed onto an alley. Thumps was already out the door before he noticed the large woman leaning against the wall.

"Well, look who's come to help."

"Hi, Roxanne."

"You look at those questions yet?"

Roxanne Heavy Runner was the secretary for the tribal council. Chiefs and councils came and went, but Roxanne endured. She was a large, fierce woman with all the social skills and compassion of a land mine.

"'Cause people are getting old waiting."

Roxanne was dressed in work clothes and covered in dust. The marks left by the safety goggles and the dust mask made her look like an urban raccoon.

Or a special forces assassin.

"Everyone is helping," said Archie. "Now that you're back, you can help too."

"Sure."

"But first," said Roxanne, "he's got to answer those questions."

Roxanne had a distinct way of phrasing a sentence that made each word sound like an exploding artillery shell.

"We finish the drywall this week," said Archie, "and next week, the stove and fridge arrive."

"Archie's going to split the main floor," said Roxanne. "His girlfriend gets the small side for her old clothes."

"She's not my girlfriend," said Archie. "Ms. Santucci is just a friend. And the clothes aren't old. They're vintage."

Roxanne made several noises in her throat that could have been ballistic missiles passing overhead.

"Guess what's going in on this side?"

"A bookstore?"

"A bookstore?" Archie frowned. "I already have a bookstore."

"A restaurant," said Roxanne. "Imagine that. A Greek opening a restaurant."

"Pappous's," said Archie. "Greek cuisine with a cosmopolitan flair."

"Pappous's?"

"It means 'grandfather,'" said Archie.

Roxanne pushed off the wall. "Six thirty tonight," she said. "Don't be late."

It took Thumps a couple of beats to realize that Roxanne was talking to him. "Me?"

"Claire's cooking your favourite meal."

"Claire?"

"Elk stew," said Roxanne. "Dress nice and bring chocolate and flowers."

"Flowers?"

"And not those cheap carnations," said Roxanne. "You can afford roses."

"Claire hasn't said anything about dinner."

"She's been trying to call you." Roxanne clicked her tongue. "But you haven't been answering."

"And Claire doesn't cook."

"Her place," said Roxanne. "Six thirty."

"Okay." Archie set the dust mask over his nose and mouth and adjusted his safety goggles. "Back to work. Place isn't going to renovate itself."

IT WAS WELL after five by the time Thumps got home. If he hurried, he could grab a shower, stop off at the pharmacy for some chocolate. He wasn't sure where he was going to find roses. Not that he wanted to buy flowers. He had always thought buying flowers was a waste. They were expensive, and they didn't last all that long. You put them in a vase, looked at them for a few days, and then threw them out.

Chocolate made some sense. At least you could eat chocolate.

Then, too, the whole dinner thing could be one of Roxanne's scams. The woman was famous for duping people into doing what she thought should be done. It wouldn't be the first time she had sent Thumps to Claire only for him to discover that Claire had not been expecting him. He'd get to her place. Claire would come to the door in jeans and a sweatshirt. There would be no dinner. There would just be annoyance and embarrassment.

In equal parts.

What he should do is call ahead. Confirm that dinner had been offered. Confirm that Roxanne wasn't just blowing smoke. Confirm that Claire really wanted to see him.

Or he could just arrive, blame Roxanne, and take it from there.

NINE

A full moon was on the rise. Claire's house sat on high ground on the western edge of the reservation, overlooking the Ironstone. Her house was a long rectangle of blue and white aluminum siding, a prefab remnant of one of the many economic ventures that the bright lights in the Bureau of Indian Affairs had insisted the tribe try.

Modular housing.

If it had had wheels, it would have been a trailer.

No one was going to photograph the place for *House Beautiful*, and Claire hadn't done much to improve its curb appeal. There was a pad of concrete slabs thrown down in front of the porch that was pretending to be a patio, and she had planted several shrubs against the low deck and a Russian olive at the west corner of the house.

The shrubs had died immediately. The tree had persevered.

Farther out, beyond the house toward the mountains, Thumps could see the shadow of the enormous slump that had taken about a mile of the coulee down into the river valley. One day, the coulee was intact, and the next, the entire edge had disappeared, forcing anyone walking the high trail to the mountains to make a long detour to get around the rip in the earth.

The Slump didn't look all that dangerous, but the raw face was unstable, and if you started to slide, there was nothing to stop you. Two hikers from somewhere in Nevada had tried to go straight across and had been swept to their deaths.

Thumps parked the car next to the tree and waited. Claire would have seen him coming along the river from a long way off, would have heard him pull into the yard.

"New car?" Claire was dressed in blue jeans and a blue work shirt. Her hair was tied back. "Honda Element?"

"It is."

She stood on the porch with her hands on her hips. "Sports jacket, slacks. You on your way to the opera?"

"Not exactly."

Claire shook her head. "Roxanne?"

"Roxanne," said Thumps.

"Let me guess," said Claire. "She said that I was going to cook dinner."

"Elk stew."

"And you were to bring chocolate and flowers."

"No chocolate," said Thumps. "No flowers."

"Good," said Claire, "because there's no dinner either."

Thumps held up a white paper bag with an overweight dragon printed in red on the front. "There is, however, takeout."

"The Fat Dragon?" Claire's face brightened. "General Tao chicken? Pork fried rice?"

"Yes," said Thumps. "And yes."

"Isn't Chinese bad for your diabetes?"

"It is."

"But now that you're here with food," said Claire, "you're thinking that we should eat."

"We'd be fools not to."

"Robert Parker," said Claire. "The Spenser mysteries."

"It worked for him."

"So, I'm Susan?" Claire smiled with just the edges of her mouth. "And you're . . . Pearl?"

"Isn't Pearl the dog?"

Claire's kitchen reminded Thumps that she wasn't the most organized of people. Nor was she the consummate house-keeper that you saw in movies from the 1950s, movies where the women waited for their husbands to return home after a hard day's work so they could bring their man his slippers, his pipe, and a martini, women whose desires were bracketed by fur coats and new appliances.

"You going to say something about my kitchen?"

There were dishes stacked in the sink, empty frozen dinner boxes on the counter, and a couple of old cottage cheese cartons on the windowsill. Thumps wasn't sure, but he hoped that the brown sludge in one of the cartons was bacon grease.

"Nope."

"If I had known you were coming, I would have cleaned the place."

"But you didn't know," said Thumps. "So there was no reason to tidy up."

Claire fished two plates out of the sink and rinsed them off. "You bring chopsticks?"

Thumps set the boxes on the table. "I did."

"You want to talk?"

"I suppose we should."

"Beer," said Claire. "If we're going to have that conversation, we should probably do it with beer."

The General Tao chicken was good, a little soggy from the ride out to the reservation, but as good as could be expected. The pork fried rice was pork fried rice. Thumps didn't think there was much that could hurt it.

"So you knew this was a set-up." Claire helped herself to a large, tangled lump of noodles.

"Educated guess," said Thumps.

"Because this isn't the first time Roxanne has pulled this stunt."

"It's her favourite ploy."

"That it is."

Thumps tried to tear open the plastic packet of soy sauce.

He had no idea what sort of malicious mind had come up with the idea of putting condiments in a plastic bomb shelter. Supposedly, there was a cut in the edge of the packet that would get you started.

"So how was the coast?"

"Great. How was New Zealand?"

Thumps had the packet twisted into a fine knot.

"You want scissors?"

"I hear you and Angie had a good time?"

"We did," said Claire. "How about you?"

Thumps took a sip of his beer. "Doesn't seem to be working, does it?"

"The beer?" said Claire. "The conversation?"

"Anything new on the adoption? The two girls?"

"Isn't going to happen." Claire helped herself to some of the pork fried rice.

"Sorry."

"But Angie has another possibility." Claire reached over and tore an edge off the soy packet with her teeth. "So, tell me about Northern California. Anything get settled?"

Thumps wasn't sure he wanted to tell Claire about Anna and Raymond Oakes. It wasn't betraying a confidence. Anna was dead. Oakes didn't count.

"How's Stick?"

"Stanley's fine," said Claire.

"His father still alive?"

Claire stopped eating. "This sudden interest in my life have something to do with your trip?"

"Nope."

"Anna," said Claire. "Was that her name?"

"It was."

"And her daughter?"

"Callie."

"You weren't Callie's father."

Thumps felt his body tighten. "No."

Claire went back to her beer. "Is that what this is about?"

"Anna had told me that Callie's father was dead."

"But he wasn't?"

"He was in prison."

"Stick's father isn't dead," said Claire. "So far as I know."

"You never talk about him."

"Nothing much to tell." Claire dumped the rest of the rice on her plate. "So Anna had a husband."

"Raymond Oakes," said Thumps. "He was in jail for life. And then he got out."

Claire put her chopsticks down. "I thought they were killed by a serial killer."

"So did I."

"But now you think that this Oakes was responsible?"

"Don't know," said Thumps. "But I'd like to talk to him."

"So, you don't know where he is?" Claire went to the refrigerator and got another beer.

"No idea."

"But you're angry. You think Anna lied to you. You think she betrayed you."

"No, I don't."

"And you think that I've betrayed you as well." Claire leaned forward on her elbows. "You don't talk about Anna or Callie."

"They're dead."

"That was cheap."

"That's not what I meant. Look, they died. They were killed. Anna never told me about Oakes. I didn't know he existed."

Claire softened a little. "And you think you could have saved them if you had known?"

"Maybe."

"And you think you can save me." Claire reached out and touched his hand. "Before I left for New Zealand, I asked you if you were interested in a relationship with me."

"You and children."

Claire nodded. "Did you ever come to a decision?"

Thumps wondered if there was another beer in the fridge. "I'd like to give it a try."

"But you have unfinished business." Claire pulled her hand away and pushed back. "Raymond Oakes. You're going after him, aren't you?"

"I need to finish it."

"And you'd like me to be waiting when you're all done playing avenging angel." Claire took the plates to the sink and put them on top of the stack.

"I need to finish it."

Claire nodded. "When you turn back out of the driveway, make sure you don't hit the tree."

THE MOON WAS HIGH in the sky, and the light lit up the land. Thumps pushed the Honda along the river road, off the reservation, and onto the main highway. Dinner had gone as poorly as he had imagined, and as he drove back into Chinook, he wondered why he had bothered to return. If all he wanted was to find Oakes, he could have just kept working the case, could have stayed on the road until he ran the man down. Maybe he wanted to see what he was giving up, a last look at what he had, an inventory of value, the cost of revenge.

It all seemed a little melodramatic. The notion of righteous retribution. Determined lawman tracks the bad guy around the countryside, and after a search that takes years, lawman finds his quarry, captures him, and brings him back for trial.

Or just kills him.

But when he returns, he discovers that the heroine has moved on, has married someone else, and is living happily ever after.

Claire had been clear. She wasn't going to wait.

And she had been right about him. He wasn't going to step away. Anna was dead. Callie was dead. No point in trying to pretend that he was doing it for them.

He was doing it for himself.

TEN

Thumps spent a restless night in a cold bed, waking up at sporadic intervals to go to the bathroom and to revisit what he should have said, what he should have done. He hadn't seen Claire in over a month, and the Fat Dragon dinner offering aside, she hadn't seemed all that thrilled to find him at her door. Thumps had hoped she would want him to spend the night, had brought his toothbrush, just in case.

Absence, it would appear, didn't necessarily make the heart grow fonder.

And how did he feel? Relationships were a team sport. What did he want? From time to time, Claire had thrown out the idea of living together. How had he reacted? He didn't remember being enthusiastic. When she had tried to adopt the two sisters out of Browning, had he jumped at the opportunity?

What did that say about him?

Thumps was willing to concede that people were not his strong suit, but maybe it was more than that. Maybe he was a closet misanthrope.

Or worse.

So now it was morning, and any reflections on interpersonal relationship theories would have to wait. The first thing on the agenda was breakfast. Two choices. He could make it himself, or he could have someone else make it for him.

Thumps opened the refrigerator. There were the end pieces of a loaf of bread and a sliver of butter that had survived the breakfast that Cooley had made.

Okay, Al's it was.

After that, he would continue the hunt for Raymond Oakes.

He and Leon Ranger had started the process, but toward the end of the second week in Eureka, Leon had had to fly to Reno, Nevada, for a conference on militia organizations and the proliferation of assault weapons. Thumps had lost his access to law-enforcement databases and had been reduced to rummaging in the boxes that Ron Peat had left for him.

Now that he was back in Chinook, he could camp out in the sheriff's office and use Duke's computer to search for Oakes, or he could go to the Aegean and talk Archie into hacking the databases he needed.

The sheriff's office would mean skirmishing with an antiquated computer and listening to the man try to talk him into returning to police work. The Aegean had the newer, faster computer, but it came with Archie, and the little Greek would want to pry into Thumps's private life while offering up volumes of advice on how that life should be lived.

Neither was a perfect solution. He'd have to make a decision, of course. And while decisions such as this were easier to make than decisions of the heart, they should only be made on a full stomach.

Thumps had just put on his jacket when the phone rang. It didn't ring all that much, and his general inclination was not to answer it. The chances were good that it was the sheriff or Archie, and they only called when they wanted him to do something. But it could also be Claire. Maybe she had had second thoughts about last evening. Maybe she had warmed to the idea of having a knight errant in her life.

"Hello."

"Is this Thumps DreadfulWater?"

The voice had the timbre and pitch of duct-cleaning services, credit-card offerings, and shopping surveys.

"Not interested."

"Not selling," said the voice quickly. "We have a mutual friend."

Thumps waited.

"Nina Maslow."

"She's dead."

"Have you had breakfast?" said the voice.

"What about Maslow?"

"We're here at the Tucker," said the voice. "It's in regard to the Obsidian Murders."

OBSIDIAN

Thumps's grip tightened on the phone. "Who is this?"

"Can we say half an hour?"

There were any number of reasons for not having a phone. Thumps could think of several without even trying. The damn thing was always too loud, always too close, always unnerving. It was like standing in a closet next to a siren. Worse, you never knew who was going to be on the other end of the line.

Sometimes, it was friends.

Sometimes, it was the past.

THE TUCKER WAS the upscale hotel in town. According to the sign next to the front door, it was number one on Trip-Advisor.

Whatever that was supposed to mean.

The original hotel had been built in the late nineteenth century and had been dragged through the twentieth century as a hospital, a general store, a warehouse, a roller rink, and a makeshift theatre for art films from France and Italy that no one wanted to watch, films that no one understood.

The voice on the phone had said breakfast, which meant the Quick Claim. The coffee shop was thinly populated. Two families with moms and dads. One with three kids, two boys, one girl, and the other with three girls. An older couple kept glancing over their shoulders to make sure none of the children got loose. Or too close.

"Mr. DreadfulWater."

The voice was sitting at a round table near the window with two other people, a man and a woman.

"Please," said the voice. "Join us."

The voice was tall with thick hair, an ex-athlete by the look of him. Broad shoulders, slim hips, a quick, neon smile. The woman was thicker, top to bottom, with clear eyes and cold hair. Viking stock, capable of throwing pigs over a shoulder with one arm and swinging a battle axe with the other.

The third member of the gang was an older man who was average in all ways. Medium height, medium weight, medium complexion. Someone you could lose in a shoebox.

"Anthony Mercer," said the voice. "This is Runa Gerson. And our somewhat taciturn colleague is Harold Shipman."

"Just Harry." The tattoo on the back of Shipman's hand was of a small black star. The ring was too large for his finger.

"My apologies for the phone call." Mercer tried to look apologetic. "Mysterious, intriguing, juvenile. It's the director in me."

Mercer, Gerson, and Shipman. It sounded as though Thumps had stumbled into a law firm. Not that the three people sitting at the table looked like lawyers. So maybe the old joke had some validity.

Why do lawyers look like psychopaths?

Because they don't want to look like politicians.

"Sit. Please," said Mercer. "Nina spoke highly of you."

"We ordered a bunch of food." Gerson waved a hand at the server. "Figured we'd share."

Part of Gerson's little finger was missing. Thumps tried not to look, but Gerson caught him.

"It's a conversation piece," she said. "I lost it to a wolf in the Yukon."

"Yesterday, it was the result of a knife fight with a Bedouin in North Africa," said Mercer.

Gerson smiled. "More exciting than getting it caught in a door jamb when I was three."

"This is a general outline of the project." Mercer took a folder out of a bag and handed it to Thumps. "You don't have to read it now."

"This was Nina's baby," said Gerson. "We're just picking up the pieces and moving forward."

Thumps looked at the title on the folder. *The Obsidian Murders.*

"*Malice Aforethought?*"

Mercer shook his head. "No," he said. "*Malice Aforethought* was cancelled."

"They lost their star and a producer," said Gerson. "There's no recovering from that."

"Maslow and Sydney Pearl were in town this summer," said Mercer. "The Samuels episode?"

"What was his name?" Shipman waited.

"Calder Banks," said Gerson. "Hosted the show. Son of a bitch killed Nina because she found out he had killed that actress in Las Vegas."

"Amelia Nash," said Mercer. "I met her once."

Thumps rubbed his temple. "So this is *Malice Aforethought, Part Two?*"

"The networks are drowning in reality shows." Mercer looked pleased with himself. "We're talking a cable movie."

"*Obsidian*," said Gerson. "It's got real punch."

Thumps could feel his defences go up. "So, you guys worked with Maslow?"

In Thumps's experience, people who answered questions too quickly were generally lying, and people who had to think about their answers were lying as well. There were even a number of theories that linked deceit with facial expressions. Eyes darting back and forth, blinking, closing for a second or two were all indicators of a lie. Right-handed individuals tended to look directly to their right when lying about something they heard, and down and to the right when they were lying about smells or sensations.

Thumps wasn't sure that any of these markers were accurate, but Mercer's eyes had begun to dart back and forth, and Gerson's eyes were blinking. Only Shipman seemed relaxed.

"We didn't actually work with Nina," said Mercer.

"But we admired her work," said Gerson.

Shipman shifted in his chair. "You've caught us."

Thumps wasn't sure he had caught anything.

"Tony and Runa didn't know Nina," said Shipman. "I was the only one who actually worked with her. I did some of the research for her projects."

Of the three, based on first impressions, Shipman was the most intriguing. Mercer and Gerson seemed eager to please. Shipman didn't seem to care.

"I brought her the Obsidian Murders. She was going to use it for *Malice Aforethought*. I talked her out of it. It was too good for a single episode. It needed more space."

"And then she was murdered."

"Yes," said Shipman. "Then she was murdered."

"Harry's right," said Mercer. "It has a great storyline."

"I understand that Sydney Pearl gave you Nina's file on the killings." It wasn't a question, and Shipman didn't wait for Thumps to respond. "But that file wasn't complete. Or at least, it wasn't up to date. At the time she died, I was following up on a couple of ideas that Nina had developed."

"I'm not working the case," said Thumps.

"You spent a month in Eureka."

"Tying up loose ends."

Shipman set a second file on the table. "Raymond Oakes?"

Thumps waited.

"Anna Tripp's husband?" said Shipman. "He got out of prison several months before the killings began."

Thumps waited some more.

"The police thought the Obsidian Murders were the work of one individual," said Shipman. "Nina had two theories that she was exploring. One that the police were right, that the killings were the work of one individual. But she also thought there was a good possibility that the killings were the work of two people. Unrelated. In the second scenario, Oakes kills Tripp and her daughter, while an unsub kills the other people. She believed that Oakes used the other murders to cover up his crime."

"A serial killer," said Gerson, "and a homicidal spouse."

Thumps and Ranger had already gotten that far. No hard evidence. Just circumstantial debris. And without Oakes, that's all it would ever be.

"Nina had me looking for Oakes," said Shipman. "I tracked him as far as Rexburg before he disappeared."

That was new. Other than the fact that Oakes had been released from prison, they hadn't been able to find any trace of the man, hadn't been able to find any hint of where he had been before the killings.

Or after.

"She also had me looking at other serial killings," said Shipman. "Nina had a theory that Northern California wasn't the first time."

All the law enforcement agencies involved had looked into that possibility and had come up empty. There had been a number of cases that had fit the same general profile of the Obsidian Murders. A series of homicides over a short period of time. Victims who had no relationship to one another. A method of marking each killing. If Thumps remembered correctly, there had been four that had looked promising. One in Arizona. Another in Colorado. Oregon. And Nevada.

But in each case, the killer had been caught or killed and the case solved.

Thumps touched the file Shipman had put on the table. "So, if I help you," he said, "you'll give me this new information."

"Figured we'd make you an offer you can't refuse," said Shipman in a better-than-average Marlon Brando voice.

"What Harry means," said Gerson, "is that the file is yours whether you help us or not. Nina would have wanted you to have it."

"True," said Shipman. "She told me if anyone could catch the Obsidian killer, it was you."

"But we'd appreciate your assistance," said Mercer.

"We're hoping you have a vested interest in getting the story right."

Thumps didn't open the folder, didn't want to create the impression that there was a quid pro quo in the making. Movies and murder investigations were two different things. They had little in common.

The food arrived. Sausage, eggs, toast, fruit, coffee. Thumps tried to remember the first rule of a diabetic. Small meals. Frequent meals.

"Harry's going to write the script," said Mercer. "I'm directing. Runa's producing."

"We're getting together tomorrow," said Gerson. "Two o'clock. Room 326."

"We're hoping you'll come and talk to us," said Shipman.

"Background about Clam Beach and the sheriff's department. Personal details about Anna Tripp and her daughter, Tally."

"Callie," said Thumps.

"Sorry. Callie."

"It would help," said Gerson, "to have an idea of who the characters are."

"But we don't want to make it a melodrama," said Shipman.

"No one wants that," said Mercer. "That's why we need you."

Shipman helped himself to the sausages and the eggs. "Of course, if I were you, I'd turn us down."

The eggs were good. So was the toast. Thumps took the two folders and put them on the seat beside him.

"I mean, who wants to be involved in a sleazy film that turns a horrific tragedy into a prime-time circus for a viewing audience of degenerate clowns." Shipman paused. "Am I right?"

"Easy, Harry," said Mercer. "Mr. DreadfulWater might think you're serious."

"And," said Shipman, "I imagine that you're going to go looking for Oakes."

"You know where he is?"

Shipman played with the ring, an emerald in a heavy gold setting. "Are you asking if I'm withholding information?"

"Are you?"

"After Tripp and her daughter were killed, you quit your job as a deputy sheriff." Shipman didn't wait for a confirmation. "And then you wound up in Chinook."

Thumps tried the sausage. It was salty and had a somewhat sweet flavour.

"I can put Oakes in Arcata just before the killings began. So, we know he was in the area. Which means he probably knew about you and Anna. He's still there after the murders. Then suddenly, he's on the road. California, Oregon, Idaho. Straight driving so far as I can tell. He finally stops the second night in Rexburg."

Thumps pulled up a map of the western states in his head.

"And then he disappears. Nada."

"You can see where Harry is going with this," said Mercer.

"What happened in Rexburg?" said Shipman. "And where was he headed in such a hurry?"

"Maybe he stayed in Rexburg."

"I checked," said Shipman. "He didn't."

"We think he was coming here." Mercer drew his fork across the tablecloth. "When Oakes left the coast, we think he was coming here."

"And the only reason he would do that," said Shipman, "is you."

ELEVEN

Rexburg, Idaho.

Thumps stood in front of the Tucker and tried to make sense of this new piece of information. Shipman had suggested that Oakes had been following him, had been on his way to Chinook when the man dropped off the map. The theory was interesting, but it didn't make much sense.

After Anna and Callie had been killed, Thumps had resigned from the sheriff's department, had thrown whatever he could into his Volvo, and had headed east. At the time, he had had no idea of where he was going or what he was going to do. A blown fuel pump had forced him to remain in Chinook while he waited for a new part. But there was no way he could have anticipated that he would stay.

Which meant that Chinook would have been impossible for Oakes to predict.

Still it was intriguing. The timing. The route Oakes had taken.

Shipman was right. Oakes could have known about Thumps and Anna, could have known that his wife was with another man. Was that it? A matter of anger? Vengeance? And then he had come after Thumps?

You could make the pieces fit. But only if you pressed hard enough.

And now, whatever the answer might be, Mercer, Gerson, Shipman, et al., wanted to make a movie out of the tragedy, out of the crime. Thumps had never understood the fascination that people had with mayhem, but he knew that violence and cruelty, along with murder in all its unimaginable forms, had become staples for the world of prime-time television.

Zombie apocalypses. Housewives from hell. Medical disasters.

People, it seemed, liked to be disgusted, liked to be terrified, and broadcasters without borders had quickly learned to mine this deep and disturbing vein in the American psyche.

MIRRORS WAS THE new kid on the block, a specialty coffee shop that had been fashioned after a famous coffee shop in Uruguay. Café Brasilero in Montevideo had been the favourite haunt of the writer Eduardo Galeano. Thumps had not read any of Galeano's work. Archie would know the man, but asking Archie about anything in print was opening the gates to literary hell.

If Galeano was a writer worth reading, the little Greek would want to know why Thumps hadn't read him already. This would be followed by a vigorous admonition to buy a book or two or at least check out several volumes from the library, followed by an intensive quiz on content and meaning.

Thumps could look the man up on the internet, get the "Galeano for Dummies" version, and hope that this modicum of knowledge would hold Archie at bay. Better yet, he should probably not even mention the Uruguayan at all.

Mirrors was crowded, but Thumps found a small table in a corner. As far as he could see, he was the only person in the place who did not have a laptop.

Sensitive electronics and hot water.

It seemed an odd combination. He wondered how many computers met their deaths each year in coffee shops around the world. A bump, a careless server, an inattentive moment over a cute animal video, and another hard drive winds up in a Nigerian landfill.

When Thumps had been in Mirrors with Nina Maslow, he had had black coffee. Maslow had had something with milk and chocolate. He wasn't sure he liked the place. It felt a little too much like a home-decorating spread in a glossy magazine.

And he didn't need any more coffee.

On the other hand, he couldn't imagine anyone looking for him here. He put the two folders on the table and opened the first one.

"Hi," said the server. "This your first time in Mirrors?"

"No."

"Great. My name is Jenny, and our special today is oliang."

Thumps tried to imagine what that might be.

"It's a Thai drink," said Jenny. "Basically, it's an iced corn, soybean, sesame coffee. You put all of the ingredients into a coffee sock, pour boiling water through it, and let it steep for about fourteen minutes. Then you add ice and condensed milk, and that's oliang."

"So, it's cold?"

"It is."

Thumps wondered why anyone would start coffee out in a sock. Or why, after they had got the coffee nice and hot, they would put in ice.

"Black."

Jenny looked somewhat confused. "Black?"

"Coffee," said Thumps. "Black coffee."

"Nothing in it?"

"Just coffee. No ice. No sock."

"Wow. That's like espresso."

"Are you bothering this young woman?"

Thumps hadn't seen Ora Mae Foreman come in, but there she was standing in front of the table, her hands on her hips.

So much for peace and quiet and anonymity.

"Hi, Ora Mae."

Ora Mae didn't ask if she was disturbing him or if she could sit down. She just did.

"I don't see any visible injuries," she said, "so I'm guessing Beth hasn't caught up with you yet."

Thumps had no idea what Ora Mae was talking about. And then he did. "Shit."

"Shit is right," said Ora Mae. "As in, you're in the shithouse."

"The appointment." Thumps tried to look repentant. "Nine thirty. For the blood test."

"Woman's not going to chase you down," said Ora Mae. "You want to die a slow, awful death, that's your affair."

"I just forgot."

"Oh yeah," said Ora Mae. "That bird will fly."

"Shit."

"And speaking of our feathered friends," said Ora Mae, "a little bird told me that you want to sell your house."

"Does that little bird run a café?"

"I don't reveal my sources," said Ora Mae, "but if you are going to sell, I certainly expect to get the listing."

"I'm *thinking* about selling."

Ora Mae took out her phone and began punching buttons. "Does that mean you're planning to leave town?"

"Maybe I just want to downsize."

"Honey," said Ora Mae, "you downsize any more, and you be in a pickup with a camper top."

The server returned. Thumps checked the cup. Yes, it was hot, and it was black.

Ora Mae stared at her phone for a moment. Then she pushed

some more buttons. "You come to a place like this and order black coffee?"

"How can you do that?"

"What?"

"Text and talk at the same time."

"Checking the comps." Ora Mae set the phone on the table. "So, you want to know what your sad sack of a bungalow is worth?"

"I'm just curious."

"Depends on what you're willing to spend to make it presentable."

"What's wrong with my house?"

"Well," said Ora Mae, "that trailer-trash yard to start."

"That's all natural biodiversity."

"That what they're calling weeds these days?"

"Just a ball-park figure."

"Don't do ball park," said Ora Mae. "Real estate is a science. For instance, why do you want to sell?"

"That would be my business."

Ora Mae gave Thumps the look that supermarket mothers reserved for their children. "Real estate agents are like doctors and lawyers and priests."

"Priests?"

"What you tell us is completely confidential."

"There's nothing confidential about real estate. It's all public record."

"For instance," said Ora Mae, "if you're selling because you have a broken heart and are wanting to get out of Dodge as quickly as possible, that's one price."

"Ora Mae . . ."

"But if you're selling to move up in the market, that's another price."

Thumps tried to slow the train. "What if I just want to sell? Maybe I don't want the responsibility of a house. Maybe I don't want a mortgage. Maybe I think renting makes more sense."

"That sounds like depression," said Ora Mae. "But between you and me, I don't think she's serious."

It took Thumps a moment to realize that the conversation had taken a right turn when he wasn't looking.

"Serious?"

"He's good-looking and all that," said Ora Mae. "But Claire's not the type of person to be impressed with muscles and a nice car."

"Claire?"

"Now me," said Ora Mae, "you can turn my head with some quality bling."

"Claire is seeing someone?"

"Well, you didn't expect her to sit around while you ran your raggedy ass around the countryside chasing bad guys."

Thumps tried to think of whom Claire might be seeing. The pool of eligible males in Chinook was not very deep. More a wading pool.

"He's from Lethbridge."

"Alberta?" said Thumps. "She's dating a Canadian?"

Ora Mae shook her head. "Women don't *date* anymore. We *see* each other. We *get together*. We *have coffee*."

"Claire's having coffee with a Canadian?"

"He's working on a water project with the tribe." Ora Mae paused and gave Thumps a slow-motion wink.

"Great."

"So, why do you want to sell your house?"

ORA MAE DIDN'T have any more information about Claire's Canadian, and by the time she left to go back to Wild Rose Realty, Thumps wasn't even sure that the man existed. Muscles and a nice car could just be another one of Roxanne Heavy Runner's romantic schemes. Ora Mae would certainly play along with that. She and Roxanne shared the same high opinion of men and their ability to manage complex emotions and interpersonal relations.

As Thumps waited for the server to refill his cup, he realized that Ora Mae hadn't told him how much his house was worth. Or how long it might take to sell it. Or what he was going to have to do to make it attractive to a potential buyer.

The yard. Ora Mae was right about the yard.

The house itself was okay. A little paint. Hard-scrub the bathtub and the toilet. Clean the windows. Replace the shingles on the back roof.

The yard was a different matter. The front had started off as a well-manicured lawn. Then the first fall, grub worms made an appearance, followed by raccoons and skunks. Thumps could remember coming out one morning to find the yard ripped up by the pesky mammals who had spent a festive evening digging up the beetle larvae and leaving the ground looking as though some deranged gardener had come through with a Rototiller.

He raked out the damage and threw down grass seed only to have dandelions, knapweed, and thistles take over. Another year of grubs, and raccoons and skunks, and more weeds, and the lawn gave way to a prairie diorama.

Thumps had seen yards in magazines that were filled with native plants, which were intended to mimic the surrounding environment. His yard was not one of those.

Still, if it meant a sale, he could always hire the folks at the Ironstone nursery to dig up the ground and put down sod. Maybe put in a tree or a couple of bushes to improve the curb appeal.

"So, what happened on the coast?"

Archie Kousoulas pulled up a chair and sat down with a thump. The little Greek had traded his dust mask and goggles for jeans and a windbreaker.

"Hi, Archie."

"Don't 'Hi, Archie' me."

"How's the construction going?"

"And don't be changing the subject." Archie turned the files around so he could read them. "Is this it?"

Thumps pulled the files back. "This is a police investigation."

"Thought you were a photographer."

"I'm also a deputy sheriff."

"Duke gave you a badge?"

"I left it at home."

Archie leaned back in the chair. "This the same home you're trying to sell?"

It took Thumps a moment to put the pieces together. "Ora Mae texted you?"

Archie held up his phone. "That's what friends do."

"Friends leave friends alone."

"She said you're depressed, that you're looking to sell your house and leave town, that an intervention is in order."

So coming to Mirrors hadn't been any safer than wandering the streets of Chinook with a sandwich board sign that said, "Help Me."

Archie lowered his voice. "How old is the case? If it didn't get solved back then, what are the chances you'll solve it now?"

"Like you said, there's new information."

"Like what?"

"Like it's confidential information."

"Does Duke know?"

"Con-fi-den-tial."

"And if Duke knows," said the little Greek, "then I should know."

Thumps wasn't about to ask what leap of logic had helped Archie to that conclusion.

"Besides," said Archie, "if you have some new information, you're going to have to check it out. And since Duke's computer isn't worth shit, at some point, you're going to want to use mine."

"I can get my own computer."

"You'll get it out of the box in one piece, maybe even get it plugged in and turned on."

"Archie . . ."

"But after that, all bets are off."

Archie ordered a *caffè gommosa*, which turned out to be a shot of espresso poured over a single marshmallow.

"A marshmallow?"

"It originated in Seattle or Portland." Archie poked the marshmallow. "It doesn't melt completely. *Caffè gommosa* is Italian for 'rubbery coffee.'"

"It looks disgusting."

"It's an acquired taste." Archie pushed the marshmallow to the bottom of the cup and held it there with his spoon. "While you were gone, I did some research into serial killings."

"Archie . . ."

"You can thank me later."

"The FBI already did that. So did the state police."

"And they came up with nothing. Right?"

"They came up with a number of cases," said Thumps. "All of them solved."

"I know," said Archie. "So, when you have time and you've

gotten your head out of your ass, stop by the bookstore and we'll talk."

"I don't do cryptic."

"You going to the car show party?" Archie settled in the chair. "Cooley said you're thinking about buying a 1956 Chevrolet Bel Air."

"Not me," said Thumps. "Moses."

"Moses doesn't drive."

Archie finished his espresso. What was left of the marshmallow lay at the bottom of the cup like a lump of white pus.

"You know that looks disgusting, right?"

"Then don't look." Archie stood up and brushed off his pants. "Gabby and I are going to go to the party in vintage attire. I'll bet she could find a nice outfit for you."

"I'm fine."

"You're not fine," said Archie. "How many friends do you think you have?"

"I've got you."

Thumps wasn't sure if Archie would smile or frown. He did neither.

"The way things are going," the little Greek said, "you're going to need more than that."

TWELVE

Aside from the periodic shrieking of the espresso machine, Mirrors was unexpectedly tranquil, a caffeine retreat filled with the low chants of hard drives and the slow benedictions of people shuffling their feet and adjusting their earbuds.

The new monastic mantra.

Thumps nursed his coffee, but he knew he couldn't stay long. Any moment, the third wave of intervention might arrive. Ora Mae and Archie had been enough for one day. If he wanted to spend his time being interrogated about his personal life, he could always go to Al's.

Thumps wondered if ventures such as Mirrors were the harbinger of things to come. A small-box store of expensive drinks and sugary baked goods with a rotating staff of well-mannered young people passing through on their way to someplace else.

Overpriced, quiet, anonymous.

He had paid the bill and was to the door before he realized he was humming the theme to *Cheers*.

THE MAIL WAS still waiting for him on the kitchen table. He set the files that Shipman had given him next to the stack of junk mail and flyers and headed downstairs to the basement. How long had it been since he had spent time in the darkroom? Two months? More? The trays were stacked in the sink on the wood racks. If he was going to do any printing, he would have to mix up new chemistry. Developer, stop bath, fix. The backlog of negatives was on the table next to the enlarger, and if he remembered correctly, there were some promising images in the lot.

Or he could just turn out the light and disappear into the blackness. If only the darkroom had a toilet, a bar fridge, and a recliner.

Thumps was trying to imagine how he might manage such a makeover when he heard the front door open and felt someone walk across his kitchen floor. The footsteps were light and cautious. It wasn't Cooley, and it wasn't the sheriff. Nor was it his next-door neighbour, Dixie Kane. They all walked as though they had elephant genes floating about in their genetic pools.

Archie Kousoulas was quicker and lighter on his feet, but the little Greek would never have come into the house with anything resembling stealth. By now, the house would have been filled with the sound of his voice, as he searched the rooms, one by one.

And then the walking stopped, and a chair was pulled out, and Thumps heard someone sit down.

Curious.

Goldilocks? Come back to check the furniture and the porridge?

Thumps opened the door quietly and slipped out of the darkroom, the heavy wood leg of his Ries tripod in one hand. In case it was the bears instead.

As it turned out, it was neither.

"Rose?"

Rose Twining was sitting at the table, opening a letter. To her credit, she didn't shriek.

"What are you doing here?"

Rose Twining lived four houses down the block, in a yellow and white bungalow. She had been born there, had lived her entire life in Chinook. At least that's what she told everyone.

"Goodness," said Rose. "You gave me a proper start."

"Is that my mail?"

"I didn't know you got home." Rose squeezed her lips together. "Who won the pool?"

Now that Thumps looked more closely, he could see that all the letters had been slit open.

Rose held up the letter she had just opened. "Dixie had to go to Denver. He asked me to look after your place."

"You've been reading my mail?"

"Had to be sure there was nothing important that needed attention," said Rose. "Maybe something from the IRS or a notice from Publishers Clearing House."

Before Thumps knew Rose better, he had believed most of what she told him about herself. That her mother was a Gypsy from Romania. That her father was a French count. That she had a brother who was a missionary in Africa.

"And your watch arrived." Rose reached into her jacket pocket and came up with a large pocket watch. "My first husband used to carry one of these."

"This came for me?"

"I would have figured you for a wristwatch guy," said Rose. "These things are a little old-fashioned."

"It's not my watch."

"And large," said Rose. "Kinda heavy to be carrying around all the time."

"You sure it came for me?"

"Had your name on the package."

"Did you happen to keep the packaging?"

"Why?"

Thumps picked up the watch and turned it over in his hand. It was heavy. Steel case with a white porcelain face. "Rockford" on the dial.

"Be handy to have the return address or the postmark," said Thumps. "See where it came from."

"If it's not your watch, why would someone send it to you?" Rose put a deck of playing cards on the table and shuffled them. "Okay," she said, "cut 'em."

"Don't need my fortune told."

"Best to know what's coming down the road," said Rose. "That way, you're not surprised when it arrives."

Thumps cut the cards.

"My mother showed me how to read the cards," said Rose. "Did I ever tell you that?"

"Yes," said Thumps, "you did."

"Look at that." Rose held up a card. "The ten of diamonds."

"Money," said Thumps. "Right?"

"Sometimes." Rose laid the cards out in a pattern on the table. "And look here. The king of hearts."

You didn't move Rose quickly. Once you let her in your house, and once she had her cards out, there was no rushing her.

"The four of hearts suggests a long trip," said Rose.

"Been there, done that."

Rose turned over the ace of spades. "And here's a problem you're going to have to deal with."

Rose didn't look much like a Gypsy. She had thin brown hair that hung off her head like wet laundry. And large, thick ears. Her face was round and when she wrinkled her nose, she looked like a mouse. As far as Thumps could tell, Rose only had two dresses. Today, she was wearing the red one with the large yellow flowers. The other dress was green with red flowers.

"You want me to do a reading for your love life?"

"Love life is fine."

"Your refrigerator is empty." Rose looked around the house. "And you're out of tea. That's never a good sign."

"Haven't been grocery shopping yet."

"And your cat ran away." Rose laid the ace of spades on top of the queen of clubs. "Maybe it's not you," she said. "Maybe it's the house."

"Rose . . ."

"Houses have personalities, you know. Maybe yours isn't cat friendly. Maybe there were dogs living here before you moved in."

Rose fancied herself the neighbourhood historian. Which was a polite way of framing a certain nosiness and an inclination to snoop.

Thumps liked Rose, though he liked her better from a distance.

"You got a couple of bills that need attention." Rose put the cards back in the pack. "And you're paying too much for your phone. That new company out of Great Falls has better rates."

"Thanks, Rose."

"You planning on staying home for a while?"

"I am."

"What about your cat?"

Thumps sighed.

"I could keep tabs on her," said Rose. "Make sure she's happy. Maybe she's having second thoughts."

"Not necessary."

Rose made her way to the door. "People are easy enough," she said. "But with cats, you never know."

THUMPS STOOD AT the sink and watched Rose make her way down the street. So far as he knew, she lived alone. According to Rose, she had been married twice or three times or once, but her husband had been killed in the war or he had run off or he had died of a nasty disease. Sometimes there were four children, all doing well in large city centres back east, or there was just one daughter with whom she did not get along, or two boys who sent her money every month.

Archie figured that Rose changed her story to suit her mood.

"It's confusing," he had told Thumps, "but there's no real harm in it."

Thumps liked the woman, but it was a bit irksome to find her in his house reading his mail. Where else had she been? The bathroom and the medicine cabinet? His cupboards and the refrigerator? Under the bed? Thumps flashed on a mental picture of Rose rummaging through the house, making notes in her book, taking photos.

Thumps had no reason to believe that the woman was lonely or depressed, but there was a suggestion of solitude, a scent of sadness. Or was he just seeing himself in Rose? The comparisons were easy enough to draw. He lived alone. He didn't have a partner, no children. He spent most of his days talking to himself. There had been a cat, but now there wasn't.

He didn't keep a notebook. He didn't sit on the porch and watch his neighbours through binoculars. But perhaps that was what was waiting for him a little further down the line.

THE BILLS WERE the usual suspects. The majority of them were paid directly out of his chequing account. He would have to remember to enter the amounts so he could keep the running balance up to date.

The letters were more junk mail. In envelopes.

An offer to increase the credit limit on a card he didn't have. An appeal from a Christian organization to help put bibles in the bowls of starving kids. A reminder from the cable company that he could get TV, internet, and phone for as little as $29.95. A personal invitation to attend a free seminar on real estate investing that promised to change his financial life forever.

He had read somewhere that, in the U.S. alone, it took over 100 million trees to produce the junk mail sent out each year. Four billion trees in the world at large.

Not a ringing endorsement for clever creatures with large brains.

Thumps hadn't intended to evaluate his life, but as he sat there at the table, he began going over what he did of a day.

Get up. Eat. Photograph a mountain. Eat. Work in the darkroom. Eat. Sit in an empty house and stare at the walls. Eat. Go to bed. Get up and repeat.

If he were to come away with anything from this schedule, it would be that his life revolved around food and little else. It didn't feel like a meaningless existence, but perhaps that's what happened when you lived alone long enough. When you no longer noticed the silence. Or felt the cold.

The answer to such malaise was action. Get out of the house. Walk along the river in the sunshine. Take in a movie. Sign up for a membership at a gym. Buy something expensive. Call Claire to see if she would like to drive over to Kalispell or Whitefish and spend a weekend in the hot tub of some swank resort.

But if the rumours of Claire and her Canadian were true, then Thumps would just have to deal with it. Being alone wasn't all that bad. And if he found isolation depressing, he could always try something like online dating. Mind you, the notion that you could find a compatible relationship by filling out a questionnaire was staggering in its comic absurdity.

And each time he got this far, the past would reach out and grab him. Anna Tripp. Callie Tripp. Eureka. The Obsidian Murders. The unfinished business of his life. Perhaps it would never be finished.

THE LATE-AFTERNOON SUN lit up the street and stretched long shadows out across the land. Thumps couldn't remember the last time he had roamed the neighbourhood. Most of the houses were quiet, the adults at work, the children in school. Thumps walked to where the sidewalk turned into prairie and turned south. How many streets could he manage? If he saw someone he knew, would he stop and talk? Exactly how many of his neighbours did he know? Dixie? Rose? Was that it?

After twenty minutes, he gave up and turned to head home. And almost missed the For Sale sign on the lawn of the blue and white house.

The Passangs. Dorjee and Tenzin. Three kids. One surly cat. Stuck to the face of the realty sign was a Sold sticker.

Thumps crossed the street. The last time he had been by, there had been curtains in the window. Now the windows were bare, and he could see parts of empty rooms. The front lawn needed to be cut, and there were flyers scattered on the porch.

So the Passangs were gone. Was Freeway gone as well? There was no reason for him to be upset. After all, the cat had left him, run off to another family. There were reasons for the infidelity, for the betrayal.

Not that a cat would need a reason.

So, where had the family gone? Across town? Out of state? Cats didn't like change all that well. Thumps wanted Freeway to be happy, but there was a part of him that hoped she would wake up one morning and realize what she had lost, would see the error of her ways and come home to him.

Romantic melancholy.

Still, the Passangs could have left Freeway behind. Maybe

she was cowering under the house, afraid and hungry, not knowing what to do. Thumps walked around the house and looked in the places a cranky cat might hide, but if Freeway was there, she wasn't showing herself. More likely she was in the back of a car with the three Passang children, heading off to places unknown, to a new life.

It was always more exciting to be the one going rather than the one left behind.

He made one last circuit, checking the bushes and the hedge. No cat. Except for the sign on the front lawn, there wasn't much difference between this house and his. World War II bungalows with clapboard siding. Two bedrooms, one bath. A small lawn that ran out to the street. A peaked roof with dark asphalt shingles.

Both ordinary in all ways. One vacant. One empty.

As he headed home, Thumps tried to imagine who had bought the house and how long it would be before they moved in.

Young family. Single mother. An older couple who were downsizing.

Maybe he should walk the neighbourhood more often, get to know his neighbours, make the strolls a part of a new social regime, a physical activity to help draw him out and put him in the world.

It was a heady idea, full of promises, and possibilities. As well as expectations and obligations. And by the time he reached his house and was safely inside, the idea, mercifully, had passed away.

THIRTEEN

By the time Thumps arrived at the fairgrounds, Anderson Cole's vintage car party was in full swing. He had called Claire, had left a message on her answering machine.

"Going to the car show. Want to meet for a burger?"

It hadn't been a particularly romantic message. More utilitarian. Serviceable. Insipid.

"Going to the car show. Want to catch dinner? I miss you" would have been better, but he hadn't thought of that until he was walking across the grass toward the roped-off area reserved for the collectible cars.

He wasn't sure why he had come. He wasn't in the market for a vintage car, and he wasn't in the mood to talk to anyone. And now, here he was, out in the open and vulnerable. So this is how social felt. Somewhere between indifferent and uncomfortable.

Thumps checked his watch. He'd stay for half an hour. No sense overdoing communal interaction the first time out.

"Thumps!"

Thumps didn't have to turn to see who had found him.

Archie was not alone. "You remember Gabby?"

Gabriella Santucci was on Archie's arm, the two of them dressed in vintage clothing. They looked like an advertisement from a 1940s Sears catalogue.

"You are invited to the grand opening." Gabby handed him a card. "We will find you something better to wear than the jeans."

"Thumps likes jeans," said Archie. "That's all he ever wears."

"Such bad habits the American man has," said Gabby.

"Had a visit from some movie people," said Archie. "You know about this?"

"Two men and a woman?"

"Mercer, Gerson, and Shipman," said Archie. "They want to do a movie on the Obsidian Murders."

Thumps glanced at his watch. Maybe he'd only stay for fifteen minutes.

"I have a pair of men's slacks. Wool and cashmere," said Gabby. "Early 1950s. Very soft, supple."

"Told them they should hire me as a research consultant," said Archie.

"You?"

"Sure," said Archie. "I know almost as much about the case as you do, and I'm not anti-social."

"Why do you not join us?" said Gabby. "Archie is going to show me his first car."

"Not the exact car," said Archie. "Just the same year and model."

Thumps checked the crowd. "I'm waiting for Claire."

"Great," said Archie. "I haven't seen Claire since she got back from New Zealand."

Gabby gently poked Archie in the ribs. "*Caro mio*, they want to be alone."

"No, they don't," said Archie.

"Yes, we do," said Thumps.

"And a hat," said Gabby, as she dragged Archie away. "You will look *bellissimo* in a Knox fedora."

ANDERSON COLE WAS standing by a 1954 Hudson Hornet, talking with Beth Mooney and Ora Mae Foreman.

"Well, look who's come out of his hole." Ora Mae was dressed all in black. Tight black slacks, a shiny black shirt, and a black leather vest.

Cole patted the car. "The old cars don't have any of the safety features that new ones have, but you don't buy these with driving in mind."

"Hello, Thumps." Beth had put on a dress for the occasion. Soft cream and teal, gathered at the waist. Next to Ora Mae, she looked small and vulnerable.

"These are sculptures," Cole continued. "Works of art. Sure, you drive them around town on good days for the fun of it, but you buy them because they're just flat-out beautiful."

"Why didn't you tell me the Passangs had sold their house?" Thumps tried to make the question sound friendly.

"Wasn't my listing." Ora Mae frowned. "Since when you been interested in other folks' real estate?"

"It's about his cat," said Beth.

"Do you know where they moved?"

"You mean that nasty old cat that ran away and left you high and dry?"

"Are they still in town?" said Thumps. "The Passangs?"

Ora Mae shook her head. "Nyingchi. Left two weeks ago."

"Nyingchi?"

"It's a city in Tibet," said Ora Mae.

"Tibet?" Thumps kept his face under control. "What about Freeway? Did they take her with them?"

"A cat?" said Ora Mae. "All the way to Tibet?"

It wasn't a reaction he had expected, but the thought of Freeway waking up on top of a mountain in the middle of a howling blizzard made him smile.

"Nobody's going to take some scruffy cat to Tibet."

"Here's a primer on car collecting." Cole handed Beth a brochure. "What are you driving?"

"Buick station wagon," said Beth. "1983, I think."

"No sense keeping it." Cole shook her head. "A hundred years from now and it still won't be collectible."

Beth turned to Thumps. "A vintage car might be fun. What do you think?"

"The trick to collecting," said Cole, "is to know which cars will increase in value and which ones won't."

"No point being upset about that ratty cat," said Ora Mae. "I'd worry more about house prices in your neighbourhood. The Passangs didn't do you any favours."

THUMPS LEFT BETH and Ora Mae and Anderson Cole to work out the distinctions between old and vintage, between junk and investment. Ora Mae was right. Why would the Passangs take a grumpy old cat all the way to Tibet?

And if they didn't take her with them, where was she? Had they just left her when they moved out of the house? Had they given her to another family? Had they taken her to the animal shelter?

She wouldn't last long there.

Thumps was surprised at the number of people who had turned out to look at old cars. He wasn't sure he understood the attraction, but he knew that there was a fascination with things after they reached a certain age. Craftsman houses, for example. Or childhood toys, furniture, ceramics, vinyl records. Now that he thought about it, this interest in the past was the very thing that Gabby Santucci was selling with her vintage clothing.

He had read somewhere that a poster for the 1927 silent movie *Metropolis*, painted by Heinz Schulz-Neudamm, had been bought at auction for $1.2 million.

So far as Thumps could tell, the only things that did not get better with age and never became collectible, no matter how old they got, were people.

DUKE HOCKNEY WAS sitting in a Cadillac convertible the size of Nebraska. The sheriff had his hands on the steering wheel and was making engine noises under his breath.

"Place is an automotive petting zoo. You bring your camera?"

Thumps smiled. "You want me to take a picture of you in this car?"

"It's a '50 Coupe de Ville," said Duke. "When I was growing up, all the successful people had Cadillacs. You drove down the street in one of these babies, the only thing you had to worry about were icebergs."

"You ever know the Passangs? Tibetan family that lived near me?"

Duke began fooling around with the knobs and sliders on the dash. "Those the folks who stole your cat?"

"They didn't steal Freeway," said Thumps.

"Not what you told me."

"I was upset then."

"So, what about them?"

"They moved," said Thumps. "Back to Tibet."

Hockney adjusted the rear-view mirror. "And you don't think they took the cat with them?"

Thumps wasn't sure what he thought. He wasn't sure that he even cared. Except he did.

"Coyote probably got her."

"What?"

"Nobody's going to take a cat to Tibet. If she hasn't come home by now, she's most likely dead."

"Thanks."

"Get another cat," said the sheriff. "You remember that sign Budd used to have in his store?"

"Duke . . ."

"'Unattended children will be given a large cup of coffee and a free kitten.'"

"Forget I asked."

Hockney took his hat off and wiped the inside brim. "So, what the hell is going on?"

"What?"

"I get a call from some movie guy who wants me to come to a meeting."

Thumps opened the passenger door and got in. The seats were comfortable, and there was decent leg room.

"Said they're doing a movie on the Obsidian Murders."

"This thing have power steering?"

"That was a California case, so the only possible reason for them to be here in Chinook is you," said Duke. "Do I need to know anything?"

"Nope."

"Nope isn't an answer."

"They want to make a movie," said Thumps. "They wanted to talk to me. End of story."

"So, you're not going to the meeting?"

The air had cooled. This was the best part of the day. When everything slowed down.

Thumps ran a hand across the leather upholstery. "You thinking of buying this?"

Duke snorted. "You kidding? I couldn't afford to drive this pig to market."

"Or to a gas station."

"That too," said Duke. "Oh, and I saw Claire."

"Here?"

"Looking at a couple of old Fords."

"Claire?"

"She's with some guy," said Duke. "You go and screw up again?"

"What'd he look like?"

"You really want to do this?"

Thumps waited.

"Younger than you," said the sheriff. "Better-looking . . ."

"Okay, forget I asked."

". . . broad shoulders, good dresser, little dimple just here . . . had a baby."

Thumps held up a hand. "A baby?"

"Five, six months old," said Duke. "Hard to tell when they're young like that."

Thumps waited for Duke to finish.

"They were right over there." Hockney pointed his chin at the field of old cars. "Checking out a '50s T-Bird."

Thumps stepped out of the car and did a slow once-over of the fairgrounds. The grandstands were in shadows now, and someone had turned on the floods. "You happen to see what the guy was driving?"

"Audi SUV. Had a baby carrier in the back seat, so you know he's the responsible kind."

"You get a plate number?"

Duke's smile held off the evening shadows for a moment. "Use of police resources for personal business is against department policy," he said with a straight face. "But because we're friends, and seeing as you're a candidate for the sheriff's position, I'll put out an all-points bulletin for your cat."

FOURTEEN

The Mustang had been a defunct Texaco gas station before Delroy "Hack" Chubby bought the property at auction and turned it into a western saloon. He left the original building intact, spliced a decrepit double-wide onto the back of the service bays, and cobbled a bar counter together out of old doors and zinc roofing panels.

Hack found a couple of pool tables in a barn near Red Lake, along with a working jukebox. He hung the station's Texaco sign from the ceiling behind the bar and nailed the grille of a 1965 Mustang to the wall just below an orphaned neon sign for the "Big Chief Motel."

In those days, the saloon was a dark, dank cave famous for its fist fights and arm-wrestling contests. Now and then someone would back their pickup into the motorcycles lined up in the parking lot like the pickets on a fence, and an all-out brawl would erupt.

There were shootings as well, but with the exception of a guy from Texas who shot off part of a buttock trying to pull his pistol out of his belt, most of the gunplay, in and around the Mustang, involved beer cans, road signs, tires, windshields, and the occasional radiator that was in the wrong place at the wrong time.

Hack was killed on his '47 Harley Knucklehead trying to pass a semi on a grade just north of Glory. His wake was held at the Mustang and lasted the weekend. And when the sun came up on Monday, Hack's daughter, Lorraine, moved the Texaco sign out of the building and into the parking lot, along with the jukebox, the pool tables, the '65 grille, and the "Big Chief Motel" neon, and burned the place to the ground.

Lorraine had her mother's looks as well as her brains, and before the ashes of the old Mustang had cooled, she bulldozed the site and began building a new bar, a red prefab aluminum building with a herd of wild horses painted across the front. Lorraine was of the opinion that a twenty-first-century bar didn't have to look and smell like a nineteenth-century brothel, that there was no reason that cowboys and bikers shouldn't enjoy a clean, contemporary ambiance with all the modern amenities.

Free WiFi, satellite TV, video gaming.

It was still the rough-and-tumble place it had been when Hack was alive, but Lorraine did have three rules. If you wanted to fight, you did it outside. Lorraine put up a rope ring in a sandpit at the back of the Mustang.

With work lights.

And to ensure that any injuries were dealt with in a timely fashion, she had set up a first-aid station stocked with bandages, antiseptic ointments, and analgesic sprays.

Lorraine's second rule was no puking in the bar. Anyone who was feeling under the weather was expected to make it to one of the bathrooms or find their way to the parking lot. Throw up in the bar, and you were gone for the rest of the evening.

Her last rule was simple and straightforward. There was to be no excessive talking or yelling when she was on stage singing karaoke. Not that Lorraine had a great voice. It was okay. But she liked to sing, and when she sang, she expected that people would have the courtesy to shut the hell up and pay attention.

THE LAST TIME Thumps had been in the Mustang, Big Fish Patek had been behind the bar pulling drinks. Tonight, the man was nowhere to be seen.

"DreadfulWater!"

The bar was packed. Cowboys and bikers were stomping their way through a line dance.

"Thumps DreadfulWater!"

Anthony Mercer and Runa Gerson shuffled off the dance floor, keeping time with Shania Twain's "Any Man of Mine."

Mercer had traded his preppy look for a pair of jeans, a white shirt, and a soft, straw cowboy hat. Gerson was still dressed in her Viking disguise.

"Bet you think we're following you." Mercer's face was glistening.

"But we're not," said Gerson. "We heard about this place and had to see it."

"You don't get this in Tinseltown."

"Except on a sound stage," said Gerson. "I'm thinking we can use this as a location for the film."

Mercer wiped his face with a checkered handkerchief. "You ever line dance?"

"Let's grab that table," said Gerson. "Before Tony falls down."

"I play a lot of tennis," said Mercer. "But this cowboy stuff is hard work."

Thumps hadn't really expected to find Big Fish still working at the Mustang. The man's real passion was upscale watches. Audemars Piguet, Vacheron Constantin, Blancpain, Jaeger-LeCoultre, Breitling. And you didn't see many of these in a cowboy bar. Thumps always expected that, one day, Big Fish would head out to San Francisco or Los Angeles or Denver, cities where such extravagance was the norm.

Big Fish liked to tell anyone who would listen that his father had named him after Patek Philippe, the famous Swiss watch manufacturer in Geneva. His real name was Patek Carpenaux. Wutty Youngbeaver thought the French sounded pretentious, so he had shortened Carpenaux to Carp, and Carp somehow became "Big Fish."

"So," said Gerson, "you coming to the meeting?"

Thumps made a space on the table for the pitcher of beer and the glasses. "Where's the other guy?"

"Harry?"

"Not a party animal," said Mercer.

"Spends all his time holed up in his room working on the script."

Thumps tried to remember the last time he had gone out at night. Maybe he and Harry had more in common than he realized.

"This your hangout?" said Mercer.

"No."

"Then you were following us," said Gerson. "How exciting."

"Should I be?"

"I'm okay," said Mercer, "but Runa's somewhat alarming."

"It's going to be a good movie," said Gerson. "But it will be better if you come on board."

There were two bartenders tonight. Thumps didn't recognize either one of them, but he'd ask about Big Fish before he left. Just in case the man left a forwarding address. Or a general direction.

Maybe Lorraine would know.

"The meeting tomorrow is to go over the ideas for the script," said Mercer. "Harry has a couple of scenarios he wants to run by us."

"It's to be a surprise," said Gerson. "Wants to get our first reactions."

"Think about it." Mercer got to his feet and tipped his hat at Gerson. "What about it, darling? Another stroll around the floor?"

"Anything you can do, I can do better."

"No, you can't."

"Yes, I can."

They continued to murder the song as they got into line with the rest of the dancers. Thumps left the pitcher where it was and made his way to the bar.

"Lorraine?" He tried to keep his voice low.

The bartender put a hand to his ear. "What?"

"Lorraine," Thumps shouted over the music. "Lorraine Chubby."

"Office."

THE OFFICE FOR the Mustang was down the hall, past the restrooms. The door was open. Lorraine Chubby was sitting in a leather lounger with her feet up. It took Thumps a moment to realize that she was pregnant.

"Doctor says I have to stay off my feet."

"Congratulations."

"Whoever came up with the logistics of human reproduction should be shot."

"You look great."

"Now I know how a cow feels." Lorraine raised the footrest.

"Hey, Thumps." Big Fish Patek was stretched out on a sofa in front of a television. "Pull up a chair. You got to see this."

Thumps stepped in behind the sofa.

"How to stalk an elk," said Big Fish. "They got videos that show you how to do it."

Thumps had been on one hunt with Cooley. All he remembered was the cold, and the bugs, and the early-season snowstorm that had come out of nowhere.

"Cooley got a new rifle, and he's going to take me and Stas over to Bear Hump," said Big Fish. "Maybe I'll get an elk. Those suckers are big. Be enough food to last me and Lorraine and the little guy all year."

It didn't register at first.

"You and Lorraine?"

"Ain't that something." Patek sat up. "Bet you never thought you'd see me settle down."

"Don't quite believe it myself," said Lorraine.

"Going to be a father," said Big Fish. "Never saw that one coming."

"You and Lorraine?"

"I'd've been your last guess," said Patek. "Am I right?"

Thumps wasn't sure he would have even thought of Big Fish as a possibility. Lorraine was smart. Big Fish was clever. Lorraine was tall and thin with soft blond hair and pale blue eyes. Patek Carpenaux was short and squat, dark, with a nose like a hammer. Lorraine was a flamingo. Big Fish was a bumblebee in a bucket.

"Don't hardly see you out here."

"Don't drink."

"Neither do I," said Big Fish. "Not anymore. Not since I'm going to be a dad."

"That's good thinking."

"So," said Patek, "you didn't come all the way out here for the halibut."

Thumps took the watch out of his pocket.

"Nice." Big Fish held the watch up to the light. "Rockford." He hefted the watch in his hand. "Steel case."

"I'm hoping you can tell me something about the watch."

"So, it's not yours?" Big Fish turned off the television and sat up. "This about a case? 'Cause you know I can be very helpful."

"This a general information question," said Lorraine, "or something that could get my sweetie shot?"

"General," said Thumps.

"'Cause I'm going to need someone to change diapers and rub my feet."

"Is there any way you can tell me who bought the watch?"

Big Fish shook his head. "Don't know much about pocket watches. Wristwatches are my thing. Now, if this were a Rolex Milgauss . . ."

"What about a serial number?"

"Got a friend in Livingston who's an expert on pocket watches," said Big Fish. "You want me to ask him?"

"Sure."

"Can you leave this with me?" said Big Fish. "Binh has a lot of contacts. If there are any records, he'll find them."

"But before you two get started," said Lorraine, "I'm going to need a sour cherry spritzer."

Big Fish slid off the sofa and rubbed Lorraine's shoulders. "You ever been married?"

"Nope."

"Nothing like it," said Big Fish. "We're due any day."

"Congratulations."

"I like it when he says 'we,'" said Lorraine. "It makes me laugh."

"Luckiest man in the world," said Big Fish. "Luckiest man in the world."

Lorraine rubbed her belly. "You and Claire ever work things out?"

"You know what the baby's going to be?"

"Naw," said Lorraine. "We want to be surprised."

"Just so it's healthy, right?"

"That's momma's job." Lorraine patted her belly. "Going to be a party here at the bar. You're invited."

"Look forward to it."

"Just be careful on the way out," said Lorraine. "You know what happens if you hit any of the bikes."

* * *

THE LINE DANCE had broken up. Mercer and Gerson had re-formed themselves into a Texas two-step. Shania Twain had been replaced with George Strait and "Amarillo by Morning."

It was after one when he walked through the parking lot and climbed into the Element. The moon was a cold sliver in a black sky, and the stars were fierce and bright. Lorraine was pregnant and happy. Big Fish couldn't believe his good luck. The neon lights on the front of the Mustang were in full flash, creating the illusion of the horse herd galloping fast and getting nowhere. Someone had found Neil Young on the jukebox. Even with the door closed and the windows rolled up, Young's soft, plaintive voice floated out into the night.

"Four Strong Winds."

Thumps sat in the car and waited to see if the melancholy would pass. And when it didn't, he leaned back in the seat, closed his eyes, and let the night hold him.

FIFTEEN

The sun came up in a rush and set the red brick of the old Land Titles building on fire. Thumps checked his watch. Eight o'clock. The second-floor windows were dark. He didn't know the kinds of hours that doctors and coroners kept, but it stood to reason that they should be early risers.

Now it was 8:01.

Thumps stepped out of the car and set the box on the roof. Maybe he should wait until eight thirty, a compromise between now and nine. Or he could be bold and take his chances. On the plus side, even if Beth was annoyed by the early morning intrusion, at least she wouldn't be in the basement.

He hadn't slept at all. He had sat in the car in the Mustang parking lot for a while and listened to the music. Then he had driven out to Red Tail Lake for no better reason than it was there.

Red Tail was a shallow lake with a state park on the south end, the tiny town of Red Tail on the western edge, and a wetland of swamps and marshes to the east. The northern end was an extended crescent of waterfront with rocky outcroppings, sporadic sand beaches, and deep-water moorings.

The Shore.

The Shore had originally been a collection of fishing shacks—large outhouses with a window and a wood stove—that the locals used during the summer and winter. Then a developer from California arrived. He bought all the buildings and the land, moved the road back away from the lake, and began putting up waterfront summer homes the size of small villages. No one actually lived on The Shore year-round. The houses here were second or third homes that were shut down for the winter, opened for the summer, and ignored in between.

Why anyone would build a house and not live in it full-time was something of a mystery, though Thumps supposed that if he had been rich enough to afford a place on The Shore, he would understand.

Some of the houses, the ones with deep-water frontage, had their own private docks, but much of The Shore was shallow, and the homeowners association had built a long dock and mini-marina to house the summer boats and to provide a place for kids to fish.

Thumps had parked the car, walked to the end of the dock, and watched the lake shift under the night sky. He had imagined that a little peace and quiet would help him think, imagined that communing with nature would help him decide what he wanted to do.

A modern variation of a vision quest.

But it hadn't. The night had stayed black. The lake rose and fell like a sleeping child. The wind kicked up and died down toward dawn. By the time he walked back to the car, the only understanding he had come to was that he was cold and that he was hungry.

And that he wasn't any smarter.

So NOW HERE he was, standing in front of the old Land Titles building. And it was 8:12. He pressed the button and waited. And then he pressed it again. The voice on the intercom didn't sound like Beth, and it didn't sound friendly. Thumps could feel the camera mounted above the door do a full body scan.

"What?"

"It's me."

"I can see it's you."

"Beth?"

"Do you know what time it is?"

"Almost nine?"

"No, it's not. Go away."

"I brought breakfast." Thumps held up the box. "Eric the Baker."

Thumps could hear Beth breathing into the intercom. Then the lock on the front door clicked open.

The family doctor–cum–county coroner was waiting for him on the second-floor landing. Beth was dressed in a pair of zebra pyjama bottoms and a Rolling Stones T-shirt. She stood like a colossus in front of the doorway, her hands welded to her hips.

"You know the phrase 'What plays in Vegas, stays in Vegas'?"

"Sure."

"Are those sour-cherry Danishes?"

"And raisin."

Beth turned and went into the apartment. "You get one cup of coffee and twenty minutes to drink it."

The apartment was warm and bright. Sunlight filled the windows, and the cream curtains glowed against the darker walls. There was a pot of coffee waiting on the table, along with two cups.

"You were expecting me?"

"Hardly." Beth went to the cupboard and took down a third cup and a large plate. "What are you doing here?"

"The blood test."

"The blood test you missed?"

"I got tied up."

"And you want me to do it now?" Beth shook her head. "That's not the way the doctor-patient relationship works."

Thumps opened the box, put a Danish on the plate, and cut it into fourths.

"Did you bring any protein?"

"Danishes don't have protein?"

"Did you ever read that brochure I gave you?" Beth closed her eyes and then went to the refrigerator. "I'll get you some cheese."

Thumps had just started to pour himself a cup of coffee when the bedroom door opened and Gabby Santucci came out, dressed in a thick terry-cloth robe.

"*Buon giorno.*"

Thumps looked at Beth.

Beth looked back. "Vegas?"

Gabby was smiling. "We have surprised our Thumps."

Thumps held up the plate. "Danish?"

The coffee was good. The cheese was a pleasant surprise. Most women Thumps knew favoured the softer, smellier cheeses. There had been a French-Canadian he had dated briefly who would only eat cheeses that had the viscosity of heavy motor oil and smelled like a condemned barn.

The cheese Beth had found was a straightforward Swiss that didn't move.

"I'm not going to do your blood work right now," said Beth. "But I'll tell Rawat to fill your prescription."

"It's okay." Thumps helped himself to a piece of Danish. "I probably can't afford it anyway."

"The medicine in this country is *molto costoso,*" said Gabby. "It is cheaper, perhaps, to die."

"And since you didn't come here at this hour for a blood test. Or free coffee"—Beth leaned back—"this must be about the break-in."

"Break-in?"

Gabby settled in the chair and helped herself to the Danish. "Someone, they come in. To this building. And then they leave."

"Okay."

"Shit," said Beth. "Have you talked to Duke?"

Thumps was having trouble keeping the conversation straight. "What about the break-in?"

"They take nothing," said Gabby.

It had been a long night. Thumps could feel his energy sag. "Then how do you know there was a break-in?"

"All the drawers in cabinets." Gabby waved a hand. "In the basement. They are pulled open."

Beth sipped her coffee. "So Duke didn't tell you?"

"Tell me what?"

Beth took a deep breath. "Whoever broke in left a black stone on my autopsy table."

Suddenly, Thumps was awake. Wide awake.

"Duke said he was going to tell you himself. After he checked it out."

"Obsidian?"

"You were on the coast," said Beth. "There was nothing to do about it until you got back."

"I've been back for . . ."

"Hardly two days."

"Three!" said Thumps. "I've been back three days."

"The first day does not ever count," said Gabby. "Jet lag."

"I drove!"

"It's probably no big deal," said Beth.

"Which is why you put in the extra security?" Thumps put his cup down with a bang. "The alarm? The camera? Because it's no big deal?"

"It's not a secret," said Beth. "We all know what happened out in California."

"Even I know what happened," said Gabby. "Archie has explained it to me. *Molto triste*."

"The Obsidian Murders," said Beth. "After all these years, you go off to the coast to look for the killer, and someone with a twisted sense of humour decides to have some sick fun."

"Was it obsidian?"

"You'll have to ask Duke."

"Damn it, Beth."

"I do bodies," said Beth. "I don't do rocks."

Gabby pulled the robe around her tighter. "Do you have such friends who would do this thing?"

"You need to talk to Duke." Beth took a cherry Danish from the box and looked at her watch. "And drink your coffee. Your time is up."

SIXTEEN

"When were you going to tell me?"

Sheriff Duke Hockney sat behind his desk and tried to impersonate a boulder.

"Sit down," said Duke. "Have some coffee."

"I've had coffee."

"It's Colombian today," said Hockney. "I'm trying out a bunch of varieties until I find one I like."

"Damn it, Duke, why didn't you tell me about the break-in?"

The sheriff heaved his body out of the chair and ambled to the coffee pot. "I did tell you about the break-in."

"You just forgot to mention the stone."

"You're supposed to hold the coffee up to the light as you pour it to check the colour." Hockney carried the cup back to his desk and opened the top drawer. "Macy got me a box of baby cookies to have with my coffee. They're not bad. You want to try one?"

"No."

Duke settled himself back in his chair. "Think like a cop for a moment."

"I am."

"No, you're not." The sheriff dipped the cookie into the coffee. "You're thinking like an avenging angel."

"The Obsidian Murders. Six-year-old cold case." Thumps held up a hand and began ticking off fingers. "Dead bodies begin appearing on Clam Beach, all with a piece of obsidian in their mouths. No one was ever arrested. There were never any suspects. Never a single break in the case. It's not just cold, it's frozen."

"And then you go back to California."

"And then I go back to California to try to pick up the pieces. I discover that Anna had a husband she never told me about."

"One Raymond Oakes," said Duke.

"Who was serving a life sentence at Deer Ridge," said Thumps. "Until he got out on a technicality."

Duke nodded. "Just before the killings began."

"And when I get back here, I discover that someone has broken into Beth's morgue and left a black stone on the autopsy table."

"You're forgetting about the movie people who suddenly show up in town." Duke shook his head. "You got a real talent for attracting the Hollyweirdies."

"Was it obsidian?"

"You look like hell, DreadfulWater."

"I didn't sleep last night, and I'm hungry, and I don't like being lied to by friends."

"Nobody's lied to you," said Duke. "What? You think that after all this time, the same serial killer from California just happens to pass through town, happens to break into Beth's place, and happens to leave a piece of obsidian for her to find?"

"So, it was obsidian."

Duke nodded. "It was. I had Scotty Jacobs at the rock store in Glory check it out."

Thumps slumped in the chair.

"Think like a cop." Hockney helped himself to another cookie. "Chances are that this is just some stupid joke. You go to the coast to try to catch a killer. Someone in town says, 'Hey, let's turn his crank.' They go to the rock shop in Glory, buy a piece of obsidian, break into the morgue, and have a good laugh."

"Someone bought obsidian at the rock shop?"

"See," said Duke. "Now you're thinking like a cop."

"Who?"

Duke waited a moment. "Wutty Youngbeaver."

"Wutty?"

"But it wasn't him," said Duke. "Wutty did buy a square chunk of something called rainbow obsidian for his girlfriend. Wasn't the same kind of obsidian that was left at Beth's."

"So why tell me?"

"To show you what's possible. Hell, it could have been the movie people. You know how they are. Stir things up. A little publicity to help their project get press."

"So, you don't know who left the obsidian in the morgue?"

Duke tapped the side of his head. "Let's say that it's the serial killer from back then. Or let's say that it's Oakes. Where have they been all this time, and why show up now?"

"So, it wasn't Wutty."

Duke chuckled. "Oh, I'm sure it wasn't Wutty."

"You lean on him?"

"Hard," said the sheriff. "It's the kind of stupid thing he might do."

"But he didn't."

"No," said Duke. "And what pisses me off is that I've got no idea who did."

Thumps was going to have to eat soon. He could feel his blood sugars dropping. The cheese and the piece of Danish had been digested and forgotten.

"In the meantime, I've got the dates for my operation." Duke took another cookie out of the tin and then put it back. "Probably need you to look after the shop for about two weeks. Cleared it with city council. You okay with that?"

"Yeah."

"In the meantime, you can use the resources of this office to try to figure out what's going on."

"Thanks."

"Don't like people fucking with my town." Duke's face went hard. "Don't like anyone fucking with my friends."

AL'S WAS EMPTY.

"You just missed everyone."

"Good."

"People didn't know you better," said Al, "they'd take you for a misogynist."

"Misanthrope." Thumps put his elbows on the counter and put his face in his hands. "Misanthropes hate humankind. Misogynists hate women."

Al brought the coffee pot over. "Got to be a reason they're spelled the same."

"They're not spelled the same."

"Too close for comfort, if you ask me."

"Did you know about the break-in at the morgue?"

"Sure."

"And about the piece of obsidian?"

"So, Duke finally told you."

"You could have told me."

"Is this the place?" Anderson Cole and George Gorka were standing at the front door of the café, not quite sure if they should come in or run away.

"This is it," said Al.

Cole spotted Thumps. "You were with the big guy."

"Cooley Small Elk."

Cole and Gorka took the stools across from the register. "DreadfulWater something, right? That Comanche?"

"Cherokee."

"Oklahoma?"

Thumps nodded.

"My daddy was part Choctaw," said Cole, "but I generally don't mention it, seeing as I've never had to walk that road. What about you, Mr. DreadfulWater?"

Al held up the pot. "You want coffee?"

George pushed his cup forward. "You remind me of my wife. Beautiful woman."

Thumps had never seen Al blush.

"Molara," said George. "She died three years ago."

"Anderson Cole," said Cole, and she stuck out a hand. "And this son of a buck is my road manager, George Gorka."

Gorka kept his attention on Al. "Maybe you'd like to come to the auction. As my guest."

Thumps had never thought he would see Al speechless. Nor did he think he would find it . . . so refreshing.

Al found her balance. "You asking me for a date?"

"George may look ordinary, but he's all Basque, and the bastard's got a silver tongue." Cole took a T-shirt out of her bag and handed it to Al. "So what's good? I'm starving, and I've got an auction to run."

"We're in your hands." George put the cup to his lips and

caressed the porcelain. "This woman knows food. I can tell. Everything will be good."

Al didn't disappoint. She grilled sausages and bacon along with the eggs and the hash browns. She even made George a waffle, something she only did for people she liked. Cole limited herself to eggs, orange, and toast.

"Turning over a new leaf," she said.

Gorka winked at Al. "She always says this at breakfast."

"He's right," said Cole. "By the time I get to lunch, I make up for lost time."

Gorka left forty dollars on the counter. "Please," he said. "I hope to see you at the fairgrounds. You can drive any car you want. Maybe we can catch coffee afterwards."

Cole stopped at the door and turned back to Al. "He's good company," she said. "Just don't mention the Battle of Roncevaux Pass."

Thumps waited for Al to come back with the pot.

"You going to go?"

"Why not." Al wiped the counter with a towel. "Vintage cars. Someone who hasn't heard any of my stories. What's not to like?"

"He seems pretty sure of himself."

"You worried about my virtue?"

"He's got a gun."

Al threw the towel over her shoulder and headed back to the grill. "This part of the country, who doesn't."

* * *

THE LAST TIME THUMPS had been in Chinook Pharmacy to buy drugs, he had had to take out a second mortgage on his house. Or at least that's how it had felt. He didn't expect this time was going to feel any better.

Rawat was all smiles in his sparkling white lab coat. "Ah, Mr. DreadfulWater, Dr. Beth has called on your behalf, and now your prescription is ready."

"Will you take a kidney in trade?"

"Oh, that is very funny. I must remember that one." Rawat set a large bag on the counter and handed Thumps a slip. "Sadly, it is also true."

Thumps looked at the figure in disbelief. "What do I pay my taxes for?"

"Bombs," said Rawat. "And missiles. You cannot keep the world safe with enlightened social programs and good health care."

"Can I set up a monthly payment plan?"

"The drug companies insist that you are to use each needle only once," said Rawat, "in order to reduce the risk of infection at the injection site. This is sound advice, but many of my customers are putting a new needle on in the morning and then using the same needle throughout the day in order to reduce the cost."

"One needle a day?"

"Others have taken to boiling their old needles and reusing them until the points are dull." Rawat shook his head. "This I do not recommend, but if cost is the issue, boiling needles is better than doing nothing."

"I'll manage."

"And if I could ask a favour?"

"Sure."

"When you see Chief Merchant, could you tell her that the talc-free baby powder she requested is here."

"Baby powder?"

"Yes," said Rawat. "For the baby."

"Was there a guy with her?"

"Indeed," said Rawat. "A friend of yours?"

"He's Canadian."

"A fine country," said Rawat. "Quite progressive."

"Just baby powder?"

"Oh my, no. Chief Merchant bought an entire baby assembly. Diapers, gripe water, no-tears shampoo, zinc ointment."

"Great."

"Such a good baby," said Rawat. "All smiles and pleasantries."

"I'll tell Claire about the powder when I see her."

Rawat handed Thumps his change. "Very good-natured," he said. "Perhaps we should insist that babies run the country."

SEVENTEEN

Anthony Mercer and Runa Gerson were sitting on a sofa. Harry Shipman was at the table. Sheriff Duke Hockney had taken up residence in a large easy chair next to the gas fireplace. The hotel's hospitality services had brought up a tray of fruit and cheese along with an urn of coffee.

The scene reminded Thumps a little of Van Gogh's *The Potato Eaters* or van der Helst's *Four Aldermen of the Kloveniersdoelen in Amsterdam.*

"Mr. DreadfulWater." Mercer stood up. "Thanks for coming."

Duke had a plate of fruit on his lap. "Coffee's just the way you like it," said the sheriff. "Weak as piss."

"Harry was just about to take us through the script," said Gerson.

"We get to be critics," said Mercer.

"Especially interested in hearing from law enforcement," said Harry.

"That's me." Duke held up his plate. "Fruit's pretty good. Try the watermelon."

Thumps took a chair at the table.

"These are ideas," said Shipman. "Nothing is set in stone. I'm counting on you to tell me what you think."

"How about that, Thumps," said Duke. "Someone actually wants your opinion."

"Okay, Harry," said Mercer. "The floor is yours."

Shipman adjusted his glasses. "The Obsidian Murders occurred in California, so you're probably wondering why we came to Chinook."

"Did wonder about that," said Duke.

"That's because I want to set the film here." Shipman paused for a moment. "And I want to start the story after the killings on the West Coast."

Gerson looked at Mercer.

"Stay with me," said Shipman. "We frame the story around a central character rather than the killings. Let's call him . . . Dick Storm for the time being."

"I can see that," said Duke. "There are times when Thumps reminds me of a Dick."

"Storm was a cop on the California coast when someone killed ten people and left their bodies on a lonely stretch of beach with a piece of obsidian in their mouths. Two of the victims were Storm's wife and ten-year-old daughter. No one was caught. Storm was devastated. He quit his job, started driving east, and wound up here in Chinook."

"How about we call the town Serenity?"

"Sure."

"Any depression or alcoholism?" said Gerson.

"Could be," said Shipman.

Mercer shifted on the sofa. "You plan to work the backstory as flashbacks?"

"Storm's only friend in Serenity is the local sheriff." Shipman made a quick note on a pad. "Let's call him Virgil 'Jerk' Johnson."

"You've always struck me as a Jerk," said Thumps.

"The film would open in the present day. Storm has put his life back together. He has a new relationship with a woman who has an eight-year-old son. For the first time in a long time, he's happy. But he's haunted by the serial killer he never caught. And that's when he makes a fatal mistake."

"He goes after the killer," said Mercer.

"Exactly," said Shipman. "He goes back to Northern California and reopens the case. Little by little, he starts to close in on the killer."

"But the killer finds out," said Gerson.

"Let's not get ahead of ourselves," said Shipman. "But yes, the killer discovers that he is being tracked and instead of running, he turns."

"Killer got a name?" asked Mercer.

"Sure," said Shipman with a big smile. "Let's call him Harold Shipman."

"Perfect," said Gerson. "I hope to hell there will be some good parts for women."

"So," said Duke, "I'm guessing that this serial killer comes to town and begins killing people close to our hero. Leaving pieces of obsidian in their mouths?"

"You're a natural-born script writer," said Shipman. "That's exactly what happens."

"We can create some really good tension," said Mercer. "A climactic scene with our hero as he tries to save the woman and her son from the killer."

"Hope to hell you're not going to kill off the sheriff," said Duke.

"*Blood Simple*," said Shipman, "meets *Silence of the Lambs*."

"More like sleazy meets sordid," said Duke.

"What about the husband? The guy who was in jail," said Gerson. "Raymond Oakes?"

"Don't need him," said Shipman. "We're not making a documentary."

"I like it." Mercer turned to Thumps. "What do you think?"

Thumps looked at his watch. "You guys going to the car auction?"

Shipman rubbed at the side of his neck. "I don't think Mr. DreadfulWater is all that impressed."

"That's just how he looks when he's overwhelmed." Hockney got out of the chair and put on his hat. "You folks let us know if we can help in any way."

"I know it sounds a bit thin right now," said Shipman, "but I've got a couple of twists in mind that'll turn lead into gold."

THUMPS RODE DOWN to the lobby with the sheriff. "Overwhelmed?"

"Something doesn't feel right." Duke crossed the lobby and pushed his way through the revolving doors. "Think I'll check up on our three musketeers. Make sure we know exactly with whom we're dealing."

"Whom?"

The day had begun to warm. Clouds were forming to the west, but they looked friendly.

"You notice Mr. Shipman's ring?" Duke stopped at the curb. "Emerald? Man's got a new car sitting on his finger."

"Tattoo's cute, too."

"You got a tattoo?"

"Nope."

"Me neither," said Hockney. "I look at kids today and wonder if I've missed out on something."

"So, what do you think?"

"What's the basic rule for serial killers?" Duke opened the door to his cruiser and let the car vent.

"They keep on killing."

"That's correct," said Duke.

"Sheriff's department and the FBI looked," said Thumps. "They didn't find anything."

"Guy could have stopped killing," said Duke. "Or he could have been convicted of another crime. Or he might have died."

"Or," said Thumps, "Maslow was right. The guy's smart."

"And he's covered his tracks." Hockney took a deep breath. "You think he killed before Eureka?"

"Probably."

"What about Oakes? Man was released from prison, what, two months before the killings began."

"About that."

"Hard to figure him for a serial killer." Hockney took a sheet of paper from his jacket pocket. "Did some checking. Oakes was in prison for murder, but technically, he didn't kill anyone. He was involved in a three-man bank robbery. Teller got caught in the crossfire with the police. The other two perps were killed. Oakes was wounded. But because there was a death and because he was the only one left standing, he caught the full weight."

Duke leaned against the car. "Here's the other interesting thing. Oakes and Anna Tripp were married three months before the bank robbery. He was eighteen. She was sixteen. These are two kids. You see what I'm saying?"

"Shipman says he can put Oakes in the area when the killings began."

"I can see Oakes killing his wife 'cause she's fooling around." Duke tightened his mouth. "Happens all too often."

Thumps jammed his hands in his pockets.

"The daughter is the part that bothers me," said the sheriff. "What kind of father kills his child?"

"It happens."

"Yeah," said Duke, "it does. Which brings us back to a single serial killer or a serial killer and a pissed-off spouse."

"And we don't know which."

Duke slid in behind the wheel. "See how much fun law enforcement can be?"

THE CAR AUCTION had already started by the time Thumps and the sheriff got to the fairgrounds. Anderson Cole was standing on a riser with a microphone and a gavel. George Gorka was beside her, taking bids.

"You going to try for that Cadillac?"

"Nope," said Duke, "but I am curious to see what some fool is willing to pay for it."

"Moses is thinking about buying a '56 Chevy Bel Air."

"Two-door convertible?"

"That's the one."

"Didn't know he drove."

"He doesn't."

"So, he doesn't have a licence?"

"Nope."

"Or insurance?"

"That too."

The sheriff thought about that for a moment. "Only place he could drive the car would be on his land. On the reservation."

"He wants to feel the wind in his hair."

"And when he runs out of gas?"

"One tank at a time," said Thumps.

Duke stopped beside the grandstands. "I better get home. Macy's making fettuccine carbonara. She picked up a couple of videos on the Amalfi Coast that we're going to watch."

"Italy?"

"That's where she wants to go first. Some town called Vietri sul Mare. She has this thing for ceramics."

"Ceramics?"

"Evidently, Vietri whatever is lousy with pottery."

"After the operation?"

"That's the plan. You know what's nice about living with an optimist?" Duke rolled his shoulders and stretched his neck. "Just about everything."

EIGHTEEN

Thumps stayed in the shade of the grandstands and watched Cole and Gorka sell cars. Every so often, he was tempted to throw up a hand, just to join in the festivities. The Cadillac went for more than he would have expected, as did the two '56 Bel Airs. Thumps looked for Moses and Cooley, but if they were somewhere in the crowd, he didn't see them.

Maybe the old man had had second thoughts about owning a car.

"Hey, Thumps."

Big Fish and Lorraine.

"You going to buy a car?"

"Just slumming."

"Lorraine has got it into her head that we should get a van," said Big Fish. "You know, for the kid and all."

Lorraine rubbed her belly. "We're going to need more room than a sidecar on a motorcycle."

"We got a sedan."

"Two doors," said Lorraine. "Hard to get a car seat in the back."

"She wants new," said Big Fish, "but I'm thinking that vintage is a better investment."

"He wants one of those station wagons with the wood sides," said Lorraine.

"There's a 1950 Ford woodie coming up. Maroon with a visor." Big Fish was all smiles. "A thing of beauty."

"And I don't want my baby riding around in a car that's older than the combined ages of its parents."

"It's not that bad."

Thumps saw Claire at the same time Big Fish did, standing next to a tall man. She was carrying something in her arms. It took Thumps a moment to realize that it was a baby.

"Hey, Claire!" Big Fish waved his arms, as though he were landing planes on an aircraft carrier. "Claire!"

And before Thumps could stop him, Big Fish jogged off across the field.

Lorraine shaded her eyes. "That Claire's new boyfriend?"

"No idea."

"Is that a baby?"

"Looks like it."

Suddenly, Lorraine was crying. "Shit."

"You okay?"

"Look at me." Lorraine was fighting hiccups between the sobs. "Do I fucking look okay?"

Thumps could feel his flight response kick in. "You look great."

Big Fish was back on the run, dragging Claire with him. "Hey, you okay?"

Lorraine wiped her eyes. "Hi, Claire."

"Lorraine."

"Is that a baby?"

"It is." Claire pulled the blanket away from the child's face.

"Wow," said Big Fish. "It *is* a baby."

Lorraine rolled her eyes. "Duh."

"Well, it is."

The man with Claire was all smiles. "Is this your partner?"

"It is." Claire stepped across the void and took Thumps's hand. "Honey, this is Melton Cobell."

"Been looking forward to meeting you," said Melton.

Claire handed Thumps the baby. "And this is the little girl I've been telling you about."

Thumps wasn't sure what exactly he was supposed to say. Or do.

"Ivory," said Claire. "Melton's niece."

"Claire's told me all about you," said Melton.

Thumps gestured toward Big Fish and Lorraine. "These are friends. Lorraine Chubby and Patek Carpenaux."

"Like the watch," said Melton.

"Exactly like the watch," said Big Fish.

"Looks like you're going to have a baby of your own," said Melton.

"Not soon enough," said Lorraine.

"Come on," said Big Fish. "Let's at least take a look at the wagon. We don't have to buy, but you don't want to have any regrets."

Lorraine put her hand in the small of her back and began moving toward the cars. "It's going to be interesting," she said, "raising two kids without a father."

The baby wiggled in Thumps's arms. Claire squeezed his hand in a way that let him know he was to keep his mouth shut. But he had already figured that part out.

"So, you're a photographer," said Melton.

"He is," said Claire.

"How long have you and Claire been together?"

"Three years," said Claire.

"I'm not married," said Melton. "Maybe someday."

"Nothing like it." Claire took the baby back and began rocking her. "She is so beautiful."

"You guys know what you're doing," said Melton. "I can see that."

Claire beamed. "This weekend still good?"

Melton nodded. "I'll bring Ivory by Friday morning." He gathered the baby into his arms and stuck out a hand. "Good to finally meet you, Mr. DreadfulWater."

* * *

THUMPS WAITED UNTIL Melton was out of hearing. "Nice guy."

"Are you angry?"

"No."

"Confused?"

"Nope."

"You should be."

"Okay," said Thumps, "maybe a little."

"Thumps!" Big Fish was standing at the edge of the crowd, shouting and waving his arms. "Thumps!"

Lorraine was doubled over.

"She was okay," said Big Fish, his voice shaking, "and then this happened."

"It's just these crazy contractions." Lorraine gritted her teeth. "It's not labour."

"How come your jeans are all wet?"

Lorraine held up a hand. "I'll just lie down in the grass for a moment."

Claire turned on Big Fish. "I think we should get her to the hospital."

Big Fish looked like an animal caught in headlights. "Okay."

"Now!" said Claire.

"I'll get the car." Big Fish turned around in a circle.

"We don't have the car." Lorraine's face was a grimace.

"Right," said Big Fish. "The motorcycle."

Claire snorted. "You brought a pregnant woman here on a motorcycle?"

"It's got a sidecar."

* * *

THUMPS LOADED LORRAINE and Claire into the back of the Element. Big Fish raced off on the motorcycle to alert the hospital in case they had never had a pregnant woman come in on the fly.

"If he gets himself hurt on that thing," Lorraine shouted between contractions, "I'll kill him."

"Drive carefully," said Claire. "Try to miss the bumps."

Lorraine began making noises that reminded Thumps of a soundtrack from a horror movie.

"Okay," said Claire. "Forget about the bumps."

Big Fish was waiting at the emergency entrance with a wheelchair. "What took you so long?"

Hospitals, to Thumps's way of thinking, were one step above morgues. They were livelier and better lighted. Some areas even had chairs and magazines and music. But the smells were just as alarming as the ones in Beth's basement, and you could hear the fear and the depression and the hopelessness in the voices that escaped the rooms and filled the corridors.

"Can you guys stick around for a bit?" Big Fish looked as though he was getting ready to run a sprint. "I got to do the paperwork, and I want to be with Lorraine."

"Sure," said Thumps. "We'll stay in case something happens."

"Like what?"

Claire groaned. "What he means is we'll be here in case you need us to do something."

"Sure," said Thumps. "Like get you coffee or something to eat."

"Cigars," said Big Fish. "I'm supposed to pass out cigars."

Claire turned to Thumps. "You need to talk to him."

"About what?"

"I'm going to get us a sandwich," said Claire. "It could be a long night."

"We're going to stay until Lorraine gives birth?"

"You got something better to do?"

"That would be great," said Big Fish. "I really appreciate you guys being here."

THUMPS FOUND A CHAIR. Big Fish walked up and down the corridor, the nervous energy bubbling out of the man.

"You ever think about having kids?"

"Sure."

"I'll bet you'd be a great father," said Big Fish. "I'm not so sure about me."

The magazine selection was limited. A copy of *People* that was almost a year old, a *Sports Illustrated*, and a *Better Homes and Gardens*.

"I mean, where do you learn to be a father? It just happens and there you are."

Thumps opened the *Sports Illustrated*. There was an article on how Eddie Lacy received a cash bonus for weighing less than 250 pounds.

"What if my kid doesn't like me?"

"Your kid will love you."

Big Fish stood in the middle of the corridor and bounced on the balls of his feet. "You think so?"

Thumps turned to an article on Richard Sherman and the Seattle Seahawks. "Absolutely."

"Oh, hey," said Big Fish, and he dropped into the chair next to Thumps. "I almost forgot."

The article was about how Sherman had not requested a trade.

"The watch you gave me?"

Thumps put the magazine down.

"No good news, I'm afraid." Big Fish took the watch out of his pocket. "It's a Rockford 905, all right. Montgomery dial. Twenty-three jewel movement. Railroad quality. I know when it was made and where, but there aren't any repair records and no sales records that Binh could find."

Thumps sighed. "Thanks anyway."

"If we knew who Ray or Anna was," said Big Fish, "that might help."

"What?"

"The inscription."

"What inscription?"

"Under the dust cover." Big Fish took out a small penknife and slipped the blade into the side of the watch and popped the back off. "See?"

On the back of the cover was a simple inscription. "*For Ray, with love, Anna.*"

"Is that any help?"

"Mr. Carpenaux?" The nurse was a large, sturdy woman. "Your wife has gone into labour. She'd like you to be with her for the birth."

"Me?"

The nurse looked at the chart. "You're Mr. Carpenaux?"

"He is," said Thumps.

"What do I do?" said Big Fish.

The nurse smiled. "You stand next to your wife and tell her how great she's doing."

"I can do that."

"And try not to get upset or pass out."

Big Fish turned back to Thumps. "Really appreciate you doing this," he said. "And I'm sorry about the watch."

NINETEEN

Claire returned with two ham and cheese sandwiches and two cups of coffee.

"Where's Big Fish?"

"Lorraine's gone into labour."

"Big Fish with her?"

"He is."

"That should be interesting." Claire pushed the magazines to one side and put the food on the table. "Pocket watch?"

"Yeah."

"When did you start carrying a pocket watch?"

"I don't." Thumps slipped the watch into his pocket. "I'm holding it for Big Fish."

Claire unwrapped the first sandwich and handed Thumps the larger half. "So, here's dinner."

"Did you get an appetizer?"

"No wine, either," said Claire. "Think of this as a poor man's picnic."

"In a hospital?"

"It is a little creepy."

"I hear that your friend is from Canada."

"Melton Cobell." Claire nodded. "Blackfeet from Standoff. He works as a water consultant for the province."

"Seems like a nice guy."

"He's not my boyfriend," said Claire.

"Okay."

"Angie Black Weasel introduced us. Melton has a sister. Ellen. She married a guy out of Edmonton. Ivory's her daughter."

"Cute baby."

"She is," said Claire. "Ellen and her husband were killed in a car crash. Ivory survived."

"Hell."

"Melton is her only family," said Claire. "He's looking after her right now, but he doesn't think he can take on the task of raising a child."

Now Thumps could see where this was going. "So, he's looking to find an open adoption for his niece."

"He is."

"To a Blackfeet family?"

"He's mentioned it."

"And you want to adopt Ivory."

"I do," said Claire.

"And Melton wants a regular family. Mom and dad. Dog. Fenced yard."

"Maybe. Maybe not."

"But you don't want to take the chance?"

"No," said Claire. "I don't."

Thumps tried the coffee. It was awful. "So, you've told him that we're together."

Claire sat in the chair and stared at the floor. "You don't have to do anything."

"He know I'm not Blackfeet?"

"You're not angry?"

"For what?"

"Using you."

"Would have been nice if you had asked."

"Would you have said yes?"

"So, Melton is bringing the baby by on Friday," said Thumps. "That means you have her for the weekend?"

"Melton has to go to Spokane," said Claire. "I told him I'd look after Ivory."

"Get to know her."

"Let her get to know me."

"Then why don't we do that?" Thumps leaned back. "You and me and Ivory."

"The three of us?"

"See how it goes."

* * *

FIVE HOURS LATER, Thumps was still awake and trying to find a comfortable position in the chair. Claire was asleep with her head on his shoulder. He didn't see the doors at the end of the corridor fly open, but he heard Big Fish.

As did the rest of the hospital.

"A boy!" Big Fish shouted. "It's a boy."

Thumps pushed out of the chair, slow and stiff. "Congratulations."

"You won't believe how small he is." Big Fish was quivering with excitement. "I got to hold him."

"That's wonderful," said Claire. "And he's healthy?"

"Shit," said Big Fish. "I didn't ask. I'll go back and ask."

"He's healthy," said Claire.

"But he's so small," said Big Fish. "Only nine pounds."

Claire made a sound like a hammer hitting a nail. "You have a name yet?"

Big Fish shook his head. "Lorraine is pretty pissed with me right now. Probably better to wait until she calms down."

Thumps tried to stop the smile. "What'd you do?"

"Got her pregnant," said Big Fish. "Would you believe it? She blames me for that." Big Fish picked up the second sandwich. "This for me?"

"Absolutely," said Claire. "You're going to need all the energy you can get."

Big Fish ripped the plastic off the sandwich. "You should hear the lungs on the kid. He's going to be a singer. I can tell."

Thumps handed him the second cup of coffee.

Big Fish took two gulps and handed the cup back. "Gotta go," he said. "They're getting Little Fish cleaned up and then I get to hold him some more."

"Little Fish?"

Big Fish started down the hall. "You think he knows who I am?"

THUMPS AND CLAIRE settled back in the chairs. The hospital was quiet. The corridors were empty and the lights had been dimmed.

"You think we should stick around," said Claire, "just in case?"

"I'll stay," said Thumps. "Call you if anything happens."

"Nine pounds," said Claire. "Small wonder Lorraine is pissed."

"What are you doing tomorrow night?"

"This about a date?"

"Dinner," said Thumps. "Just the two of us?"

Claire stood up and stretched. "I hear there's a film company in town that wants to do a movie on the Obsidian Murders."

"Yeah," said Thumps. "There is."

"You helping them?"

"Not really."

"But you're still working the case," said Claire. "California. Here. Paris."

"Paris?"

"If you thought you'd find answers in Paris, you'd go to Paris," said Claire. "Wouldn't you?"

"Always wanted to see that city."

"So, you'll be at my place Friday? When Melton drops Ivory off?"

"I will."

"And you'll stay the weekend?"

"What about dinner?"

Claire put her jacket on. "Sure," she said. "We can start there."

THE COFFEE WAS GONE. So were the sandwiches. Thumps wandered down to the vending machines before he realized that he didn't have the right change. He went back to the chair and read the rest of the articles, everything from the new design in soccer cleats to the ten ways to keep ants out of your kitchen.

Big Fish didn't return. He and Lorraine were probably trying to figure out a name for the baby. Thumps should have suggested that they do what many of the tribes did. Wait to see what the child was like before giving it a name. Nothing worse than being saddled with "Bobby" when you turn out to be a "Winslow."

Claire was right. He couldn't be counted on. The Obsidian Murders would always be there, waiting in the shadows. And yes, he would go to Paris if that's where the answers lay.

Life being what it is, one dreams of revenge.

Thumps had always wondered exactly what Gauguin had meant, whether the painter had thought that revenge should remain in dreams or if he was arguing that living in the waking world was reason enough for retribution.

Of course, Thumps could change all that. If he wanted. As with so many other things in life, it was a matter of choice. Drop the case. Put the killings behind him. Forget about justice or vengeance. Get on with the life he had.

There it was. The simple answer. Maybe even the right one.

A SQUALL HAD SNUCK in out of the northwest. The ground was wet, and the Element was glistening. The rain had washed all the dust out of the air, and the stars looked as though they had been scrubbed and polished.

Five-fifteen.

Too early to be up. Too late to go to bed. Just enough time to sit in his house in the dark and feel sorry for himself.

TWENTY

Thumps parked the Element at the curb and tried to imagine a For Sale sign on his front lawn. How would he feel about that? What would he do once he had slipped that mooring? Would he stay in Chinook? Claire was offering an alternative, but she had her reasons, and they didn't necessarily include him.

No house. No Claire. No cat.

Not the end of the world.

The weekend was going to be interesting. Claire and a baby. Thumps and Claire and a baby. What did you do with a baby? You carried it. You put it in a stroller and took it for a walk. You would certainly have to feed it, change its diaper, give it a bath. Thumps tried to think of something fun he could do with a baby, and came up empty.

Claire had done this before. She would probably have some ideas.

Lorraine and Big Fish were going to have to learn on the fly.

Thumps opened the front door and stepped inside. There was something to be said for coming back to an empty house. Everything quiet and calm. He remembered an old television show that his mother had liked where the husband came home every day and would sing out, "Lucy, I'm home." Before she ran away, Freeway would have been here to greet him. Sure, he understood it was because the cat wanted to be fed, but she had been there waiting for him nonetheless. And that's what had counted.

"Freeway," Thumps sang out to the refrigerator, "I'm home."

"In here."

Thumps froze. In the early morning silence of the house, the voice was startling.

"Living room, Tonto."

"Leon?"

Leon Ranger was sprawled out on the sofa, a bath towel thrown over his shoulders. "Door was open."

"No, it wasn't."

Leon ran a hand through his hair. "Then get better locks."

"What are you doing here?"

"Your fridge is empty," said Leon. "You're going to have to buy me breakfast."

"You drove all the way out here?"

"That Roadtrek I bought," said Leon. "Sweet ride."

"Why?"

Leon sat up. "After you left, I began looking into Raymond

Oakes. Amazing what you can find when you know where to look. And whom to look for."

"Okay."

"But the captain felt that my looking at an old case was getting in the way of my real duties."

"Such as sitting on your ass in a basement, collecting dust."

"Exactly," said Leon. "So when he suggested that I should think about my career in law enforcement, I did."

Thumps waited.

"You know the nice thing about retirement?" Leon grinned. "Just about everything."

"So you're retired," said Thumps, "and you're here . . ."

"And we got work to do, Tonto. I got all sorts of new shit."

"You do the tests on the obsidian?"

"I did," said Leon. "But you're probably not going to like the results."

Thumps nodded. "Couple of things I need to tell you as well."

"Well," said Leon, his attention on something over Thumps's shoulder, "I hope the first thing you're going to tell me is that the guy standing behind you with a gun is a friend."

Sheriff Duke Hockney was in his civvies, his service revolver in his hand. "You know," said the sheriff, "I ask myself that question every day."

"Morning, Duke."

"Wouldn't be 'Morning' me if I were you."

Leon Ranger. And now Sheriff Duke Hockney. Thumps wondered when Moses Blood and Cooley Small Elk were going to show up and they could start the party.

"Rose Twining called me," said Duke. "At home."

"Rose?"

"Woke Macy," said Duke. "Said some shady character in a moving van had broken into your house and was trying to rob the place."

"That would be me and the RV," said Leon. "I parked it out back."

"Told Rose it didn't make much sense," said Duke, "'cause you don't have anything worth stealing. But I came anyway."

"Duke," said Thumps, "this is Leon Ranger."

Duke put his gun back in its holster. "Charmed."

"Leon and I used to work together on the coast."

Duke nodded. "So, I don't get to shoot him?"

"You had breakfast yet?" said Leon. "Tonto here is buying."

THE CAFÉ WAS OPEN. There was one customer, a woman in a floral print, hunched over at the counter, but Al was nowhere to be seen. By now, the place should have been jumping with piles of hash browns on the grill and the steam spread out along the ceiling like a storm front.

Leon looked around. "Neat place. Can you get a waffle?"

The woman turned on the stool. "I'll tell you three the same thing I told Wutty."

"Al?" Thumps had never seen Al Couteau on the customer side of the counter.

"Today is make-your-own-breakfast day."

"I'll be damned," said Duke.

And Thumps had never seen her in a dress. "Is that lipstick?"

"Shut up, DreadfulWater."

"And eye shadow?" said the sheriff. "What'd you do to your hair?"

Al fixed all three men with a lethal glare. "You really want to go there?"

"You know," said Duke, "I don't think Al's been to bed."

Thumps remembered. "She had a date last night. With the guy from the car show."

"A date?"

Leon leaned around the sheriff. "Hi," he said. "I'm Leon Ranger. You must be Al."

Al squinted. "You with these two?"

"Never saw them before in my life."

Thumps settled himself on a stool. "I like your hair."

"Yeah," said Duke. "Wearing it long like that, makes you look younger."

"What he means," said Leon, "is that it makes you look younger than you normally look."

"Right," said the sheriff, "that's what I meant."

"I was up all night," said Al. "All right? Yes, it was a date. George Gorka. We had dinner and stayed out late. Went dancing at the Mustang."

The sheriff shook his head.

"I drank too much. I haven't had any sleep." Al let her shoulders sag. "Is there anything else you boys want to know?"

Thumps looked at the sheriff and at Leon. "Nope."

"No interest in whether George and I had sex?" Al waited. "Or whether he's taking me out again tonight?"

"Nope," said all three men in unison.

Al cocked her head at Leon. "I'm guessing you're something that DreadfulWater dragged back from the coast?"

"Guilty."

"He and Thumps used to work together," said Duke.

"A cop?"

"Retired," said Leon.

"So," said Al, "you here about that piece of obsidian?"

Leon turned to Thumps.

"That's one of the things I was going to tell you." Thumps rubbed his eyes. "There was a break-in. At the coroner's office here in town. Nothing taken, but someone left a piece of obsidian on the autopsy table."

"The hell you say."

"Most likely a stupid prank," said the sheriff.

"And then there's this." Thumps took the watch out of his pocket.

"Since when did you start carrying a pocket watch?" said Al.

"It's not mine." Thumps popped the dust cover so everyone could see the inscription. "Found it in my mailbox. Or to be exact, Rose Twining found it and opened the package."

"Rose?"

"She was collecting my mail. She was worried it might be something important."

"Postmark?" asked Leon.

"Let me guess," offered Duke. "Rose threw the packaging away."

"She did," said Thumps. "So we have no idea where it came from."

"*For Ray, with love, Anna.*" Leon read the inscription slowly, pausing at each comma. "Oakes's watch."

"Maybe."

"No maybe," said Leon. "When I was looking at Oakes and Deer Ridge, I saw the inventory record. There was a large pocket watch listed among his personal belongings."

"Raymond Oakes," said Duke. "Someone sent you Oakes's watch?"

"While you're at it," said Al, "tell your buddy about the movie company."

Thumps was tired and he was hungry. "Maybe you should turn the grill on."

Al didn't move. "Be my guest," she said.

The grill was not nuclear physics. Find the knob for the gas.

Light the gas. Let the grill get hot. He had seen Al do it enough times. And he knew where she kept the hash browns. In a bowl of water in the refrigerator. Along with the eggs and the juice.

It was actually fun standing on the cooking side of the counter. He didn't have to talk to Duke or Leon or Al. The sizzle of the potatoes drowned out whatever conversation was happening at the counter, and, for the moment, all Thumps had to worry about was getting the toast to come up at just the right moment.

He gave the first plate to Al.

"Son of a gun," she said. "It appears the man can cook."

"Is it too late to ask for eggs over easy?" said the sheriff.

Thumps gave himself extra hash browns and extra salsa.

"Pretty generous portions," said Al.

"I did all the work."

Al turned on the stool to face Leon. "So, you drove all the way out here to help our Thumps solve a cold case."

"That was the idea," said Leon.

"And you've got a bunch of new clues."

"We do," said Duke.

"And no idea what they mean."

"There's that," said Thumps.

Al smiled at Leon and smoothed her hair. "I've seen these two geniuses in action," she said. "I wouldn't hold my breath."

TWENTY-ONE

Lance Packard was sitting behind the sheriff's desk when Thumps and Duke and Leon got to the office.

"We got a 503 out at the fairgrounds," said the deputy.

"English," said Duke.

"Stolen car." Lance was on his feet and reaching for his jacket. "You want me to take it?"

"Who called it in?"

"Woman." Lance checked his book. "One Anderson Cole."

"The car auction people?"

"I guess."

"I'll take it. Can use the fresh air." Duke pointed his hat at Thumps. "Why don't you come along? Get some practice in law enforcement."

"I have to entertain Leon," said Thumps.

"Bring him along," said Duke. "Law enforcement is endlessly entertaining."

* * *

THE FAIRGROUNDS WERE DESERTED, and the only evidence that there had been a vintage car show was the transport truck parked at the far end of the grandstands. Anderson Cole and George Gorka were standing in front of the barn.

"Sheriff," said Cole. "Mr. DreadfulWater. Handsome stranger."

"Leon Ranger," said Leon. "Humboldt County Sheriff's Department."

"Multinational police presence," said Gorka. "Nothing like small-town hospitality."

"Be nice, George," said Cole.

"No, I mean three cops for one stolen car. I'm impressed."

"Just one cop, I'm afraid," said Duke. "These two are retired."

"So they're just, what, observing?"

"Why don't we start at the beginning." Duke took his book out.

"Our cars were in two areas," said Cole. "The ones for auction were in a roped-off area in front of the grandstands. Our more expensive cars and our display vehicles were in the barn."

"What kind of car we talking about?"

"A 1967 Mustang," said Gorka. "We came out this morning to put the cars on the truck and the Mustang was missing."

"Barn locked?"

"No," said Gorka. "Fire code."

"Security?"

"Cars were locked," said Cole. "We're not exactly Fort Knox."

Duke made notes. "The Mustang the most expensive car in the barn?"

"Not by a long shot," said Gorka. "We have a 1932 Packard Twin Six and a 1946 Packard Super Clipper Club Coupe."

"So, they hot-wired the car?"

"Didn't have to," said Cole. "They took the keys."

Duke frowned.

"We keep the keys in a lockbox," said Gorka. "Box was broken."

Thumps shaded his eyes. "The cars on the transport. They look to be all 1940s and '50s."

"They are," said Cole. "That's our specialty."

"So, why a '67 Mustang?"

"Ford began making the Mustang in 1964," said Leon. "The '67 was the first redesign."

"You know your Fords," said Gorka. "You ever hear of Autoworks International?"

"Can't say that I have," said Duke.

"A few years back, they rebuilt a 1967 Ford Mustang." Gorka lowered his voice as though he had just stepped into a church. "Tremec TKO 600 five-speed transmission, fuel-injected 392 cubic inch V8 with twin Rotrex superchargers and a pair of custom intercoolers. Zero to sixty in four seconds. Custom paint job."

"Sounds expensive," said Duke.

"Supposedly cost over a million to build."

Duke stopped writing. "That's one expensive car."

"One of a kind," said Cole. "It first appeared at the 2006 SEMA."

The world ran on acronyms. CIA, IBM, CEO, IRS, CPA, AT&T. But try as he might, Thumps had no idea what SEMA stood for.

"SEMA," said Cole. "Specialty Equipment Market Association."

"Okay," said Duke. "So you guys lost a million-dollar car?"

"No," said Cole. "Our car's a replica."

"Doesn't have the engine or the transmission or the rest of the expensive goodies," said Gorka. "Just the paint job. The paint job is the same."

Thumps had lost track of the conversation back at SEMA. He looked at Duke and Leon to see if they had been able to keep up.

"So, your car," said Duke, "the replica, isn't worth a million?"

"Our Mustang was a 427 V8," said Gorka. "Book is high thirties. With the paint job, it's low forties."

"Because it has a nice paint job?"

Gorka smiled. "Not just any paint job. Sikkens Obsidian."

Suddenly, Thumps was back with the conversation. "Obsidian?"

"Sure," said Gorka. "That's why they called it the Obsidian Mustang."

"Because of the colour." Duke looked at Thumps.

"That's right," said Gorka. "Sikkens made a custom colour for the Autoworks Mustang. Obsidian black. The deepest black you'll ever see. Beautiful. Like falling into a well."

"And your Mustang was painted the same colour," said Thumps. "Obsidian black."

"It was a damn expensive paint job," said Cole. "Let me tell you that."

"How many people knew about the paint?"

Cole shrugged. "Anybody who read the write-up on the stand next to the car."

Okay, Thumps had run out of patience with coincidences. The break-in at the Land Titles building, the pocket watch, and now a missing Mustang painted obsidian. Someone was having a good time at his expense.

"Licence plate?" said Duke.

"OBSIDIAN," said Gorka. "What else?"

"Okay," said the sheriff. "Let's run through it again. From the top."

THUMPS AND LEON left the sheriff to the business at hand and wandered over to the transport truck to look at the cars that were stacked up on the ramps.

Leon settled in next to a maroon Plymouth. "Who wants to go first?"

"Someone's screwing with us," said Thumps.

"With you," said Leon. "I'm retired."

"It's as though I hit a tripwire on a land mine. I go back to the coast, and all hell breaks loose."

"Are you asking me?" Leon took the silver dollar out of his pocket.

"You're not going to solve the case with that?"

"Nope," said Leon. "But I figure to keep it handy for when you ask me to do something and I have to make a decision."

"I'm not going to ask you to do anything."

"I've heard that before."

Thumps organized the elements in his head to see if he could make any sense out of the pieces.

"Three scenarios, so far as I can see," said Thumps. "One, our serial killer has resurfaced here in Chinook."

"After all this time?" Leon shook his head. "Why?"

"Second, Raymond Oakes has resurfaced here in Chinook."

"Again," said Leon. "Why?"

"And third," said Thumps, "someone is playing a sick game."

"A break-in, a pocket watch, and a stolen car. That's some game."

"So, we still have nothing."

"Not necessarily," said Leon. "We can't do much about the break-in or the pocket watch, but a car is an entirely different critter."

"Okay."

"If the guy who stole the car is the guy who did the break-in and sent the pocket watch, then we can suppose that he's still in town."

"Because why go to all that trouble and then drive away."

"So we find the car," said Leon, "we find our perp."

"Harder to hide than a pocket watch."

"You know the town," said Leon. "Where would you hide a car?"

THE SHERIFF TOOK another twenty minutes with Cole and Gorka. He didn't look particularly happy as he stomped across the broken ground, his hat pulled down tight on his head.

"You two solve this thing yet?"

Thumps waited for Duke to get all the way to the transport truck. "Did Cole have a tracking device on the car?"

"That would be too easy," said Duke.

"Thumps thinks the car is still in town."

Duke nodded. "Lots of places to hide a car."

Thumps took the watch out of his pocket and let it hang by the chain. "Why steal a car?"

"You going somewhere with this, Tonto?"

"I can see the break-in," said Thumps. "Low risk. The watch is low risk as well."

"But the car isn't," said Duke.

"You have to steal the keys, sneak into the barn, drive the car away, and hide it." Thumps took a deep breath and let it out. "And there's no guarantee that Cole or Gorka would have mentioned the paint job. So far as they're concerned, it's just a stolen '67 Mustang."

"Maybe the car was stolen for two separate reasons," said Leon.

"The paint job," said the sheriff. "So we'd make the connection."

Thumps nodded. "And our perp needed a car for something else."

"And even if we didn't tumble to the symbolism of the paint, our perp would still have the car he needs," said the sheriff. "Win, win."

"Pretty weak," said Leon.

Thumps walked away from the transport, and then he walked back. "Common denominator in all this is me."

"Someone is trying to get at our Thumps," said Duke. "Get inside his head."

"That's the way I read it," said Leon.

"Still could be a prank," said Duke.

Thumps nodded. "Could."

"So what do we do?"

"Only thing we *can* do," said Thumps. "Wait to see what happens next."

Leon flipped the silver dollar. "Call it," he said. "You win, and you and Marshal Dillon get me as a free consultant."

"Sure as hell can't pay you," said Duke.

Leon caught the coin and peeked under his hand. "Damn," he said. "You are one lucky son of a buck."

"He like this all the time?" said Hockney.

"No," said Thumps. "Sometimes he can get really annoying."

TWENTY-TWO

Hockney went right to the table by the filing cabinets and touched the side of the old percolator. "Ready to go."

"Never turn down coffee," said Leon.

Thumps felt somewhat aggrieved that Duke had started making drinkable coffee. After years of drinking the glop that had come out of the sheriff's coffee pot, it didn't seem fair that Leon should miss that minor rite of passage.

"Sheriff's coffee," said Thumps, trying to keep the edge out of his voice. "Not what it used to be."

"Sarcasm is the last refuge of a scoundrel," said Duke.

"Patriotism," corrected Thumps. "'Patriotism is the last refuge of a scoundrel.'"

"Here," said the sheriff. "Make sure you keep it charged."

"I don't need a cellphone."

"It's not yours," said Duke. "It belongs to the city."

"I don't want the city's cellphone."

"You have to carry one when you're acting sheriff," said Duke. "You might as well practise."

Leon grinned. "You're going to be acting sheriff?"

"Temporary," said Thumps.

Leon turned to Duke. "Vacation?"

"Something like that," said Duke. "You want cream or sugar?"

"Just black," said Leon.

"Good," said Hockney, "'cause we don't have cream or sugar."

What Thumps wanted was to go home and crawl into bed. He wasn't particularly tired, but since he had arrived back in Chinook, he hadn't had much time to himself. It would be pleasant to lock the door, crawl under the covers, and just lie there in the dark. He didn't think it was depression. It was more the exhaustion that comes with being alive.

"Damn," said Leon. "Now that's coffee."

"Hear Lorraine had a boy." Hockney pulled the tin of cookies out of his drawer and set them on the desk. "But they can't agree on a name."

"My sister has one of those baby-name books," said Leon. "Must have close to a thousand names in the damn thing."

"Word is that Lorraine wants a name that's imposing."

"Imposing?"

"You know," said Duke, "something with at least three syllables."

"Edward," said Leon.

"Only two syllables."

"Percival," said Leon. "He was some kind of knight."

"According to Dora Manning, whose niece works at the hospital, Lorraine is considering Orlando, Leander, and Jeremiah."

"Lotta name for a baby to be dragging around," said Leon.

"While Big Fish," said Duke, "wants something that people will remember. Memphis, Yancey, Ishmael."

"Ishmael?"

"Right now, Big Fish is calling the baby Little Fish, and according to Dora's niece, that isn't going over so well."

Thumps tried to imagine in what universe Big Fish thought he would win an argument with Lorraine.

"And all this before they even decide on whether the boy is going to have Lorraine's last name or Big Fish's or if they're going to do that hyphenated thing that turns the kid into a zip code."

Big Fish would be better off just to agree with whatever Lorraine wanted, amass as many air miles as he could in the process, and live to lose another day.

Duke yawned and closed his eyes. "So, what do you want to do?"

"About Big Fish?"

"Big Fish is on his own," said the sheriff. "Man fool enough to take on Lorraine Chubby is beyond help. What do you want to do about our little mystery?"

"How about we start over," said Leon. "Put the whole thing together piece by piece."

"You make it sound like a puzzle," said Duke.

"It is," said Leon.

"Sure," said Duke. "Except we don't even know if we have all the pieces."

"So we work with the pieces we have," said Leon.

"Be my guest," said the sheriff. "I'll sit back and referee."

"Late summer on the coast," said Leon. "Tourist season is almost over. Then suddenly, we're up to our necks in bodies."

Hockney held up a hand. "Bodies with a piece of obsidian in their mouths."

"That's right," said Leon.

Duke nodded. "Were they all killed the same way?"

"Bludgeoned," said Leon. "The killer used pieces of driftwood and rocks, anything that he could find at hand."

"Up close," said Duke.

"And smart," said Leon. "He doesn't have to bring a weapon with him or take it away."

"Were you able to arrange the victims in order of killing?"

"No," said Thumps. "By the time we found all the bodies, there was no way to establish the timeline."

Leon looked at Duke. "In most cases, we knew they were dead before their families knew they were missing."

"So they weren't all discovered right away?"

"Best we can figure," said Leon, "is that they were killed over two days, three at the most."

"The bodies were left in the dunes and the seagrass. Above the high-tide mark," said Thumps. "A lot of people walk the beach, but they stay near the water. Nobody much goes into the deep sand."

"Ballsy," said Duke. "Each trip to the beach would expose him."

"Sure," said Leon, "but the chances he'd be noticed were slim."

"Still, you put out queries?"

"We did," said Leon. "Ads in the local and state papers. Television. The internet."

"And you got nothing?"

"Worse," said Leon. "One guy swore that he had seen his next-door neighbour at the beach with an axe."

"Let me guess," said Duke. "A neighbour with whom he had a beef."

"Lawsuit," said Leon. "Then there was the mother of two who fingered a secretary in her husband's office. Said she was walking on the beach when she saw the secretary come out of the seagrass with blood on her hoodie."

"And?"

"We checked. The secretary was in Mexico on vacation at the time of the killings."

"Nothing like a serial killer to bring out the best in people." Duke ambled over to the coffee pot. "So, no leads. No timeline. The wild card is Raymond Oakes, and you guys didn't know about him until a couple of weeks back."

"All correct," said Leon. "But Thumps had an interesting idea."

"He gets one of those every so often," said Duke.

"Once we knew about Oakes, we went back to the evidence and tested the obsidian that was found in the mouths of the victims."

Duke poured himself a cup of coffee and let the steam flow over his face. "Because if Oakes had killed Tripp and her daughter, and a serial killer had murdered the other people, then the obsidian would be different."

"That was the thinking," said Leon.

"And?"

"Inconclusive."

"Which brings us to Nina Maslow and her research," said Thumps. "Maslow dug up Oakes, and she did a rough profile of the serial killer."

"Let me guess," said Duke. "They don't match."

"Not even close," said Thumps. "Maslow believed that the Obsidian killer was well educated, wealthy, and extremely intelligent. She was sure that Northern California wasn't his first."

"Whereas Raymond Oakes didn't even graduate from high school," said Leon. "He was in jail before he was twenty and barely out when the killings took place."

"Okay," said Duke. "Let's back it up a bit. Maslow would have been able to do a full background check on Oakes, but she had no way of doing a reliable profile on a ghost. Our serial killer could have been a woman for all Maslow knew."

"Possible," said Leon. "But not likely."

"And profiling isn't a hard science," said the sheriff. "Mostly, it's a good guess."

Thumps took the two files out of his bag and handed them to Duke. "You remember John Douglas and Robert Ressler?"

"Names ring a bell."

"FBI agents," said Thumps. "In the late '70s, they looked at thirty-six serial killers to try to figure out what made them tick."

"Split them up into organized and disorganized," said Leon.

"Not much of a profile," said Duke.

"Disorganized criminals were generally young, drunk or high, or mentally ill. They were sloppy, left all sorts of trace evidence lying around."

"And generally got caught," said Leon.

"Whereas organized criminals were smarter," said Duke. "That's pretty much common sense."

"Douglas and Ressler's general premise was that behaviour reflects personality."

"Now there's a T-shirt," said Duke. "'Behaviour Reflects Personality.'"

"Anyway," said Thumps, "that's what Maslow did. She looked at the crime itself and then began working her way back to the criminal. What triggered the crime? Who were the victims? How were they killed? What happened to the bodies? Was there any post-offence behaviour?"

"You mean such as writing letters to the press or phoning investigators?"

"Right," said Leon. "Evidently, that happens a lot. Nothing like a little publicity to float a serial killer's boat."

"But in the case of the Obsidian Murders," said Thumps, "the killer made no attempt to insert himself into the investigation."

"Okay," said Duke, "I get that Maslow figured the guy for organized. Killing ten people takes some planning, but there's no way she would have known what triggered the killings. And, as I remember, there didn't seem to be any rhyme or reason as to how he chose his victims."

"True," said Leon. "The victims ranged in age from twenty-two to seventy-one, men, women, and one child. Some were local. Some were tourists passing through. The only constant was that their bodies were arranged in the sand and each victim had a piece of obsidian in their mouth."

"I get the organized and smart part," said Duke. "Guy commits multiple murders and gets away without leaving a trace. But how did Maslow come to the conclusion that the guy was well educated and wealthy?"

Thumps could feel his shoulder tightening. "Maslow saw the obsidian as a clue. A number of cultures, such as the Olmecs and the Aztecs, would put stones in the mouths of the dead. Jade, pearls, obsidian. That kind of symbolism wouldn't be common knowledge."

"Our perp could have looked that up on the internet," said Duke. "Wouldn't have to go to university to play Aztec."

"No," said Thumps, "he wouldn't."

"And he could just have a thing for obsidian."

"He could," said Leon.

"Which brings us to the wealthy part." Duke leaned back in the chair and rested his hands on his stomach. "Impress me."

"I think Maslow was guessing," said Thumps.

"No shit," said Duke.

"None of the victims were robbed. Nothing was taken. Credit cards, jewellery, cash. One of the victims, a lawyer out of San Francisco, had a forty-thousand-dollar watch on his wrist."

Duke snorted. "What idiot takes a forty-thousand-dollar watch to the beach?"

"Better question," said Leon, "is what idiot kills the guy wearing it and leaves the watch?"

"You know," said Duke, "I can't tell an expensive watch from a cheap watch."

"Another of the victims had $2,000 cash in his pocket," said Leon.

"Thin," said Duke. "Very thin."

"Hell," said Leon, "thin is all we've got."

"So, what about this Raymond Oakes?"

"Oakes doesn't fit the profile," said Thumps, "and Maslow couldn't see him leaving an expensive watch and that much cash behind."

"But she thought he could have killed Anna Tripp and her daughter."

"Yeah," said Leon. "Maslow thought that was a possibility."

Duke sighed. "So we've either got a brainy, rich serial killer spreading joy wherever he goes, or we have a serial killer *and* a homicidal spouse. Is that about it?"

Leon nodded. "I think that covers it."

The sheriff stood up and stretched. "You want more coffee?"

"Sure," said Leon.

Duke brought the coffee pot over. "Today, it's a Brazilian blend with black cherry overtones and hints of tobacco."

"Perfect."

"But what I don't get," said Duke, "is the time delay. When you went back to the coast to poke around, did you find anything new?"

Thumps pushed his cup forward. "Just Raymond Oakes."

"While here in Chinook, we get a break-in at the county morgue, where someone leaves a piece of obsidian on the autopsy table," said Duke. "You get a pocket watch in the mail that supposedly belonged to Oakes. And someone steals a car that is painted black."

"Obsidian black," said Leon. "And don't forget the movie folks."

Duke shook his head. "What kind of people go around making films out of someone's misery?"

"Like you said," said Leon, "it could be a bad joke."

Duke put the pot on his desk. "We even know what this Oakes character looks like?"

"Got a photograph," said Leon. "Mug shot. I can email you a copy."

"We'll show it around," said Duke. "I'll have the boys check the motels north to Glory and east to Red Tail Lake."

"But if we're looking at a serial killer," said Thumps, "we're blind."

"Nonsense." Duke pushed his glasses up his nose with one finger. "He's a psychopath. He looks just like the rest of us."

TWENTY-THREE

Thumps was fine with the idea of a house guest. In the abstract. The reality of having someone in his personal space was a different matter entirely. Not that Leon turned out to be a house guest in the strict sense of the term.

"No offence," Leon said, "but I'll stay in the Roadtrek. More comfortable. Private. My own bed. Bathroom. Television. Kitchen."

Leon took him on a tour of the RV, and Thumps had to admit that the amenities and the finishes were impressive.

"And I won't have to listen to you snore."

Leon unrolled a long extension cord that they hooked into an outlet on the back porch. "Got solar panels on the roof," said Leon, "but a plug-in is more reliable."

There was a laptop on a fold-up table.

"Got satellite WiFi. Can write my novels anywhere in the world. Do all the research online."

"What about the toilet and sink?"

"Fresh water reservoir and the toilet dumps into a holding tank." Leon rambled on like a proud parent. "Can go at least a week before I have to find a dump station and drain the black water."

"Black water?"

"That's what they call the . . . you know."

Thumps tried to put the picture out of his mind.

"There's enzymes you have to put in the tank that help break down the solids, but all in all, the maintenance is pretty easy."

"You need any blankets or pillows?"

"Nope, brought everything with me." Leon opened the small refrigerator. "Beer, nuts, and hard-boiled eggs."

"Major food groups."

Leon tapped the sofa with his foot. "You press this button, and the darn thing turns into a bed. You believe that?"

"Nice."

"Ron always thought you'd come back. He didn't fill your position for over a year." Leon took a beer from the refrigerator. "What happened?"

There it was, the question for which Thumps didn't have an answer.

"I mean, I can understand why you never came back. But we never heard from you again. Nothing. You had a lot of friends on the force."

"Herb and Paul?"

"Those assholes." Leon's laugh was sharp and cold. "No, they thought you quit, thought you gave up, that you ran away."

"Maybe I did."

"Paul mouthed off once too often, and Ron decked him."

"Ron?"

"Wouldn't have thought it," said Leon. "But all that home repair, swinging a framing hammer. Hell of a right. One shot, and Paul didn't get up."

"Jesus."

"Mind you, getting cold-cocked didn't change his opinion," said Leon, "but after that, he kept his thoughts on the matter to himself."

"I'm sorry I didn't call."

"Damn straight you are. You don't treat friends like that." Leon went back to the fridge. "You want a beer?"

"You want me to try to explain?"

"Do you want to?"

"Not really."

"Then have a beer," said Leon. "I hate explanations, and I hate drinking alone. Makes me feel like some pathetic alcoholic."

THE REST OF the afternoon was taken up with stories, stories they had told each other when they were cops on the coast, stories they knew by heart.

"You remember Guy Dixon?"

"Sure."

"You remember that charity golf tournament we went to in Truckee?"

"Greenwood something."

"That's the one," said Leon. "Sixth hole, Guy puts the cart in the lake."

"And tries to get you to pull him out with your cart."

"So I back up my cart . . ."

"And you backed it up too far."

Leon put his beer on the table and let the silence fill the room. "Always thought it was strange that you and Anna never got married."

Thumps tried smiling. "Thought we were boring each other with old stories."

"Or even moved in together." Leon worked on a burp. "I mean, hell, you were Callie's father for all practical purposes."

"How about we take the RV for a spin."

"But now we know," said Leon. "Anna was married already and didn't want to tell you."

"We could take it along the river road," said Thumps. "Give you some pointers on photography."

"Anna could have divorced Oakes while he was in prison. But she didn't."

"I could get a photo of you and the RV with the mountains in the background."

"She loved you, but I'm guessing she still had feelings for him. Or she felt sorry for him. And there was the child." Leon picked up the bottle and swirled the beer around. "Women are strange that way."

Thumps could see that he wasn't going to be able to move Leon off his line, so he sat back and let the man run.

"You didn't know any of this," said Leon, "but you must have wondered why she kept you at arm's length?"

"She didn't keep me at arm's length."

"She didn't tell you about Oakes."

"Again. What difference does it make?"

"And when they were killed, you fell apart."

Thumps could feel the anger rising. "You going somewhere with this other than in circles?"

"Thought you indigenous types liked circles."

"Fuck you."

"That's the spirit," said Leon. "Good to see you have some fire left."

Thumps set his beer to one side. "Maybe this isn't such a good idea."

"What?" said Leon. "My being here? Reopening the case? Dredging up the past? All of the above?"

"Me drinking."

"Call this drinking?" Leon finished the bottle. "Look, you want to solve the case. You want to find who killed Anna and Callie. I want to find who killed all those people. Maybe we're looking for the same person. Maybe we're looking for two different people."

Leon paused for a moment. "We used to be good at this.

You and me. Six years ago, we got blindsided, and we screwed up. Ten bodies was a load to deal with. Along with state and federal cops and the press and the public all screaming at us to do something."

"We tried."

"Sure, we tried," said Leon, "but we also got swept up in the hysteria. We didn't do our job. At least, we didn't do it well enough."

"And I ran away," said Thumps. "Is that what you're trying to tell me?"

"You left. Can't say I understood your reasons. But that was then. This is now."

"And you think we can finish this."

"I'm not the one who drove all the way to California." Leon saluted Thumps with the empty bottle. "I was happy rotting away in that basement."

"So," said Thumps, "what kind of mileage does this thing get?"

"Changing the subject isn't going to save you."

"Why don't we try."

"Okay." Leon helped himself to another beer. "Where might a lonely brother go to find wine, women, and song in this one-horse town?"

"Wine, women, and song?"

"Okay," said Leon, "booze and dancing."

"The Mustang."

"Good manners dictate that you show me around, introduce me to the populace."

"Busy tonight."

"A date?"

"Dinner."

Leon reached into his pocket and came up with his silver dollar. "Flip you."

"For what?"

"Heads, you come to the Mustang with me," said Leon. "Tails, I go to dinner with you."

Thumps opened the door of the RV and stepped out into the fading light. "You need to get a life."

"Tomorrow"—Leon followed Thumps into the yard— "tomorrow, we work the case from the beginning."

"Sure."

"You up for that?"

Thumps nodded. "Yeah, I'm up for that."

"'Cause this time, I need to know that you're in it till the end."

TWENTY-FOUR

Thumps took his time in the shower. Not a rub-a-dub-dub kind of shower with soap and a washcloth, but rather a stand-under-the-hot-water shower. Until it ran cold. Not a bad way to live a life.

Alone.

In the dark.

The water drowning out all sound.

If it weren't for the limits of hot-water tanks, standing in the shower long enough might just wash away the past and leave you clean and ready to start over again.

THE MOTHER LODE was busy.

"I have a reservation."

"Name?"

"DreadfulWater," said Thumps. "For two."

Thumps hadn't expected Claire to be on time. And she didn't disappoint.

The server was an older man with a heavy accent that sounded authentic. Italy perhaps. Or maybe somewhere in Germany where they spoke French as a second language.

"Would you care for a drink while you wait for the rest of your party?"

"Water, please."

"We have American Summits, Apollinaris, Badoit, Berg, and, of course, Evian and Perrier."

"Of course."

"I would recommend the American Summits, which is sourced from springs high in the Beartooth Mountains of Wyoming, or the Berg, which is harvested from icebergs off the coast of Newfoundland and Labrador."

"Tap water."

The man didn't miss a beat. "Ah," he said, "Château Chinook."

"No ice."

"Excellent choice."

Al Couteau and George Gorka were at a table in the corner. Thumps was tempted to wander over, just to be annoying, but he knew that Al was not the forgiving type, and only a fool messed with breakfast. Al was wearing a dark dress with bright white stars. Her hair was down, and she was smiling. George was holding her hand. The two of them were bent over, their heads close together as though they were exchanging state secrets.

"Mr. DreadfulWater."

Mercer, Gerson, and Shipman.

Mercer brushed his hair off his forehead. "You dining alone?"

"No."

"Aha," said Shipman. "And she's late."

"God, Harry," said Gerson. "That is such a cliché."

"Late is late," said Shipman.

"Archimedes Kousoulas," said Mercer. "Great guy."

"Spent the afternoon with him," said Shipman. "All sorts of good background information. Man's a walking encyclopedia."

"Says that the two of you are working the Obsidian murder case together," said Gerson.

Thumps could only imagine what Archie had told the movie people.

"Said the two of you were about to crack it wide open."

"Archie mention the Aztec treasure?" Thumps kept a straight face.

"The fortune in gold that Antonio Garcia de la Vega is supposed to have brought north out of Mexico?"

Thumps nodded. "That's the one."

"Wants us to do a film about it," said Shipman. "After we're done with Obsidian."

"He wants to play himself," said Gerson. "He's really kinda sweet."

Mercer picked at a spot on his jacket. "You have any luck with Oakes?"

Thumps tried to read the man's face. "Thought you weren't going to use Oakes in the script."

"We're not," said Shipman. "But curiosity is a powerful thing."

Over Shipman's shoulder, Thumps saw Claire come into the restaurant.

Thumps stood as she got to the table.

"Am I late?"

"Mercer, Gerson, and Shipman," said Thumps by way of introduction. "Claire Merchant."

"Lawyers?" asked Claire.

"Close," said Mercer. "Entertainment."

"They're thinking of making a movie about the Obsidian Murders."

"Ah," said Claire.

"That's what most people say," said Shipman. "We should leave you be."

"We didn't make a reservation," said Mercer, "so it looks like it's fast food."

"That's disgusting, Tony."

Thumps smiled. "The sheriff did mention something about a giant squirrel."

"Try Shadow Ranch," said Claire. "Stay away from the squirrel."

"The script is almost done," said Shipman. "I'll get you a copy when it's locked."

* * *

THE SERVER ARRIVED with a menu. "May I bring the lady something to drink?"

"House white," said Claire.

"The specials are on the insert at the front," said the server. "I'd recommend the prime rib."

Claire had dressed for the occasion. Thumps was so used to seeing her in jeans and a work shirt that Claire in a dress and heels was somewhat of a shock.

"You look great."

"Well, aren't you the charmer."

"No," said Thumps, "you look . . ."

"Stunning?"

Thumps quickly ran through the synonyms for "stunning." Spectacular, striking, fabulous, magnificent, gorgeous, exquisite.

"You look beautiful."

Claire blushed. "It's been a while since we did this."

Thumps tried to remember the last time they had gone out to dinner. Before Seattle and the cancer treatments. Long before that.

"We should do it more often."

"Yes," said Claire, "we should."

The server was back, and he waited patiently while Claire looked at the menu one last time.

"Rabbit," said Claire. "I'm going to have the rabbit ravioli. And the bruschetta appetizer."

"And for the gentleman?"

"Prime rib," said Thumps. "Medium rare."

Claire sat back and willed her shoulders to relax. "This is nice."

"It is."

"Is that Al?"

"It is."

"With a man?"

"George Gorka," said Thumps. "He's with the vintage car auction."

"Good for her," said Claire. "I suppose you know about Beth and Gabby Santucci."

So he hadn't imagined Santucci in Beth's apartment.

"But that's not why you invited me to dinner." Claire unfolded her napkin and spread it on her lap. "Is it?"

"Thought we should talk about us."

"Really?"

"Absolutely."

"Maybe you want to talk about Victor."

Thumps tried to play dumb.

Claire cocked her head. "Moses didn't mention Victor?"

Thumps shrugged. "He might have."

"Want to see a picture of him?"

"No."

"Men," said Claire. "Not sure what separates you guys from buffalo."

"Buffalo don't take beautiful women out to dinner."

"Victor was good-looking. He was exciting." Claire played with the wineglass. "He was the bad boy that mothers warn their daughters about."

"Maybe I'm a bad boy."

Claire started laughing. Tears began streaming down her face.

Thumps waited, hoping she would stop. "There's lots you don't know about me."

It was somewhat embarrassing. People at the other tables began glancing in his direction, and Thumps realized that they were probably thinking that Claire was crying, that he had said something brutish or unkind.

Even Al and George were looking at him.

"God," said Claire, "but you do make me laugh."

"So what about Ivory?" said Thumps, trying to change the subject.

Claire wiped her eyes with her napkin. "Well, you'll get a good dose of baby."

"Great."

"Screaming. Feedings every two hours. Dirty diapers. More screaming. Singing, rocking, burping, more dirty diapers."

"I'll be fine."

"Sure," said Claire. "For the weekend. I figure you're good to get through that."

"What do you need me to do?"

"I want to adopt her," she said. "Can you help me do that?"

"I can."

"Callie," said Claire. "You thought of her as your daughter, didn't you?"

The food arrived. Thumps put his napkin on his lap and went to work on the prime rib. It was slightly overcooked, but good.

"What time should I come by on Friday?"

"Any time," said Claire. "I'll make something for dinner."

"I could bring Chinese."

Claire cocked her head to one side. "The salmon stuffed with wild rice was a mistake anyone could make."

Thumps nodded.

"The instructions didn't say anything about cooking the rice first."

Thumps smiled. "You want to split a dessert?"

"And when you find him," said Claire, her voice soft and sad. "When you find Raymond Oakes, will that be the end of it?"

THUMPS HADN'T EXPECTED that Claire was going to stay over. And she didn't. They said good night at her truck.

"Last time you were looking at an adoption, you almost bought a Subaru from Freddy Salgado."

"I'll stay with the pickup."

"Too bad you don't have a club cab."

"Single cab will work for the time being," said Claire. "See how it goes."

CASH AND CARRY was open, and Thumps spent a leisurely hour wandering the aisles. Eggs. Potatoes. Shredded wheat. Bread. A six-pack of beer for Leon. There was a sign on the wall above the produce that said, "Buy Local." The grapes were from Chile. The melons from Turkey. The peaches were from the Okanagan Valley in British Columbia.

The bananas weren't marked, but Thumps was sure they hadn't been grown on a plantation in West Yellowstone.

Cash and Carry had changed some of their food offerings. Not long ago, the store had had an organic section. Now the space had been taken over by an enormous freezer with glass doors that was filled with microwave meals in bright, appealing cartons. Thumps read the nutritional guide on a box that contained Salisbury steak, green beans, and mashed potatoes. No wonder Americans were obese. Sugar, fat, salt, unpronounceable chemicals. The ready-to-eat food industry was the new cartel, its CEOs the new drug dealers.

He had put two quarts of vanilla ice cream into the cart, wheeled them around the store for a while, and then put them back, a somewhat astonishing triumph of self-restraint and good sense that he would mention to Beth the next time she asked him about his diet.

THE RV WAS GONE.

Thumps considered driving out to the Mustang to make sure that Leon had made it there safely and was not annoying anyone unduly. He was reasonably sure that a retired deputy sheriff was not going to impress the regulars who called the bar home. There was something about club colours and motorcycles that made such men feel invincible.

If Big Fish was back at work, Thumps could call and ask him to look after his friend. Or Leon could try taking out his silver dollar and flipping himself out of trouble.

Thumps took his time putting the dry goods into the cupboards and the perishables into the fridge. Tomorrow, he'd make an omelette. Onions, peppers, a little sausage meat, tomatoes, Swiss cheese. Multi-grain toast. A pot of black coffee.

Then he and Leon would open the boxes, spread the files out, and go back to work as though they had just caught the case that morning.

TWENTY-FIVE

Thumps was up with the sun. He had wanted to sleep in, had pulled the covers over his head, had rolled himself up in the blankets, had even taken a stab at that technique where you relax your toes and work your way up.

But in spite of his best efforts, here he was, standing in front of the refrigerator with the morning light at the window, trying to decide whether Leon was a bacon or sausage man.

The RV was back. So, Leon had survived an evening at the Mustang, though in what condition remained to be seen. Thumps shredded the potatoes and began cooking them in olive oil and butter. He laid the bacon strips on the grill, arranged the sausages in the fry pan, and turned the oven on to 200. The meat would beat the potatoes done, and he'd put the bacon and sausages on the lower rack while he waited for

Leon to appear. Then he'd fold the eggs into the skillet and put the toast down.

The other day at Al's, working the grill, had been fun. And it had reminded him of Eureka. Anna and Callie. He had been the primary cook in the relationship. Dinners, for the most part. Always at his place. They had never moved in together, and Anna had never offered to have him stay overnight.

He had thought it had been because of Callie.

Thumps took two plates out of the cupboard and set them on the counter when he heard the back door open.

"Hope you made enough for two, Tonto," Leon shouted from the laundry room. "'Cause we are hungry."

"Yes, we are," Thumps shouted back.

Leon was partially dressed, pants, T-shirt, no socks, no shoes. His hair was stuck against the side of his face as though he had spent the night with his head in a steam press. Thumps had seen better-looking eyes on a dead rat.

"Bacon *and* sausage." Leon crowded in against the stove. "You must be my mother."

"I thought *I* was your mama." Ora Mae Foreman was standing in the doorway, looking as though she had just stepped off the pages of *Forbes* or *Elle*.

It took Thumps a moment to digest the scene.

"Your mouth is open." Ora Mae pinched two fingers together. "Two eggs over easy, dry toast, and coffee. Please."

"I'll take the works," said Leon. "Got to recharge the old battery."

"The man's an Energizer Bunny," said Ora Mae. "But his taste in movies stinks."

"*The Naked Prey*. 1965," said Leon. "Cornel Wilde as a big-game hunter in Africa."

Ora Mae rolled her eyes.

"He's captured by the natives, and they give him a chance to run for his freedom."

"This is where it gets really stupid," said Ora Mae. "They shoot an arrow and where it lands is the guy's head start. You believe that?"

"Soon as he reaches the arrow, the chase begins." Leon notched an imaginary arrow into an imaginary bow. "Indians ever do that?"

Thumps got out two more eggs.

Ora Mae shook her head. "Ain't no way some skinny White guy outruns that tribe. Those men were in great shape."

"The foreman here tells me you going to sell your house."

Ora Mae slugged Leon on the shoulder. "I told you not to call me that out in the open. Thumps here will get the wrong idea."

"You should think about an RV," said Leon.

"No, he shouldn't," said Ora Mae. "They're no better than a car. Drive it off the lot and you lose half the value."

"Less than a third," said Leon. "And there's no guarantee that a house will appreciate. I have friends in Arcata who bought at the top of the market. They won't get their money back."

"Sure," said Ora Mae. "Shit happens. Difference is an RV is *guaranteed* to depreciate."

Leon tried to peel his hair off his face. "You got indoor plumbing?"

"Down the hall," said Thumps. "First door on the left."

Thumps could feel Ora Mae looming behind him.

"I expect you've got some questions," said Ora Mae.

"Nope." Thumps stayed at the stove and kept his head down. "I'm good."

"For instance, what's a good-looking lesbian doing with a junkyard dog?"

"Opposites attract?"

"That the best you can do?"

"Food's almost ready."

"Psychology 101," said Ora Mae. "Sexual activity depends on the availability of a partner."

Thumps put the potatoes and the meat on the table and began buttering the toast.

"And he's a good dancer," said Ora Mae. "He ain't much to look at, but the man has got some moves." Ora Mae helped herself to a taste of the hash browns. "And he makes me laugh."

Leon was back, and he didn't look much better. His hair was still stuck to the side of his face, and now it was wet.

"A yellow sink?"

Thumps shrugged.

"And a yellow toilet?" Leon shook his head. "Enough to put a man off his business."

"It's lime-green," said Ora Mae. "All the rage in the '60s."

"Food's ready," said Thumps.

"What happened to those over-easy eggs and dry toast?" said Ora Mae. "Hell of a world when a gorgeous woman can't get over-easy eggs and dry toast."

CONSIDERING THE PEOPLE sitting around the kitchen table, breakfast was a quiet affair. It was Ora Mae who finally broke the silence.

"Is that the serial killer stuff?" Ora Mae nodded toward the stack of banker boxes.

"That's it," said Leon.

"And you two think you're going to catch this guy."

Thumps sighed. "We don't even know whom we're trying to catch."

"Leon told me there was an ex-husband."

"Not ex," said Thumps. "They were still married."

"Anna Tripp," said Leon, as though this explained anything. "And Raymond Oakes."

"There's married," said Ora Mae, "and then there's married."

"He may have nothing to do with the killings."

"So, you're chasing a husband," said Ora Mae, "or you're chasing a ghost. This husband own real estate?"

Leon looked at Thumps.

"'Cause if he owned any real estate before he went into prison," said Ora Mae, "he may still own it."

Thumps poured himself another cup of coffee. "Oakes was nineteen when he went to prison. No family. Grew up in foster care. Doubt he owned much of anything."

Ora Mae helped herself to the last sausage. "There was this old woman in the neighbourhood. Us kids thought she was crazy and maybe she was. Anyway, she always wore this blue sweater. Robin's egg blue. Button-up with a little collar. Wore that damn sweater every day of the year. Hot. Cold. Didn't matter. You see what I'm saying?"

Thumps looked at Leon.

"Well, that sweater got real ratty. Moth holes. Falling apart. Didn't smell so good either. And one night, when she was asleep, her son sneaked that sweater away from her and threw it out. Figured that she'd forget about it over time."

"But she didn't?" said Leon.

"Nope," said Ora Mae. "Every day after that, she'd wander through the neighbourhood looking for that sweater."

"Her son get her a new sweater?"

"He did," said Ora Mae. "But he wasn't fooling his mother, and she just kept on looking until the day she died."

There were a few hash browns left and one piece of toast.

"That's a sad story," said Leon. "Flip you for that last piece of toast."

"You eat the toast," said Ora Mae. "I got to get back to selling houses. They don't sell themselves, you know."

"You never told me how much you thought my house is worth."

"That's 'cause you're not serious," said Ora Mae. "You're just feeling sorry for yourself and looking for sympathy."

"No, I'm not."

"You want a bunch of strangers coming through your house, opening drawers, checking closets, turning the taps on and off, asking questions about heating and cooling costs?"

Thumps could feel a shot of sharp panic shoot through his body.

Ora Mae stood and brushed off her suit. "Yeah," she said. "That's what I thought."

"We going dancing again tonight?"

Ora Mae smiled her bright smile at Leon. "A walk on the wild side?"

"Call it." Leon flipped the silver dollar into the air and caught it on his wrist.

"See." Ora Mae turned to Thumps. "He makes me laugh."

TWENTY-SIX

Thumps carried the dishes to the sink.

Leon stayed at the table, relaxing in the chair. "She's right about the depreciation," he said. "But what you get with an RV is the freedom to go wherever you want to go, whenever you want to go. With a house, you're staked to the ground."

"Not sure that I want a house or an RV."

"Some people think that renting is the best of all worlds. No mortgage, and the landlord is stuck with the leaky roofs and the wonky appliances."

Thumps slipped the dishes into the soapy water.

Leon picked up a banker box and set it on the table. "But, if you ask me, living in an apartment is like wearing someone else's underwear."

"So, what do you want to do today?"

"What I want," said Leon, "is to go back to bed. I'm not as young as I used to be and that woman is a pistol."

"You know she's a lesbian."

Leon took the lid off the box. "And?"

"Nothing."

"Wouldn't have taken you for a puritan."

"I'm not."

"You sound as though you don't approve."

"I'm just surprised," said Thumps.

"With all the shit that happens, that's the one thing that makes life bearable," said Leon. "Being surprised."

Thumps wiped his hands and sat down. "So, what surprises do you have for me today?"

Leon pulled out a file. "Well, let's start with Raymond Oakes. This Maslow of yours and Shipman-what's-his-name say they can place Oakes in the area at the time of the murders."

"Nina Maslow," said Thumps. "Harry Shipman."

"Whatever." Leon opened the file. "These are the records for every motel from Crescent City to Garberville. And there's no record of Raymond Oakes. So the question is, how did Maslow and Shipman find Oakes when the entire Humboldt County Sheriff's Department, the state police, and the FB of I could not?"

"We didn't know about Oakes at the time."

"Sure." Leon tapped the file. "But we know about him now, and surprise, surprise, his name still doesn't appear anywhere."

"Maybe we should talk to Mr. Shipman."

"Cop 101. See?" said Leon. "It's like riding a bike."

"They're staying at the Tucker."

"Already called." Leon held up a cellphone. "It appears your movie people are up with the chickens and on the move."

"On the move?"

"Nice woman at the front desk said they were asking directions to the reservation."

"She have anything more than that? Reservation is a big place."

"Moses Blood," said Leon. "The name she heard was Moses Blood."

THE FIRST PART of the trip was made in silence. Leon leaned against the door and went to sleep. Thumps would have done the same thing, except he was behind the wheel, and cruise control had its limits.

"We there yet?" Leon's eyes were still closed, but the rest of him was awake.

"You have a nice sleep?"

"I think you hit every pothole in the road."

"Missed the big ones."

Leon straightened up. "You got any idea why the movie folks want to see this Blood guy?"

"Nope."

"You think Oakes is Indian?"

"You mean Blackfeet?"

"He doesn't look Indian," said Leon. "But you can never tell. Maybe he was originally from around here."

"Maybe."

"His prison record lists him as White," said Leon, "but that doesn't tell you much. He could be part Indian and doesn't want to admit it. You remember that seminar on race and gender we had to take?"

"Sure."

"Dr. William Brock," said Leon. "He said that race and gender were constructs. That they didn't really exist."

"What about him?"

"Man was White," said Leon. "And he was male."

"I think he was speaking theoretically."

"Problem is we don't live in a theoretical world." Leon took out his cellphone and snapped a photo of the passing panorama. "If he had been Black and female, he might have had a different theory."

The road to Moses's place had been graded not too long ago by an oil company that was trying to run a pipeline through the reservation. The pipeline had stalled in a series of court cases, and the road had been left to its own devices. Thumps picked his way through the ruts all the way to the bottomland along the river that Moses called home.

There was a black SUV parked in front of the house. Moses and Cooley were sitting at the big picnic table. Along with Mercer, Gerson, and Shipman.

"That Blood?"

Thumps eased the car into the shade of a big cottonwood. "Moses Blood and Cooley Small Elk."

"I got to get me a name like that," said Leon. "What do you think of Leon Shadow Runner?"

"Not much."

"Leon Dark Wolverine?"

"Even less."

Anthony Mercer was holding court at the table. Moses and Cooley were looking on gravely, nodding and grunting every so often to let Mercer know that they hadn't fallen asleep.

Cooley got up and stretched. "You guys can sit here," he said, gesturing to the bench. "I'll get a chair."

"Yes," said Moses. "You're just in time for the big finish."

"Mr. DreadfulWater," said Shipman. "Mr. Blood said you'd be along."

Thumps had given up trying to figure out how Moses seemed to know what was going to happen before it did.

"This is Leon Ranger," said Thumps. "Leon's a Humboldt County sheriff."

"Retired," said Leon.

"The Leon Ranger," said Cooley. "That's a really cool name."

"You think so?"

"Absolutely," said Cooley. "And since you're Black, you could wear a white mask."

"Shit," said Leon. "That's a good idea."

"No, it's not," said Thumps.

"Mr. Mercer wants to use my house for the big shootout," said Moses. "Maybe even have a car chase along the river."

"Nina had talked about Mr. Blood," said Shipman. "I think she was planning on using him on camera."

"Then I could watch TV," said Moses, "and see me."

"I'll have to be there with him," said Cooley. "Moses might get nervous when the director says, 'Action!'"

"I think we can find a place for the both of you," said Gerson.

Moses turned to Thumps. "Maybe they could find a place for you and Claire and the baby."

"Everybody likes babies," said Cooley.

Shipman looked surprised. "You have a baby?"

Thumps let the question slide by. "So, you're going to have a shootout?"

"And a car chase," said Cooley.

"The serial killer lures our hero to a place like this," said Shipman. "Somewhere secluded. Primeval."

"*Prime Evil*," said Cooley. "That would be a pretty good title for the film."

"It would," said Shipman, "but we're going to call the movie *Obsidian*."

"That's a good name too," said Moses. "Some of the tribes farther west used obsidian for arrowheads and knives."

Cooley nodded. "And the Aztecs used obsidian knives to cut the hearts out of people they didn't like."

"Jesus," said Leon. "You guys got any vampires in this film?"

Gerson smiled. "And no zombies."

Shipman shifted on the bench. "But I don't think that Mr. DreadfulWater and Deputy Ranger came all the way out here to check on the film."

"Loose ends," said Leon.

"Ah," said Shipman. "Raymond Oakes."

"The husband?" said Mercer. "The ex-con who disappeared."

"Let's walk and talk," said Shipman. "I need to stretch my legs."

"Go ahead," said Gerson. "Tony and I will wrap up the details with Mr. Blood."

"Maybe Moses can run the bad guy down on a horse," said Cooley. "That would be a surprise ending."

SHIPMAN LED THE WAY along the riverbank. Thumps and Leon followed along behind. Leon was the first to speak.

"We went back over the motel records and couldn't find Oakes's name anywhere. No record he had ever stayed in Humboldt County."

"Nina found him under an alias," said Shipman. "Check your records for a Charles Cullen at the Bayview Motel."

"Okay," said Leon. "She happen to mention just *how* she found him?"

"Not exactly," said Shipman. "I know she was especially interested in single men in generic motels, motels where you didn't have to go through a lobby to get to your room."

"That would be the Bayview," said Leon. "But how did she know that Oakes was Anna Tripp's husband?"

"Don't know that," said Shipman. "Sorry."

Thumps tipped his hat back. "And how did she know that Cullen was Oakes?"

"Don't know that either," said Shipman, "but I expect that she put all the single men into a pile and began sorting through them, checking names and addresses, ages, professions, credit card and phone records."

"Is that how you'd do it?" said Thumps.

"That's one way," said Shipman.

"Until she discovered that Charles Cullen didn't exist?"

"That's what I'm guessing," said Shipman.

"So, it was Charles Cullen whom you tracked to Rexburg?"

"That's right," said Shipman.

"Motel?"

"Motel 6."

"You see, what bothers me," said Leon, "is why this Maslow didn't share this information with the police."

"You'd have to ask her that," said Shipman.

"Except we can't."

"No," said Shipman. "You can't."

Thumps hadn't known Maslow all that well, but what he did know of the woman told him that she wouldn't have shared her information freely.

Leon took out his silver dollar. "Let me guess. Heads, you didn't go to the cops. Tails, you didn't go to the cops."

"Maslow didn't tell me about Oakes until just before she was killed," said Shipman. "I figured you guys already knew about Oakes."

Leon caught the dollar and peeked under his hand. "Try again," he said.

"Look," said Shipman, "I don't know for sure that this Cullen was Oakes or that Oakes killed anyone. It was Maslow's theory, not mine. And frankly, I don't give a shit about Oakes. He's not even in the script."

"And you're not looking to solve the case," said Thumps. "You just want to make a movie."

"Sue me," said Shipman. "I'm an asshole."

"Naw," said Leon, "being an asshole is my job."

Shipman's smile was friendly but tired. "I've given you everything Maslow gave me. You have the research I did for her. You've got all the original evidence from the case. You know about Oakes. All you got to do is turn lead into gold."

Leon turned to Thumps. "What about it, Tonto? How's your alchemy?"

"Second time you've said that," said Thumps.

"What?"

"Lead into gold," said Thumps. "You said that you had a couple of twists in mind that would turn lead into gold."

"That's right," said Shipman. "I do."

"You want to share?"

Shipman shrugged. "Maslow had an interesting idea that the Obsidian Murders could be the work of a killer who was evolving."

Leon frowned. "Evolving?"

"She thought he had killed before, but rather than honing his technique, he was feeling his way through different methods and maybe even a different set of victims."

"So there wouldn't be a pattern."

"More than that," said Shipman. "Maslow thought he was learning that there were no limits to what he could do, that the killings were becoming a complex game."

"Like chess?"

"More like Go," said Shipman. "But without the board and without the rules."

"Never played Go," said Leon. "So, Maslow thought this guy was killing people as part of a game? Serial killers versus the police?"

"No," said Shipman. "Maslow was worried that this guy was becoming so skilled and confident that he was beginning to play against himself."

"And you're going to incorporate this 'evolving serial killer' idea into the plot?"

"You should go to Rexburg," said Shipman. "See if you can find what happened to Oakes. Boots on the ground and all that."

"You didn't go?"

Shipman shook his head. "That's what the phone and the internet are for. Had Cullen at the Motel 6 for one night."

"And nothing after that?"

"Checked all the towns between Rexburg and here," said Shipman. "Zero."

Moses and Cooley had left the picnic table. Mercer was heading back to the car. Gerson was waving and shouting something that Thumps couldn't hear.

"Time to go," said Shipman. "We still have a ton of work to do before we lock the script. Who knows, with any luck, by the time we get to the first day of shooting, you guys will have solved this thing."

MOSES MADE A POT of coffee, and the four of them took chairs down to the river.

"It doesn't get any better than this," said Moses. "Come evening, you can watch the bats dance in the sky."

"Bats?" said Leon. "Those buggers got nasty teeth."

"They just eat bugs," said Cooley, "and sometimes fruit. But they are a little on the ugly side."

"I hear Al has a boyfriend," said Moses. "That guy with the cars."

"George Gorka."

"That's the one," said Moses. "Al says that they are going to go to that fancy lodge north of Glory. The one with the big pool and hot tub."

"Gorka has to drive the transport down to Cheyenne for the next auction," said Cooley. "Then he's coming back, and the two of them are going to spend the weekend just eating and swimming."

"They might do other things," said Moses, "but that would be their business."

"A whole weekend," said Cooley. "Gorka seems nice enough, so I hope that Al isn't leading him on."

"Yes," said Moses. "Personal relationships are tricky."

"Al said she's going to close the café," said Cooley, "so it looks serious."

Thumps sat up. "Close the café?"

"Just for the weekend."

"Any fish in the river?" asked Leon. "I've got a pole in the RV."

"You bet," said Cooley. "Some good-sized trout."

"You can bring your RV down," said Moses. "Park it right over there. But the first fish you catch, you have to let it go, so it can tell all its relations that you're trying to catch them."

"Give the fish a fighting chance?"

"That's right," said Moses. "Then if you catch one, you know that the fish don't mind being caught."

Thumps turned toward the river and let the wind find his

face. In the distance, the mountains ranged along the horizon, soft shadows in the morning light. What was it Claire had told him any number of times? If you could see the mountains, you knew you were home.

"Look at that," said Moses.

"Sweet," said Cooley.

A squadron of white pelicans appeared on the river, skimming the surface of the water.

"They get all nice and fat on the coast," said Moses, "and then they come here to nest and raise their young. First sign of cold weather, they head out for someplace warm."

Thumps watched the pelicans disappear in the distance. Maybe the birds were on to something. It wasn't a bad idea when you thought about it. Moving from one place to another, following the good weather, never staying too long.

"That's why I bought the RV," said Leon. "So I could be a pelican."

TWENTY-SEVEN

As Thumps drove back to Chinook, he tried to imagine living with Claire and Ivory. The idea was appealing, but then ideas were generally more attractive than realities. Leon, for example. When Ranger had shown up, Thumps had been delighted to see him. Now that Leon had moved in, Thumps wasn't sure what he was going to do with him. Take him out for dinner? Show him the sights?

And if Leon complicated his life, what would Claire and a baby do?

"You know what we should do, Tonto?"

"Solve the case."

"Sure," said Leon, "we should do that. But maybe we could do a little photography."

"Photography?"

"You're a photographer," said Leon. "I'm a writer. Be a step up if I could take pictures as well."

"The magazine work."

"That's right," said Leon. "Nothing like a photograph to brighten a story."

Thumps rolled down the window and let the air rush in. "Well, first you'll need a camera."

"Got one," said Leon. "Sweet little camera. Fixed lens. Real quiet."

"You have it with you?"

"Back at the RV."

"First rule," said Thumps. "You have to carry the camera with you."

Leon nodded. "So how about it?"

"How about what?"

"How about showing me how to take pictures?"

"Now?"

"Sure," said Leon. "We can take photos and solve the case at the same time. You got something better to do?"

No, Thumps thought to himself, he didn't have anything better to do. Which was depressing all by itself.

"We could work the town," said Leon. "Do some street photography. Let me get the hang of the camera. You can give me pointers and critique my shots."

There were probably a good many reasons why this was a

bad idea, but off the top of his head, Thumps couldn't think of any.

"Which version of Photoshop do you have?"

"Photography is more than just Photoshop."

"You're still shooting film?" Leon banged his hand against the side of his head. "Darkrooms and nasty chemicals?"

"Nothing wrong with film."

"You do know," said Leon, dropping his voice an octave, "darkroom fumes are what killed the dinosaurs."

THE FUJI REMINDED THUMPS a little of an M series Leica.

"It's what they call a rangefinder," said Leon. "The soft shutter-release button and the thumb rest are accessories. Had to pay extra for them."

"Red?"

"Yeah," said Leon, "but you can get the buttons in green or bronze or blue with birds and lizards."

"Designer accessories."

"Youth market," said Leon. "The kids are the ones with the money."

"So, what do you want to shoot?"

"I was thinking something with western character," said Leon.

"Seedy?"

"Seedy's good," said Leon. "And I'm a little hungry. This town got any good doughnut joints?"

GOOD DOUGHNUTS WERE, to Thumps's way of thinking, an oxymoron. For a diabetic, they were poison. Beth had been very specific about doughnuts. And pizza and hot dogs and pasta, and most of what you would find at popular places such as the Golden Harvest Chinese-American buffet.

Still, if you had your heart set on doughnuts, there was only one place to go.

Dumbo's.

As they drove across town, Thumps tried to prepare Leon for Morris Dumbo.

"Dumbo's," said Thumps. "The proprietor is one Morris Dumbo. Morris is a man of specific opinions."

"Bit of a racist?"

"Nothing 'bit' about Morris."

"He going to refuse to serve me?" Leon started smiling. "You know, I've never been refused service."

"You've led a sheltered life."

"Sometimes, in a good week," said Leon, "I even forget I'm Black."

"Morris will probably mention it."

"Hot dog," said Leon. "Can I shoot him?"

* * *

Dumbo's was at the end of Main Street. It was a one-storey clapboard rectangle, about the size of a double-wide trailer. The building itself was a particular shade of brown that reminded Thumps why he didn't want a dog.

As Thumps waited to turn left into the parking lot, he could see that Dumbo had been hard at work. For reasons known only to the man himself, Morris had painted a bright yellow stripe all around the building. From a distance, the place looked like a present tied up with a ribbon.

Leon looked out the side window. "You're kidding."

"Nope."

"I'm bringing my pistol."

"You wanted seedy."

"I wanted good doughnuts."

"Best in the state."

"If this is a joke," said Leon, "I'll shoot you."

The interior of Dumbo's was unremarkable. Tables with plastic cloths, chairs that weren't related, worn wood floors, small windows that were so dirty you couldn't see out. Even on a bright day, the light that came in through the panes was no more than a soft glow.

Leon stopped in the doorway. "I hear a banjo and we're out of here."

Thumps had forgotten about the smell that rose off the floor and hung in the air like a haze.

"Is that mildew?"

Morris Dumbo was behind the counter, stretched out in his Naugahyde recliner. Under the big Budweiser clock was a handwritten sign that said, "I Don't Serve Those I Don't Like."

Morris looked up as Thumps and Leon stepped into the shop.

"Afternoon, Morris," said Thumps.

"That you, chief?" Morris sat up. "Who's your shadow?"

"Friend of mine," said Thumps.

Morris was a thin, grizzled man with a bony face and a head of short brown hair that looked as though you could use it to scrub pots and pans.

"Cop?"

"Retired," said Leon.

Dumbo kept his eyes on Thumps. "Your friend armed?"

"He is."

"So am I," said Morris. "You see that sign?"

"You make it yourself?" said Leon.

"It means what it says."

Thumps bent down and looked at the baskets of doughnuts. "How about an old-fashioned and coffee?"

"You still diabetic?"

"More or less," said Thumps.

"Then you'll be wanting the plain," said Morris.

"I'll take a chocolate cake," said Leon. "And coffee."

Morris stood behind the counter with his arms crossed. "I don't know you."

Leon nodded. "Where'd you serve?"

Morris squinted in the dim light. "You a vet?"

"'Nam."

"Shit."

"You can say that again," said Leon.

"Marine?"

"Army," said Leon. "Company B, First, Twenty-second Infantry, Fourth Division."

"You sorry son of a bitch." Morris started laughing. In the dank confines of the doughnut shop, it sounded as though someone was banging on a dumpster with a steel pipe. "You got drafted."

"Way it was."

"Didn't have no rich daddy to save your ass."

It was Leon's turn to smile. "Didn't have no daddy at all."

Morris opened the case and put two chocolate cakes on a plate. "First two are on me," he said. "For your service. Coffee too."

Leon nodded.

"But the chief pays his own way."

"Always do," said Thumps.

"And don't go spreading rumours about how generous I am," said Morris. "Just gives people ideas."

Thumps took the table in the corner, near the window, as far away from Dumbo and his recliner as he could get. Morris's eyesight might be suspect, but his hearing was twenty-twenty.

"Interesting guy," said Leon.

"As in the Chinese proverb?"

"Maybe I should take his picture," said Leon. "You know, one of those candid portraits."

"That's Morris," said Thumps. "Candid."

"But he makes a good doughnut."

"The best," said Thumps.

"And cops would know."

Thumps wondered if two old-fashioned plains would have less sugar than one old-fashioned glazed.

"You know there's something not right about our Mr. Shipman." Leon broke the doughnut in half and dipped it in the coffee.

"He seems to know more than he should."

"There's that," said Leon. "We looked hard and came up empty."

"We didn't know about Oakes at the time," said Thumps. "And he was using an alias."

"Charles Cullen at the Bayview Motel."

"Easy enough to check out," said Thumps. "We've got the motel records."

"Let's say he shows up," said Leon. "What I don't understand is how he did it."

Thumps waited.

"I mean, the guy is just out of prison."

"Motel would want to see ID," said Thumps. "Major credit card. Driver's licence."

"Fake IDs are expensive."

"And then he shows up in Rexburg, Idaho."

"How'd he get there?" said Leon.

"Bus?" said Thumps.

Leon shook his head. "The way I see it, he comes out of prison with no money and no prospects. The only thing he has going for him is Anna Tripp, and yet a few weeks after he's released, he seems to have found a new life as Charles Cullen."

Thumps tried his doughnut. He could feel the sugar rush through his body.

"I think we want to talk to Mr. Shipman again," said Leon. "And this time, we might want to squeeze a little harder."

Morris came over with the coffee pot. "You get one refill," he said. "After that, it's a buck per fill-up."

Leon leaned back and smiled. "Maybe Mr. Dumbo can help us."

"Don't do much helping," said Morris. "Especially cops. No offence."

"None taken," said Leon. "But let me ask you a question. Let's say you just got out of prison."

Morris stiffened. "You calling me a crook?"

"Nope," said Leon. "We just need a third opinion."

Morris's face brightened. "You guys are working that serial killer case."

Thumps sighed silently to himself. He wondered if Dumbo had had money in the pool.

"What's the first thing you would do?"

Morris set the coffee pot on the table and pulled up a chair. "I get out of prison, and you want to know the first thing I'd do?"

"Yes."

"How long I been in?"

"Let's say . . . twenty years."

"Get laid," said Morris. "No question."

"And after that?"

"A good meal."

"And after that?"

Morris's face darkened. "Twenty years. Man could lose a lot of friends in that time. Family too. Be like starting over. What was I in for?"

"Bank robbery," said Leon. "Murder."

"So, I'm a badass."

"No," said Thumps, "you were just a kid when you went in."

"Am I Black?" said Morris. "Like you? Or Indian like the chief here?"

"No," said Leon. "You're poor White trash."

Morris threw his head back and cackled. "I guess I'd try to find a job. Or I'd rob something. I've got a sister in California. Place called Roseville, just east of Sacramento. I'd go there."

"Roseville?"

Morris nodded. "Yeah, first thing I'd do is go see Franny."

"Because she's family?"

"I'd be starting over," said Morris. "When you start over, family is where you begin."

TWENTY-EIGHT

It was a short drive from Dumbo's to the bookstore. Thumps wasn't sure whether Archie would be at the Aegean or supervising the renovations at Budd's, but given that the one was clean and bright and the other was noisy and dirty, he'd start with the bookstore.

And hope for the best.

"A bookstore?" Leon got out of the car and stretched his back. "You read?"

"Let me do the talking," said Thumps.

"Sure," said Leon.

"This another Dumbo doughnut moment?"

"Not exactly."

Leon shook his head. "You got some interesting friends."

"Whatever you do," said Thumps, "don't mention Aztecs."

"Damn," said Leon. "Aztecs were on the tip of my tongue."

* * *

THINGS WERE ON the move in the bookstore. The last time Thumps had been in the Aegean, there had been racks of vintage clothing against the far wall. Now, the racks were gone and Archie had added a long table with four computer monitors.

"This looks like one of those old libraries."

"Used to be," said Thumps. "Archie bought it and turned it into this."

"Archie?"

"Archimedes Kousoulas," said Thumps.

"Greek?"

"Every inch."

Leon looked around. "And we're here . . . because?"

"Thumps!" Archie stood in the doorway of his office. "About time."

Leon leaned in. "Seems he's upset with you."

"He's always upset with me," said Thumps.

"And you must be Leon Ranger." Archie rushed forward and took Leon's hand. "Deputy sheriff. Retired. Parents with a sense of humour."

Leon smiled. "My mother had a thing for guys in masks."

"Who doesn't," said Archie. "Come on. I don't have all day."

* * *

ANDERSON COLE WAS relaxing on the sofa near the window. She didn't get up.

"Mr. DreadfulWater," she said. "George tells me Mr. Blood decided against a car."

"This is Leon Ranger," said Archie. "Friend of Thumps from the coast."

"East or west?" said Anderson.

"West," said Leon. "Northern California."

"Ah," said Anderson. "The Obsidian Murders."

"Anderson's car show was in Redding at the time of the killings," said Archie. "How's that for a coincidence?"

"The story was in all the papers," said Anderson. "Terrible."

Thumps hadn't expected to find Cole in Archie's office. "Thought you were off to Cheyenne."

"George will set it up," said Anderson. "I'll drive down in a couple of days."

"Ms. Cole is going over to Black Swan."

"The thermal springs?"

"I figure a girl's entitled to a little R and R," said Anderson. "George doesn't need me, and I could use some downtime."

Black Swan was just north of Glory. Thumps had never been to the resort, but now that he thought about it, maybe Black Swan was something that he and Claire and the baby could do. A quiet drive in the country, a day in warm water. Something slightly romantic. Something slightly domestic.

"Sell many cars?"

"Enough for a night at the resort." Anderson smiled at Leon. "You look like a man who would appreciate a vintage car."

"RV," said Leon.

"Pity," said Anderson. "I could never get used to having to drain the you-know-what."

"You guys find her car yet?"

"You'd have to ask the sheriff," said Thumps.

"Good chance it's in pieces by now," said Leon.

"Don't think so," said Anderson. "Got a feeling we'll get lucky."

"Lot of money to lose if you don't," said Archie.

"They say there are more important things than money," said Anderson. "I'd like to think they're right."

"Good books," said Archie. "Good food."

"And a soak in hot water." Anderson pushed off the sofa. "I should get going. If you change your mind about a car, we'll be in Cheyenne. Just a short drive from here."

"Six hours," said Thumps.

"More like seven," said Archie.

"Archie says he's solved the Obsidian Murders," said Anderson. "So that should free up some time."

THUMPS WAITED UNTIL Anderson had left the store. "You've solved the murders?"

"Generally speaking," said Archie.

"That's impressive," said Leon. "You want to share?"

"I didn't tell Anderson that I had solved the murders," said Archie. "I said that I have a theory that may lead to the case being solved."

"A theory." Leon suppressed a yawn. "Is that like an educated guess?"

"A theory is a type of contemplative and abstract thinking." Archie pushed his glasses up his nose. "For instance, the police look for and consider physical evidence."

"This theorizing," said Leon, "is this something the ancient Greeks did?"

"Exactly," said Archie. "Socrates. Plato. Aristotle."

"The big three," said Thumps, trying to head off the lecture that was coming.

Leon nodded. "So you want us to think like Socrates?"

"It couldn't hurt," said Archie.

"Didn't the Greeks kill him?" Thumps couldn't help himself.

"What has that to do with anything?"

"That's right," said Leon. "The Greek government made him drink arsenic."

"Hemlock," said Thumps.

"All right," said Archie. "Stop. You want to hear my theory or not?"

"Is there any coffee?" said Leon.

* * *

It took Archie a few minutes to arrange the large library table. Archie sat at one end, and he had Leon and Thumps sitting across from each other.

"Here's what I've been able to put together so far." Archie handed each man a folder. "The research isn't complete, but I think it's pretty significant."

Thumps started to open the folder.

"Not yet," said Archie. "First, we need the background and the premise."

"Premise?" Leon rubbed his face.

"A statement that is assumed to be true for the purpose of an argument," said Archie.

"Background and premise," said Thumps.

"Okay," said Archie. "We're all in agreement that the killings on the coast, what the press called the Obsidian Murders, were the work of a serial killer."

"Me and Socrates here would call that a fact," said Leon.

Archie made a face. "Are all your friends as annoying as you?"

"There's this Greek guy," said Thumps, "who runs a bookstore . . ."

"Very funny."

"The premise?"

"Right." Archie shifted in the chair. "What do we know about serial killers?"

"They kill people."

"And they don't stop," said Archie. "Once they begin, they don't stop."

"Is this going to take long?" said Leon. "'Cause I got a date with a dancing fool."

"Annoying," said Archie, "and impatient."

"Serial killers," said Thumps. "They kill people. They continue killing until they're caught."

"The Obsidian Murders could have been his first kick at the can," said Archie, "but I'm betting it wasn't."

"Yeah," said Leon. "We went through all this in the original investigation."

"Then we're in agreement," said Archie. "Clam Beach wasn't his first rodeo. Ten killings in a matter of a few days is the work of someone who knows what he is doing."

"And we looked at other serial killings," said Leon. "FBI, state, locals. We looked hard and came up empty."

Archie began to fidget. Thumps wasn't sure if it was nervous energy or if the little Greek was excited.

"That's because you asked the wrong question," said Archie. "You asked about unsolved serial killings that matched the Obsidian Murders."

"That would be the question, all right," said Leon.

"What you should have asked," said Archie, "is, of the reported serial killings in North America, which ones had commonalities."

"We asked that question too."

"And then what did you do?" said Archie.

"We looked at all the cases," said Leon, "to see if we could find any, as you say, commonalities."

"So, you looked at the unsolved cases," said Archie, "and discarded the solved ones."

Thumps suddenly saw it. The point that Archie was trying to make. "You think that our serial killer is among the solved cases?"

"That's a little crazy," said Leon. "I like it."

"All right, children," said Archie. "Now let's open our folders to page one."

TWENTY-NINE

Thumps and Leon spent the next twenty minutes reading through Archie's research, while the little Greek made coffee.

Leon was the first to speak. "You got one hell of an imagination."

"So, you think it's possible?"

Thumps closed the folder and leaned back in the chair. "All of these cases were solved."

"That's the link," said Archie. "And they were all solved because the person responsible died."

"Suicide," said Leon. "Another suicide. Another suicide."

"All suicides," said Archie. "Five serial killers and five suicides."

"Okay."

"How many serial killers do you know who commit suicide?"

"You know," said Leon, "I hadn't really thought of it."

"Ted Bundy," said Archie. "Lonnie Franklin, Israel Keyes, Anthony Sowell, Gary Ridgway, John Wayne Gacy."

"FBI estimates that there are probably twenty-five to fifty active serial killers in the U.S. at any given time," said Leon.

"Sixty-eight percent are White. Twenty-three percent are Black," said Archie. "No offence."

"None taken," said Leon. "Once again, I'm a minority."

"And what do they all have in common?"

"Serial killers?"

"No," said Archie, "just the ones who get caught."

Thumps took in a deep breath. "They don't kill themselves."

"*Vero nihil verius*," said Archie. "Nothing is truer than the truth."

"Jesus," said Leon. "Now we're quoting Plato?"

"Not Plato," said Archie. "It's the motto for the Mentone Girls' Grammar School in Mentone, Australia. They translate it as 'Nothing is truer than truth,' but it's close enough."

"Archie . . ."

"The point is, you have five serial killings that match the Obsidian Murders and in each case, the killer committed suicide. Five serial killers. Five suicides."

"Okay," said Leon. "Let's back up. You've arranged these cases together because the killings took place over a short period of time."

"Two to three days," said Archie. "Max."

"And because they occurred at the same time each year."

"Between late summer and early winter."

"And because each of the killers killed himself."

"If they actually were the killers," said Archie.

"Another conspiracy theory," said Leon. "Well, why didn't you say so?"

Thumps tried to remember who had said that you couldn't invent a conspiracy theory so absurd that someone somewhere didn't already believe it.

"Not theory." Archie waved the folder at Leon. "Evidence."

Leon rubbed the back of his neck. "What time is it?"

"Time to solve this case," said Archie.

"Leon has a date," said Thumps.

"You just got to town," said Archie.

"Ora Mae Foreman," said Thumps.

"Ora Mae?"

"Yeah, I know," said Leon. "She's a lesbian. And she's a great dancer. And she's fun."

"Fun?"

Leon got to his feet. "And you guys are boring."

"You're going?"

"Have to shower and shave," said Leon. "Looking good. Feeling good."

"You can't just leave," said Archie.

Leon took the silver dollar out of his pocket. "Call it."

"What?"

Leon caught the dollar on the back of his hand and peeked

at it. "Mustang time," he said. "If you two solve the case, you can tell me over breakfast."

ARCHIE SAT AND POUTED. Thumps went through the research again, going over the cases one by one.

"This is good work," he said.

Archie brightened. "You think so?"

"Yeah," said Thumps. "The pieces fit. The FBI wouldn't have looked too long at cases they considered solved. Neither would we. The general details of these five are close enough to have warranted a look if the killer hadn't been dead. But for all of them to have committed suicide is more than a little odd."

"I knew it."

"There's only one problem." Thumps closed the folder and tried the coffee. It was cold. "In the Obsidian Murders, we never found the killer, and as far as we know, no one killed himself."

"What if he was *supposed* to kill himself?" Archie opened the folder and spread out the pages. "Each one of these supposed serial killers had the same sort of background. High school education at best. Minor run-ins with the law. Some even spent time in jail. Minimum-wage jobs. Thirty-six to forty-eight. White. Anger issues. And most important, loners. No family. No friends to speak of."

"A fall guy."

"It's beautiful," said Archie. "You're a serial killer who kills and then dumps the blame on a patsy."

"That takes planning," said Thumps.

"Maybe that's why all these killings are a year apart," said Archie. "Maybe it takes that long to put everything in place."

"So, he hires someone to come to Eureka?"

"Maybe for a job," said Archie. "Or the possibility of a job. Or maybe he's getting paid as part of a study. Hundred ways to do it."

"And then our killer does his thing and arranges to blame it on this poor slob."

"It would be interesting to find out how the police got on to each of these individuals."

"As in anonymous tips?"

Archie nodded. "As in."

"And when the police arrive, they find their suspect dead with incriminating evidence in their possession."

"Game, set, match."

"Pretty elaborate," said Thumps.

"Not if you like the long game," said Archie. "I think this guy's smart."

"So did Maslow," said Thumps. "Smart and rich."

"There," said Archie. "All the pieces."

"Then what happened on the coast?"

"Okay." Archie was on his feet and pacing. "Let's call our serial killer 'Obsidian.'"

"Let's not."

"So, Obsidian hires a guy to play the patsy. But when he goes to kill the guy, make it look like suicide, and plant the incriminating evidence, he discovers that said patsy has flown the coop."

"Run away?"

"Or maybe, just maybe, he was taken off the board." Archie stopped in his tracks. "Maybe he goes out and gets drunk or gets into an altercation."

Thumps rubbed at the back of his neck. "And is thrown in jail."

"And Obsidian doesn't know about this until it's too late. Because now, the man who was supposed to take the fall has an ironclad alibi."

"And Obsidian is out in the open."

"Or at least he doesn't have the cover he had planned."

"Leon," said Thumps. "We're going to need Leon."

"They won't give you the information?"

"On prisoners who were in county jail during the time of the murders? Probably not. But Leon still has friends on the force. He'll be able to find out."

"Except he's out dancing with a lesbian."

"I'm pretty sure lesbians dance."

Archie looked hurt. "That's not what I meant. You think it's a racial thing?"

"You mean because Ora Mae is Black, and Leon is Black?"

"It doesn't sound very enlightened when you say it like that."

"You're wondering if lesbians and straight men have sex."

"I'm wondering if Leon is straight." Archie looked pained. "Does Beth know?"

Thumps supposed that Archie knew about Beth and Gabby. The little Greek knew about everything else that happened in town. But maybe he didn't.

Thumps stood up. "I'll get Leon to call Eureka in the morning."

"Even if I'm right," said Archie, "we won't be any closer to finding out who Obsidian is."

"New clues are new directions," said Thumps.

Archie sat on the sofa and put his feet on the coffee table. "What are you going to do about Claire and the baby?"

Thumps looked at Archie.

"What? You're going to have to talk to someone who understands these sorts of things."

"You don't understand these sorts of things."

"I read," said Archie. "And I spend a lot of time on the internet."

Thumps stopped at the doorway. "What if the trip to the coast wasn't the catalyst?"

"What do you mean?"

"What if something else was already in play? What if the break-in and the watch and the stolen car are all part of a larger plan?"

"And the movie company?"

"And the movie company," said Thumps. "What if all of this is connected?"

"To the Obsidian Murders?"

"Yes," said Thumps. "To the murders."

Archie stayed on the sofa, looking a little flat, as though someone had let the air out of him. "That," he said, "would not be good."

Thumps picked up the folder. "Can I take this with me?"

"Sure." Archie revived a little. "So, what do we do next?"

"We aren't going to do anything," said Thumps. "It's late. I'm going to go home, read a book, and go to bed."

Archie shook his head. "Your buddy goes out dancing. You go to bed. There's a killer out there. He may even be right here in Chinook."

"Good news," said Thumps. "If he's in town, at least we know where he is."

"That's the good news?"

Thumps yawned. "Ask me that in the morning."

THIRTY

The night was black. Thumps eased the car away from the curb and drove until he was out of sight of the bookstore. Then he turned north. Archie wasn't going to be happy when he found out that Thumps hadn't gone home, that he had ditched the little Greek.

THE MUSTANG PARKING lot was full. The birth of a baby hadn't slowed business. Thumps wondered if Big Fish was back behind the bar or home with Lorraine, up to his neck in fatherhood.

Leon was at a corner table by himself. "Took you long enough."

"He's a friend."

"He's a civilian," said Leon. "And if he's right, he could be in a world of danger."

"No Ora Mae?"

"Just an excuse," said Leon. "If I had stayed, we'd still be there."

Thumps put the folder on the table. "It's pretty compelling."

"He really figure it out?"

"Most of it," said Thumps. "Archie's thinking that Obsidian arranged for suspects to be in place at each of the killings."

"Complicated, but effective." Leon nodded. "One-stop shopping."

"And then along comes Eureka."

"Only this time," said Leon, "something happens, and the plan winds up in the toilet."

"Archie's figured that part out too."

"Shit," said Leon. "He's smarter than he looks."

"We need to call Eureka in the morning."

"To check to see who we had in lockup at the time." Leon sipped his beer. "It's a long shot, but I can call Sam and have her check it out."

"Sam?"

"Samantha Tupper," said Leon. "You met her. She said you were cute."

"Cute?"

"But she's got no taste in men."

"Archie figures that Obsidian is in town," said Thumps. "That all of this—the break-in, the watch, the car—is part of a long plan."

"Nothing I see to say the little guy is wrong. Big question is why?"

"That's the question, all right."

"And the other question," said Leon, "is what any of them have to do with this."

Thumps followed Leon's eyes.

"They were already here when I arrived."

Anthony Mercer, Runa Gerson, and Harry Shipman were at a table by themselves.

"Didn't take the old guy for a party animal."

"You think one of them is Obsidian?"

"Why not?" said Leon. "It's a perfect cover."

"Did Ora Mae really sleep with you?"

"Jesus," said Leon. "You've been living in a small town too long."

Thumps looked over at the table. "So, you think we should join them?"

"Beat the bushes?" said Leon. "See what flies out?"

"You got any better idea?"

SHIPMAN WAS THE first to see them coming.

"Mr. DreadfulWater," he said, "and Mr. Ranger."

"Join us," said Mercer. "We're celebrating."

"We've got the script in order," said Gerson. "Another six months and we'll be on set."

"Too bad," said Leon. "Thumps and I had worked out some interesting plot points for the film."

"Really?" said Mercer.

Leon pulled out his silver dollar. "Heads, you tell him," he said. "Tails, I get the honours."

Shipman smiled. "You guys practise this shtick? Dumb and dumber?"

Leon looked under his hand. "I guess it's me."

"You discovered something?" said Gerson. "About the case?"

Mercer sat up. "You solved it?"

"That could help the film," said Gerson. "Or it could hurt it."

"We haven't solved it," said Leon. "But we're thinking that we know why no one has caught Obsidian."

Mercer looked at Thumps. "Obsidian?"

"Archie's name for the killer."

"It's not bad," said Gerson. "Obsidian. Might be able to use it in the film."

"If you haven't solved the case," said Shipman, "just what have you accomplished?"

"Modus operandi," said Leon. "We've got Obsidian's pattern."

"Okay," said Mercer. "Let's have it."

"Ongoing investigation," said Leon. "Can't share the details with you right now."

"That's not nice," said Gerson. "No one likes to be teased."

"What we can tell you," said Leon, "is that there are a series of serial killings that everyone thought were solved."

"But they're not solved?" said Mercer.

"In each case, the person thought to be responsible committed suicide."

"And the case was closed," said Shipman.

"That's right," said Leon. "We're thinking it was a set-up. That the real killer walked away and left somebody else to take the blame."

"Too complicated for a movie," said Shipman. "But it is intriguing. You know who the real killer is?"

"We're talking about the killings on the coast?" said Gerson. "Right?"

"That and more," said Leon. "We expect to break the case in a couple of days."

"Well, this is exciting." Mercer turned to Shipman. "We may have to rewrite the script."

"Frankly, my dear," said Shipman in a reasonable impersonation of Clark Gable, "I don't give a damn."

Gerson yawned. "I'm going to call it a night, Scarlett. Big day tomorrow."

"You can't go," said Mercer. "Dancing's just about to start."

"I'm with Runa." Shipman got to his feet. "I need my beauty sleep."

"All right, party poopers," said Mercer. "But don't wake me before ten."

* * *

MERCER ORDERED ANOTHER pitcher of beer and some nachos. "I think we look a little desperate."

Leon scanned the room. "Three guys sitting by themselves?"

"Three's not a good number," said Mercer. "One is okay. Two is fine. But three . . ."

"Because?"

"I've done a study of bars," said Mercer. "When women come into a drinking establishment by themselves, they're either depressed or looking for someone to drink with. Two women in a bar are looking for a party."

"Sounds scientific," said Thumps.

"Experience," said Mercer. "But you see a group of three or more women, you know that they've brought their party with them and that you don't stand a chance."

"Whereas," said Leon, "when you see three guys, you know that they're desperate?"

"Exactly," said Mercer. "You think we should get some chicken wings?"

Big Fish was nowhere to be seen. Which made sense. Thumps imagined that a newborn would take all the energy of two adults for quite some time. This was the world to which Claire was committed, the world that Thumps was about to enter.

Or not.

"So," said Leon. "Just how does this film business work?"

Mercer looked blank.

"I mean, do you use your own money?"

Mercer snorted and then started to cough. "Are you kidding? No one uses their own money."

"But someone has to pay for the production."

"Sure," said Mercer. "In the case of *Obsidian*, it's Dustan Schwarzstein Ltd. Spells Dustan with an *a*. That's the money pot."

"He easy to work for?"

"Not a 'he,'" said Mercer. "Dustan Schwarzstein is an *it*. A holding company."

Leon nudged Thumps with his foot. "So, you guys are just the hired help?"

"I'm a filmmaker," said Mercer. "A damn good one."

"And this is your big break?" said Thumps.

"I've made other films," said Mercer.

Thumps waited.

"Okay, mostly commercials," said Mercer. "But that's all going to change."

"Congratulations," said Leon.

Thumps got up. "I'm going home."

Mercer turned to Leon and brightened. "You're going to stay, aren't you?"

"Sure," said Leon. "Two guys aren't as desperate as three."

"Two guys are perfect." Mercer ran a hand through his hair. "See those two at the bar? The blonde and the redhead? As soon as you stood up, they looked our way."

Thumps moved past Leon and put his hands on the man's

shoulder for a moment. "Maybe Mr. Mercer can fill you in on the film business."

"You ask me any question," said Mercer, "and I'll answer it."

"Best offer I've had all day," said Leon.

"The redhead," said Mercer. "If it's all the same to you, I'd like the redhead."

"In my experience," said Leon, "that's not the way it works."

THUMPS STOOD OUTSIDE the Mustang and took in the night sky and the stars. Thumps had loved the coast. The fog. The damp. The soft, deep greens of the old-growth forests.

What was left of them.

But the high prairies had their own grandeur, and a clear sky at night was high on Thumps's list of marvels.

He strolled through the parking lot on the off chance that whoever had taken the black Mustang had a sense of humour and had parked it outside the bar in plain sight.

Thumps took his time as he walked past the Chevys, the Dodges, the Hondas, the Hyundais, the Fords, and the Jeeps. As well as an entire tribe of pickups. To be sure, there would have been a certain poetry to finding the Mustang at the Mustang.

But in the end, all he found was the sound of the land at night.

THIRTY-ONE

For the first time since he had returned from the coast, Thumps got to bed in good order and was up the next morning with the dawn. Leon's RV was parked in the backyard. The curtains were drawn, and there were no signs that anyone was home. He considered knocking on the side of the vehicle, but there was something to be said for having the morning to himself.

Yesterday's mail was on the kitchen table, each letter carefully slit open. Thumps was going to have to talk to Rose. He just couldn't think of what he would say. He checked the envelopes. Bills. An offer of another free credit card. Thumps shuffled through them again on the off chance that there was a postcard from Freeway.

Having a wonderful time in Tibet. Wish you were here.

* * *

AL WAS IN FRONT of the grill, working a pile of hash browns. Wutty Youngbeaver, Jimmy Monroe, and Russell Plunkett were on their usual stools. There was an older couple with cameras draped around their necks at the far end of the counter. Tourists, by the look of them, not sure that coming to the café was a good idea but bold enough to take the risk.

"Hey, Thumps." Jimmy Monroe got off his stool and put his hand on Wutty's shoulder. "May I introduce Wutty Youngbeaver, Baron of Sealand."

"Grand Baron," said Wutty. "Grand Baron."

Thumps found his favourite stool and sat down.

"So from now on," said Jimmy, "we have to address Wutty as 'your Baronship.'"

"If you ask me," said Russell, "it sounds stupid."

"You can buy a knightship," said Wutty. "But knights are below barons."

"Maybe Thumps would like to be a knight," said Jimmy. "A knight in shining armour and all that."

Thumps tried to imagine how he was going to stay out of this conversation. Al came to the rescue.

"You want breakfast?"

The cold snap in her voice caught Thumps by surprise.

"Al's grumpy," shouted Wutty. "We should have warned you."

"I'm not grumpy," said Al, her voice sharper than before.

"She got stood up," said Wutty. "By that car guy."

Thumps tried to look sympathetic. "George Gorka?"

"You want breakfast or not?"

"I want breakfast."

"And coffee?"

"Yes," said Thumps. "I'd like coffee as well."

"Then you might want to keep your opinions to yourself."

"I don't have any opinions."

Al poured coffee into a cup. "Keep it that way."

"The car guy was supposed to take Al to that fancy place in Glory," said Wutty.

"Détour," said Russell. "It's supposed to be French."

"It's got one of those funny marks above the *e*," said Jimmy. "That's what makes it French."

"Marilyn Travers over at the credit union says that their specialty is awful," said Wutty. "So you probably didn't miss much."

"Offal," said Al, her face shaping itself into a tornado. "O-f-f-a-l."

"That's not how you spell 'awful.'"

"Offal is the entrails and internal organs of an animal," said Al. "Tongue, bone marrow, cow heart, pig's lungs."

Wutty blanched. "Jesus!"

Thumps took a chance. "That doesn't sound like George. I'll bet he got hung up in Cheyenne."

"That's what phones are for," said Al.

"No man in his right mind would miss a date with you."

"Is that because I'm so ravishing," said Al, "or because I'm armed and dangerous?"

Thumps was working on the right answer when Leon came through the door of the café in a rush.

"Hey, Tonto. What's the big idea?"

Thumps couldn't think of any big idea he had had lately.

"Ditching me."

"Didn't ditch you," said Thumps. "You were asleep. Thought you might have company."

Leon slid onto the stool next to Thumps. "I did have company. Judy. Nurse at the hospital. That friend of yours who had a baby?"

"Lorraine and Big Fish?"

"Judy says they still haven't figured out what to call the kid," said Leon. "Judy spent most of the night on my computer, looking up names."

Thumps made a sympathetic noise. "Sounds romantic."

"Judy thinks they should call the kid Ragnar after some show about Vikings." Leon made a face. "What kind of a name is Ragnar?"

"Wutty has a new name." Jimmy raised his coffee cup to show Al that it was empty. "Baron Youngbeaver, Lord of the Realm, Keeper of the Prissy Purse."

"Privy Purse," said Wutty.

"What's a Privy Purse?" said Russell.

"It's the allowance that royalty gets for their private expenses," said Leon. "I saw this documentary about Queen Elizabeth."

"You get an allowance?" said Russell. "If you sign up with this Sealand outfit?"

"Hope you didn't buy that off eBay," said Jimmy, "'cause those bastards are a bunch of crooks."

"So," said Russell, "how much do you figure a baronship is worth?"

"Hey!" Al whacked the counter with her hand. "Do I look like I want to listen to this shit?"

Wutty held his hands out. "Hey, Al," he said, "say the word, and the boys and I will have a talk with the asshole."

"Yeah," said Russell. "No one messes with our friends."

Al smiled at Thumps. "They're sweet," she said, "in a Cro-Magnon sort of way."

"He'll show up with roses and a good explanation," said Leon. "Man didn't strike me as a fool."

"I'm guessing you want breakfast too."

"Yes, ma'am," said Leon. "I'll have whatever Tonto is having."

"Tonto?" Al looked at Leon sideways. "What's Thumps call you?"

"Leon," said Leon. "What else would he call me?"

BREAKFAST ARRIVED IN good order, and Thumps and Leon ate without talking. Wutty and Russell and Jimmy were busy drinking coffee and dreaming up ways to spend Wutty's privy purse.

"You get any land with your baronship?"

"Naw," said Wutty. "I just got my allotment."

"Too bad," said Jimmy. "If you're going to be landed gentry, you're going to need more land than that."

"You can buy land on the moon," said Russell. "You get an authentic certificate and a map that shows just what part you own."

Thumps spread the hot sauce on his eggs. It was good to be back. He hadn't realized how much he had missed the café and its regulars until now.

"You mind me calling you Tonto?"

"No big deal."

"Is it the same thing as you calling me 'boy'?"

"No," said Thumps, "not the same thing."

"I could call you Little Beaver," said Leon. "You could call me Red Ryder."

"How's your breakfast?"

"Or you could call me Friday, and I could call you Robinson Crusoe."

"How about you call me Thumps," said Thumps, "and I'll call you Leon."

"I like Tonto better," said Leon. "When I was a kid, Tonto was my hero."

Thumps didn't notice the sheriff until Duke was standing at his shoulder.

"You going to eat all that toast?" Hockney didn't wait for an answer. "What's on your schedule for today?"

"Wutty's a Baron of Sealand," said Thumps.

"Sealand?" said Duke. "Is that that abandoned offshore oil platform in the middle of the North Sea?"

"That's the one," said Leon.

"We have to call him Grand Baron Youngbeaver," said Thumps.

Duke looked over at Wutty. "Not happening in my lifetime."

"You find that Mustang yet?" said Leon.

"Not yet," said the sheriff. "But I just caught something almost as much fun. You two about done eating?"

Thumps knew a trap when he heard one. "Nope. Diabetics are supposed to eat slow."

"Except when it comes to doughnuts," said Leon. "With doughnuts, you have to eat them fast."

"You two went to Dumbo's?"

"Yesterday," said Leon.

Thumps pointed a finger at Ranger. "It was his fault."

"They were good doughnuts."

"Morris served you?"

"He did."

Wutty and Russell and Jimmy were paying their bill at the register. Wutty held up a twenty so that it caught the light.

"The Grand Baron is generous," he said.

"You should get a T-shirt that says that," said Russell.

"Bill comes to $19.75," said Al.

"Keep the change," said Wutty.

* * *

AL BROUGHT THE coffee pot with her.

"You want coffee?" she asked. "Or breakfast?"

"Neither," said Duke.

"Then you're just taking up space."

"George Gorka stood Al up last night," said Leon. "She's pissed."

"I'm not pissed."

"Man must have a death wish," said the sheriff. "You two about ready?"

"You know," said Thumps, "maybe we should get Duke a dukeship. What do you think?"

"Grand Duke Duke," said Al. "Karma is such a bitch."

The sheriff put a beefy hand on Thumps's shoulder. "Forget karma," he said. "We got a date with destiny."

THIRTY-TWO

Destiny, it turned out, was the Tucker hotel. Duke led the way through the lobby to the elevators.

"I read about this place on the internet," said Leon. "Built in 1876."

The sheriff pressed the button for the third floor.

"Same time as Crazy Horse was kicking Custer's butt at the Little Bighorn."

"If you say so."

"Top floor burned off in 1890," Leon continued. "When they rebuilt it, they added two new floors."

Duke set up a low grumble in his throat. "What are you? A tour guide?"

"History's interesting," said Leon. "After that, the place fell on hard times. First floor was used as a hospital for a time and then as a warehouse."

Hockney kept his eyes on the floor indicator above the door. "Fascinating."

"One article said that when McAuliffe Moran bought the place, a local group was showing art movies in the lobby."

A bell dinged, and the doors opened. Duke was the first one off.

Leon turned to Thumps. "There's someone who doesn't watch the History Channel."

ROOM 326 WAS a small suite. Deputy Lance Packard was standing at the small bar. Anthony Mercer was pacing between the remains of a potted plant and an overturned sofa.

Duke took a moment to appraise the room. "I'm guessing that this isn't a housekeeping problem."

Mercer kept pacing, his hands flapping at his side. "What the hell is going on?"

Lance held up an evidence bag. "You're going to want to look at this."

Inside the bag were two small black stones.

"Okay," said Duke, "let's take it from the top."

Lance nodded. "Well, Mr. Mercer here came in and found the place as you see it."

"This your room?"

"No," said Mercer. "It's Harry's."

"Harold Shipman."

"Right."

"So you wouldn't know if anything is missing," said Duke.

"Harry," said Mercer. "Harry's missing. Runa too. We were supposed to meet for breakfast, but they never showed."

Lance looked at his notebook. "When Mr. Mercer couldn't find his two friends, he came to Mr. Shipman's room."

"I tried their cells," said Mercer. "I went to Runa's room. She wasn't there. I came here, and this is how I found the place."

Duke raised his head as though he were testing the air. "You have a key for the room?"

"Sure," said Mercer. "It's Harry's room, but it's also our production office."

"Any indication of foul play?" said Leon. "Signs of a struggle? Blood evidence?"

"None that I could see," said Lance.

"Blood?" Mercer took a step backwards.

"Is there a chance," said the sheriff, "that they're together somewhere?"

"You mean like . . ."

"Yes," said Duke. "I mean like that."

"Harry and Runa?" Mercer snorted. "You're kidding."

Thumps walked the perimeter of the room. "Not a robbery. Smash and grab would have taken the laptop."

Duke rocked back and forth on his heels. "When was the last time you saw Mr. Shipman and Ms. Gerson?"

"Last night," said Mercer. "We all went out to the Mustang."

"Drinking?"

"Those stones," said Mercer, pointing to the evidence bag. "They're obsidian, aren't they?"

Duke turned to his deputy. "Why don't you take Mr. Mercer over to the office. Get a detailed statement while everything is fresh."

HOCKNEY TOOK HIS TIME. Bedroom, bathroom, and then back to the living room. "Okay," he said, "who wants to go first?"

"You figure this for a crime scene?" said Leon.

"Who knows," said Duke. "Maybe Shipman's a real slob."

"Feels staged," said Leon.

"This the same room?" asked Thumps, even though he knew the answer.

"It is," said Duke.

Leon looked at both men. "You two want to share?"

"Nina Maslow," said Thumps. "This was her room."

"The dead woman?" said Leon. "The one who did the research on the Obsidian Murders?"

"*Malice Aforethought*," said Duke. "Reality program that was in town a while back. Maslow was staying in this very room."

"And there was a break-in?"

"Same as this," said Duke.

Thumps held the evidence bag up to the light. "Except for the stones."

"Yes," said Duke. "Except for the stones."

"You know," said Leon, "for a small town, you have more than your fair share of creepy."

"If I find out that this is all a publicity stunt," said Duke, "we're going to have us a lynching."

"Mercer's right about the Mustang," said Thumps. "Shipman and Gerson were there."

"And they left together," said Leon. "Thumps took off a little later. Mercer and I stayed."

"By yourselves?"

"Nope," said Leon. "We were joined by two lovely women."

"Names?" said the sheriff.

"There was a blonde," said Leon. "Cynthia, Stephanie. She decided on Mercer. The other woman was a nurse. Judy."

"The four of you close the place?"

"Mercer and the blonde were still there when nurse Judy and I left."

Duke tried to work up a smile. "I can't tell you how pleased I am to know that you've been able to avail yourself of our local hospitality."

"Hospitality's okay," said Leon, "but the shit's beginning to pile up."

Thumps considered raising the question, but Duke beat him to it. "So, what do we think of our Mr. Mercer?"

"Seems harmless enough," said Leon. "In a goofy sort of way."

"You were going to check out our merry band of movie-makers," said Thumps.

"Lance looked into it," said the sheriff. "Would appear our folks are not on the A-list of entertainment notables."

"Or on the list at all?"

"Yes," said Duke, "there's that."

"You think this movie thing is a con?" said Leon.

"Don't know what it is," said the sheriff, "but something's rotten in Denmark. I had Lance check *Variety* and the other entertainment blogs for any hint of a movie about the Obsidian Murders."

"Nothing?"

"You want to know anything about the new spate of reality shows," said the sheriff, "or find out what's happening on *Game of Thrones*, just ask Lance."

"Could be a small, independent production," said Leon.

"We could ask Mercer," said Thumps.

"But we don't want to do that just yet," said Duke. "Do we?"

"Shipman and Gerson," said Thumps. "Doesn't feel right."

"I don't think that they're shacked up in some motel," said Duke, "but I'm going to go ahead and waste the time and man-power, just in case I'm wrong. You two want to help?"

Leon fished the silver dollar out of his pocket. "Well," he said. "Since you asked."

THIRTY-THREE

Duke locked the room down with crime-scene tape and went back to the office to continue his chat with Anthony Mercer. Thumps and Leon stopped at the hotel's business centre and used one of the computers to check on the lodging possibilities in the vicinity.

"Why would they go somewhere else," said Leon, "when they have perfectly good rooms right here?"

"Privacy?"

"I figure Shipman for cheap," said Leon. "What do we have?"

"Motel 6."

"Anything cheaper?"

"The Wagon Wheel."

"Okay," said Leon. "Let's start there."

* * *

SHIPMAN AND GERSON weren't at the Wagon Wheel, and they weren't at Motel 6.

"Maybe I was wrong," said Leon, after they struck out at the Holiday Inn. "Maybe the guy is classier than he looks."

"At the Mustang," said Thumps, "did they feel as though they were interested in each other?"

"I'm not sure they realized they were in the same room," said Leon.

"Yet they left together."

"They shared the same car," said Leon. "There's a difference."

"And," said Thumps, "so far as we know, they never made it home."

"So where are they?" Leon rolled down the side window and let the air rush in. "They're in the middle of a movie project, and they decide to disappear."

"There's always foul play."

"There you go," said Leon. "Always with the negativity."

"Old habits."

"Besides the Tucker," said Leon, "where's the fanciest place for eating and quiet contemplation?"

"Are we back to food and sex?"

"We are," said Leon.

"Shadow Ranch," said Thumps. "Buffalo Mountain."

"Best food?"

"They're both expensive," said Thumps. "Shadow Ranch has the golf course. Buffalo Mountain has the casino."

"Never saw the sunshine in golf," said Leon. "Let's try the casino first."

"Okay."

"And just so we're on the same page, lunch is on the sheriff's tab."

There were, Thumps discovered, several motels perched on the outskirts of town that he had never noticed before.

"The Dew-Drop Inn?" Leon made a face. "You're really going to stop?"

"The authentic motel experience," said Thumps. "Maybe Shipman and Gerson like seedy."

The motel was painted a disturbing shade of yellow with a green trim that reminded Thumps of old asparagus.

"The last one was seedy," said Leon. "This is squalid."

"It's your turn to go in and ask."

"I'm not armed."

"Mention Duke's name."

Leon quickly took the silver dollar out of his pocket. "Call it."

IT WAS AFTER two by the time they got to Buffalo Mountain.

"I may need a shower," said Leon.

"You didn't even get out of the car."

"And I'm hungry," said Leon. "This place do buffet or à la carte?"

"Both."

"We eat first," said Leon, "and ask questions later."

Buffalo Mountain had been designed by Douglas Cardinal

and was organized into three distinct parts. To the north and west, set in the trees with views of the mountains, were the condominiums. The conference centre with its reception area and restaurant was to the east. At the south end was the large copper-domed casino.

"Pretty fancy," said Leon. "They do rentals?"

"They do."

"If it was me," said Leon, "this is where I'd come."

Thumps guided Leon to the dining room with its floor-to-ceiling windows that overlooked the river and White Goat Canyon.

"I could get used to this."

"Look at the menu," said Thumps. "I'll check with the front desk."

"Check-out at most places is around eleven," said Leon. "So unless they got a late check-out or they decided to stay another night, they're long gone."

"If they were ever here at all," said Thumps.

"Yes," said Leon, "there's always that."

"Just so you know," said Thumps, "the prairie oyster appetizer is just deep-fried meatballs."

THUMPS DIDN'T RECOGNIZE the young woman at the front desk. But he did know the family name.

"Welcome to Buffalo Mountain."

"Heavy Runner," said Thumps. "Any relation to Roxanne?"

"My auntie." The woman had a badge that said ARLENE
HEAVY RUNNER. "You're DreadfulWater."

"I am."

"My auntie has told me all about you."

"Roxanne has a great sense of humour."

Arlene smiled. "No, she doesn't."

Thumps smiled back. "I'm hoping you can help me."

"Ms. Merchant is in the Canyon Room."

"Claire's here?"

"Council meeting," said Arlene. "She should be out in the
next half-hour."

"Actually," said Thumps, "I'm checking on something for
the sheriff."

"Aren't you a photographer?"

"I am," said Thumps, "but I'm wondering if you have a
Harold Shipman or a Runa Gerson staying here."

"That's confidential."

"It's police business."

"It's still confidential."

"You'd tell your auntie," said Thumps, "if she asked."

Arlene's smile faded. "That's not very nice."

"And," said Thumps, "if they aren't staying here, then you're
not breaking any confidence."

"When would they have checked in?"

"Last night," said Thumps.

Arlene worked the keyboard. "Nope. No Shipman. No
Gerson."

"Maybe they checked in under an alias."

Arlene went back to the keyboard. "Nobody checked in last night."

"Gerson is about thirty-six or so, five foot seven. Blonde. Viking warrior type." Thumps tried to remember what Shipman looked like and couldn't. "The guy is older."

"We're slow this time of the year." Arlene looked at the monitor. "The only arrival we've had in the last two days has been a party of six. All women."

Thumps tapped the reception desk with his fingers. "It was a long shot."

"What about those questions?"

"What?"

"Auntie is going to want to know if you've answered those questions," said Arlene. "What should I tell her?"

LEON WAS AT the table by the windows where Thumps had left him, but he was not alone.

"Ora Mae is going to show me a couple of condos."

"You can't afford a condo."

"Don't be telling my clients what they can afford and what they can't." Ora Mae was dressed in a dark navy suit with a white blouse. "You'd be surprised what is possible with some creative financing."

"Any luck?" said Leon.

"Not here," said Thumps.

Leon considered the news for a moment. "Then we might as well see the condos."

"I thought you were hungry."

Ora Mae's glare had weight. "You guys think of other things besides food and sex?"

"Absolutely," said Leon. "For instance, right now I'm thinking that Thumps can handle the mystery of Shipman and Gerson on his own, while we look at the potentials of real estate."

"Let's start with the one-bedroom," said Ora Mae, "and work our way up."

"After that," said Leon, "we'll probably grab something to eat. Maybe visit the casino."

Ora Mae straightened her jacket. "Gary Diggins and the Essex Alleycats are playing at the Mustang tonight."

Thumps looked at Leon. "More dancing?"

"You got something against dancing?" said Ora Mae.

"What I'm saying," said Leon, "is don't wait up."

"Don't worry," said Ora Mae. "I'll get the Ranger back to town. Wild Rose Realty provides door-to-door service."

THUMPS STAYED AT the table and sorted through his options. He could get back in the car and drive over to Shadow Ranch on the off chance that Shipman and Gerson were enjoying the amenities of the resort. Or he could sit and watch the river run down the canyon, eat something light, and wait for Claire to emerge from her meeting.

Or he could keep things simple and just go home.

"Arlene said you were here."

Tribal council meetings could be bloodbaths, but Claire looked none the worse for wear.

"Hey."

"You eat yet?"

"Nope."

"Mind if I join you?"

"Please."

"Arlene says the sheriff has you looking for a couple of adulterers."

Thumps shook his head. "Missing persons."

"How long they been missing?"

"Since last night."

"Thought the police liked to wait seventy-two hours before they released the hounds."

"That's a myth," said Thumps. "There's no waiting period for missing persons."

"I'll remember that next time my nephew runs off." Claire sat down with a sigh. "Have you ordered?"

"Nope." Thumps opened the menu. "What's good?"

"Just so you know," said Claire, "the prairie oyster appetizer is just deep-fried meatballs."

THIRTY-FOUR

Thumps settled on the pasta special. Claire ordered a salad.
"That's not much to eat."

"There was coffee and pastries at the meeting," said
Claire. "And I'll eat some of yours."

"Interesting meeting?"

"Regulations for cattle grazing on the extension lands. I
could hardly contain myself."

The pasta was disappointing. It was supposed to have been
farfalle with roasted autumn vegetables and garlic sausage, but
what arrived was penne with green peas and a marinara sauce.

"So, what are you up to?"

Thumps tried to think of a right answer.

Claire pushed on without him. "I just figured that since
you're here, maybe you'd like to stay."

"Stay?"

"Here," said Claire. "I have a condo. We could go for a walk. Talk. Have a late dinner."

"Like a date?"

"Sure," said Claire. "Like a date."

"You have a condo?"

"Bought it when Buffalo Mountain opened," said Claire. "Tribal members got first crack at the units."

"Good view?"

"The best," said Claire. "Finish your autumn vegetables, and I'll show you."

CLAIRE HAD BOUGHT one of the three-bedrooms. The Cascade. The Cataract. The Confluence. All the units had names, but Thumps could never remember which was which.

"Big unit."

"I rent it out during the season," said Claire. "It almost pays the mortgage."

"Hell of a view."

"I'm going to get into something comfortable."

Thumps kept his face under control. "Okay."

"Not that comfortable," said Claire, and she disappeared into one of the bedrooms.

Thumps walked out onto the balcony. The view was the same

as the view from the dining room. He sat in one of the wrought-iron chairs, stretched his legs, and watched the river rush away through the canyon.

"How's the case going?"

Claire had reappeared. She had lost the suit and found a pair of shorts and a loose top.

"It's not."

"Still trying to find the husband?"

Thumps shook his head. "Don't even know where to look. He gets out of prison. He disappears."

Claire pulled up a chair. "Did he have any place to go?"

"Like family?"

"Family," said Claire. "Friends. A favourite part of the world."

"Don't know."

"He had Anna."

Thumps started to say something and then stopped.

"I'm surprised that he didn't try to see Anna," said Claire. "She was his wife. Callie was his child."

"Nina Maslow thought that Oakes might have killed them."

Claire shook her head. "Why?"

"Because she was with me."

"Then he would have killed you."

"Maybe Anna was easier," said Thumps. "Maybe I was supposed to be next."

"Sure. If this were a movie." Claire took the other chair. "So, tell me about it."

"What?"

"Anna's murder. The sooner you get it solved, the sooner you can get on with the rest of your life." Claire stretched out one leg and touched Thumps's foot. "Maybe I can help."

Thumps looked down at the river. His field camera and tripod were in the car. He could set it up just inside the sliding doors and wait for the sky to lose some of its high glare.

"I'll go first." Claire shifted in the chair. "Victor Brandt."

Thumps started to object.

"Just shut up and listen." Claire closed her eyes for a moment. "Anna and I had quite a bit in common."

Thumps frowned.

"Not just you." Claire made a face. "We were both young. Single mothers whose partners left them."

"Okay."

"Women with children, on their own," said Claire. "You following this?"

"I am."

"Make a noise every so often, so I know you're awake."

"Okay."

"Victor came along one summer, and I ran off with him. It was exciting. We rode all over the country." Claire stretched her legs. "And then I got pregnant."

"Stanley."

"I had Stanley in a small town in Utah," she said. "Monticello. Mormon country."

Thumps had seen pictures of the Great Salt Lake and Canyon-
lands. John Ford had filmed his westerns in Monument Valley
on the Navajo Nation.

"But we didn't stay long. Victor got a line on a job in Arizona.
Place called Holbrook." Claire stretched her legs. "Then one
morning, Victor got on his motorcycle and disappeared. Stanley
was about nine months old. I waited for him to come back.
End of the second month, I called Moses. He sent me money
for a bus ticket."

"So, you came home with a baby."

"Six months later, Victor showed up on the reservation.
Wanted to get back together. Make a new start."

"And you said no?"

"No," said Claire. "I said yes."

Thumps waited.

"He stayed a week. And then he was gone again. Don't think
he liked a crying baby or the smell of a dirty diaper." Claire
paused and stared out at the view. "Or me."

"Man was a fool."

"I was hoping you'd say something like that."

"It's the truth."

"Every six months or so, he'd show up, a little worse for
wear. I think he was doing drugs by then. You know why he
kept coming back?"

"Money?"

"I was his touchstone," said Claire. "It took me a while to
figure it out. I was the only constant thing in his life."

"Must have been tough on you."

"Not really. He came back again when Stanley was two, and this time, Moses and my uncles talked to him. Made it clear that he wasn't to come back again."

"They beat him up?"

Claire laughed. "No, they didn't beat him up. And they didn't threaten to kill him or anything like that. God, you watch too much television."

"So, what'd they discuss?"

"Motorcycle insurance," said Claire. "Okay, your turn."

"Nothing to tell," said Thumps. "I was at a conference in San Diego when the killings started. By the time I got back, Anna and Callie were dead."

"A serial killer."

"So far as we know."

"Or the husband."

"Perhaps."

Claire sat back and closed her eyes. "What was Anna doing there?"

Thumps rubbed the back of his head.

"I mean, did you guys ever go to the beach?"

"Anna was a nurse," said Thumps. "I was a cop. We both worked shift."

"So you go to San Diego, and she takes her daughter to the beach." Claire opened her eyes. "What time of the day?"

"What?"

"What time of the day did she go to the beach?"

"Evening."

"Were most of the victims killed at night?"

Thumps cocked his head. "You're beginning to sound like a cop."

"I am a cop," said Claire, "but just for this one case."

"Yes," said Thumps. "They were killed at night."

"So why was Anna at the beach? At night. With her daughter." Claire stood up and leaned against the railing. "And what was she wearing?"

"Wearing?"

"It might tell us why she was there." Claire paused. "Would you rather we didn't talk about Anna?"

"I'm okay."

"You seem to know less about this case than you should."

"How about we talk about us."

"And the baby?"

"Sure."

"Or we could do something else. For instance, we could lie down and hold each other."

"A nap?"

"And if that doesn't work out," said Claire, "I'm sure we'll be able to find alternatives."

"Maybe he'll come back."

"Victor?" Claire snorted. "It's been twenty years. There's nothing to come back to."

"Does he know that?"

"Doesn't matter." Claire took Thumps's hand. "All that matters is that I know."

WHEN THUMPS WOKE, he was lying on the bed by himself. His shoes were gone. So were his socks. As well as his pants and shirt. He could vaguely remember climbing onto the bed with Claire, could remember holding her.

Or did she hold him?

So, where was she? Thumps waited in case she had gotten up for a drink of water or to go to the bathroom. He listened for the sound of someone moving about the condo. Nothing.

And it was night. How long had he been asleep? "Hello."

Claire was sitting on the balcony, bathed in moonlight. Well, not moonlight. There was no moon. Just the overhead balcony light. But the effect was much the same.

"Look who's awake."

"What happened?"

"You passed out."

"Passed out?"

"My uncle was diabetic," said Claire. "Whenever he had a heavy meal, he'd pass out."

Thumps tried to remember where he had put his diabetes kit.

"You had pasta. Did you take any insulin?"

In the car. The testing kit and the insulin were in the car. "What time is it?"

"Almost midnight. I poked you a few times to make sure you weren't dead."

"Did I take my clothes off?"

"My uncle didn't take his diabetes seriously either," said Claire, "and he wound up losing a foot."

"Did we . . . ?"

"Oh, and your cellphone's been buzzing."

"I don't have a cellphone."

"In your jacket."

The cellphone Duke had given him. Thumps had forgotten about it. And now that he remembered, he wished he hadn't.

"Someone's trying to find you," said Claire. "And they sound serious."

"The sheriff. He gave me a cellphone."

"Why would Duke give you a cellphone?"

"It's a long story."

"Is this about his prostate operation?" Claire caught Thumps's reaction. "Is it supposed to be a secret?"

"Guess not."

"So, you're going to what? Be the sheriff?"

"Acting sheriff," said Thumps. "Just until Duke is back on his feet."

"Well, Mr. Acting Sheriff," said Claire, "you better answer your phone."

Claire's ears were better than his. Thumps fumbled in the jacket pocket until he found the phone.

Duke did not sound happy. "Where the hell you been?"

"It's almost midnight."

"The law doesn't sleep. You still at Buffalo Mountain?"

"What do you want?"

"I want you," said Duke. "In town. ASAP."

"No can do," said Thumps.

"Get your ass to the fairgrounds." Duke didn't frame it as a question.

"I'm busy."

"Are you with someone?"

"None of your business."

"Claire?"

"I. Am. Occupied."

"She'll understand."

He could hear the sheriff arguing with someone in the background. For a moment, Thumps thought he had lost the connection.

"Hey, Tonto. You better get in here. We found Shipman and Gerson. Sheriff says to bring your camera."

"Shit."

"Worse than that," said Leon. "But if you hurry, there may be some doughnuts left."

THIRTY-FIVE

Claire had been understanding.

"The sheriff or sex," she had said. "It's an easy choice."

Thumps had tried to defend himself. "You heard me," he said. "I told him I was busy."

"You better put on some clothes. A make-believe lawman in his underwear isn't all that intimidating."

"Technically," said Thumps, "I'm not make-believe. I have a badge."

Claire walked him to the door, undoing her blouse one button at a time. "Someday," she said, "you'll have to explain the statutes on indecent exposure."

THE DRIVE BACK to Chinook was made at speeds exceeding the limit. By the time he got to the fairgrounds, the place was ablaze in lights and activity. Hockney's cruiser was parked against the barn. Beth's station wagon was next to it. The sheriff and the county coroner in the same spot at the same time eliminated the possibility of this being a social occasion.

One of the sheriff's other deputies, Bob or Bruce, Thumps could never remember, was controlling the traffic.

"Sheriff's expecting me."

The name tag said "Fred." Thumps tried to come up with some kind of mnemonic reminder.

Deputy Fred was skinny with a small pot that hung over his utility belt like a small bag of potatoes.

Fred, Fred, potato head.

"DreadfulWater!" Sheriff Duke Hockney and Leon Ranger were standing at the entrance to the barn. "About time."

The sheriff had work lights set up, but the barn swallowed most of the illumination, leaving the interior in a disturbing pattern of half-light and long shadows.

The black Mustang was parked in the centre of the barn. Most of the lights were trained on the car. Beth Mooney was standing beside the driver's door.

"There he is," she said, with no happiness in her voice.

Thumps caught the sharp, copper smell before he got anywhere near the car. "Shipman and Gerson?"

"In the car," said Leon. "And it's not pretty."

Thumps stayed where he was.

"You can't see anything from there," said the sheriff.

"Don't need to see anything," said Thumps. "I know a dead body when I smell one."

"Two dead bodies," said Leon.

Beth came over. "Don't want to tell you law-enforcement types how to do your job, but the crime scene is over here."

"I'm a photographer," said Thumps.

"Who is going to photograph my crime scene?"

"How about I lend you my camera?"

"We going to have to listen to your 'Navajo sensibilities' whine?" said Beth. "Again?"

"Murder?"

"Is that really a question?" said Duke.

"Someone bashed their heads in," said Leon. "Did a fine job."

"Mr. Mercer has already identified the bodies."

Thumps looked around.

"He's sitting in Lance's cruiser," said Duke. "He looked as though he was getting ready to throw up."

"And better Lance's cruiser than yours."

"I'm the sheriff," said Duke. "Can't drive around in a vehicle that smells like puke."

"He under arrest?"

"Maybe," said Leon. "Maybe not. Duke hasn't decided yet."

"Maybe you want to flip for the answer," said the sheriff.

Leon already had the silver dollar out.

* * *

HAROLD SHIPMAN WAS behind the wheel. Runa Gerson was in the passenger's seat. Thumps took shots from both sides of the car. He shut down the flash, turned up the ISO, and shot through the windshield. Both bodies were intact, but the faces were gone. Someone had pounded their heads into pulp. The attack had been violent, excessive, and focused.

"Thoughts?" said Beth.

"We haven't looked in the mouths yet," said Leon.

"I want to get them back to the morgue first," said Beth.

"So, someone kills Shipman and Gerson, puts their bodies in a stolen Mustang, and parks the car in the barn from which it was originally stolen."

"We found blood over here." The sheriff pointed toward the high stack of hay bales. "Drag marks from there to the car."

Thumps walked to the bales and then back to the car. "So, how does the killer get Shipman and Gerson to come out here?"

"That's exactly what we've been asking ourselves," said Duke.

"And we don't have a good answer yet," said Leon.

"While you boys are thinking about it," said Beth, "how about you bag the bodies and put them in my wagon."

Duke jammed his hands in his pockets. "You and Leon okay with that?"

"Not happening," said Thumps.

"I got prostate cancer," said Duke. "I'm not supposed to lift anything heavy."

"That's hernia surgery," said Beth.

* * *

THUMPS TOOK SEVERAL photographs of the sheriff and Leon loading the bodies into Beth's station wagon.

"Was DreadfulWater really a cop?" asked the sheriff.

"So far as I can remember," said Leon.

"We'll finish up here," Duke told Beth. "Meet you back at the morgue."

"I'll be waiting." Beth shut the door and started the engine. "It'll be the high point of my evening."

Anthony Mercer was sitting in the back seat of Lance Packard's cruiser.

"He puke yet?" asked the sheriff.

"Nope," said Leon, "but he's not happy."

"Not my problem," said Duke.

"That's what I told him," said Leon.

Thumps suddenly felt as though he were moving in slow motion. "Wait a minute. Who found the bodies?"

"Wondering when you were going to get around to that," said Duke.

"Mercer?"

"You're slowing down, Tonto," said Leon.

"Man says he got a call," said Duke. "Voice told him to come here."

"And he did?"

"According to our Mr. Mercer," said Duke, "that's exactly what he did."

"An anonymous call? To go to a deserted barn in the middle of the night?"

"Appears our Mr. Mercer is an adventurous fellow."

Anthony Mercer didn't look adventurous. He looked ill. He was genetically pale to begin with, but now he was almost translucent. His eyes were ringed in red, and his nose was dripping. Thumps wasn't sure whether he felt sorry for the man or was just put off by his appearance.

Duke squatted down by the open door. "Well," he said, "we got a whole bunch of questions. Where would you like to start?"

Mercer sat in the back seat of the cruiser and looked straight ahead.

"Okay," said Duke, "I'll start. Did you kill Mr. Shipman and Ms. Gerson?"

Thumps could see the man's lips moving.

"Didn't hear that," said Duke.

"No," said Mercer. "I didn't kill them. What kind of a monster do you think I am?"

"You do work in the film industry," said Leon.

"Was that supposed to be funny?" Mercer stared at Leon.

"Yes," said Leon, "it was."

"All right," said Duke. "Now that you've recovered some of your nerve, let's take it from the top."

"I got a call," said Mercer. "At the hotel."

"Male? Female?"

"Couldn't tell," said Mercer. "They didn't chat."

"And this voice said?"

"'The barn at the fairgrounds has the answers.'" Mercer wiped his nose. "I thought it was Shipman."

"Shipman?"

"He liked to be mysterious," said Mercer. "I thought it was a joke."

"But you went."

"Sure," said Mercer. "I mean, maybe he and Runa had actually found something."

"And when you got here?"

"I found them in the car." Mercer's nose began dripping again. "Jesus."

"Then what?"

"I called you guys."

"You didn't look around?" Duke glanced at Thumps and Leon. "You didn't search the barn? Check to see if the killer was still here?"

"Oh, Christ," said Mercer, visibly shaken. "I didn't even think of that."

"Evidently not," said Duke.

"I could have been killed as well."

"Why?"

"Why?" Mercer began hitting the back of the seat. "We're doing a movie about a serial killer. It's pretty obvious, isn't it?"

"I tend to be a bit dense," said Duke.

"He's killing us off," said Mercer. "One by one."

"Actually," said Leon, "he's doing two at a time."

"You're not fucking funny!"

Thumps waited to see if the sheriff was going to pick up the conversation. "You said you thought the voice on the phone was Shipman."

"Who else would call me at the hotel?" Mercer sat back in the seat. "We don't know anyone in town. Shipman liked to do voices. And to be honest, the man could be an asshole."

"Hard to work with?"

"Thought he was in charge of the project."

"But he wasn't."

"You ever hear of a writer being in charge of anything?"

Duke shook his head. "He's got a point."

"Producer, director, writer," said Mercer. "That's the pecking order."

Leon kept his voice level. "So, you two didn't get along?"

"What?" Mercer got out of the car. "Of course, we got along. It's Hollywood. Nobody likes anyone, but we all get along."

"Don't mind Mr. Ranger," said Duke. "He's just looking for a motive."

"That's me," said Leon. "But you don't have to worry. I'm retired."

"Am I under arrest?"

"Nope." Hockney tipped his hat back. "Would appreciate it if you didn't leave town just yet."

"And if I do?"

"Damn," said Duke, "but I hate the hard questions."

"Then I'm going back to the hotel."

"That's a good idea," said Duke. "Have a drink. Get a good night's sleep. Maybe stop by the office in the morning."

"Why?"

"Just routine," said the sheriff. "Since you identified the bodies, we'll need a signed statement."

HOCKNEY WAITED UNTIL Mercer drove off in his car. "Ideas?"

"Autopsy," said Thumps.

"Autopsy isn't an idea," said Duke.

"Smart money says Shipman and Gerson have obsidian in their mouths," said Leon.

"Because there's a serial killer in town?" The sheriff looked skeptical.

"None of this makes much sense," said Thumps.

"I was good with the 'doesn't make sense' answer," said Duke, "before the bodies turned up."

"Why were they killed?" said Leon. "Did they find something? Wrong place, wrong time? Strikes me they were more of a threat to themselves than to a serial killer."

"Or an angry husband."

"Wasn't Raymond Oakes," said Thumps.

"And you know this how?"

"It's Obsidian," said Thumps. "You're right. He's here in town."

Duke grunted. "Obsidian?"

"Our clever name for the serial killer," said Leon.

"Sounds like a character from *Game of Thrones*," said Duke.

"Good show," said Leon. "I really like the little guy."

"Okay." Duke pulled his gun belt up. "Let's do this the old-fashioned way."

"Wait for an anonymous phone tip?" said Leon.

"The autopsy," said Duke. "We'll start with the autopsy."

THIRTY-SIX

Thumps followed the sheriff back into town. Leon rode with Duke. Which gave Thumps time to go over the original case, page by page, in his head. Claire was right. He knew less about the case than he thought he knew.

How had that happened?

What was Anna doing on the beach that night? Why was Callie with her? The three of them had only gone to the beach once. To watch the big race. The Trinidad to Clam Beach Run and Walk.

THE SHERIFF'S CRUISER was already parked in front of the old Land Titles building. The place was dark, but that was because the basement windows were at the back, in the alley. Thumps pressed the button for the morgue, and the door snapped open.

Abandon hope, Thumps thought as he stepped inside, *all ye who enter here.*

Beth was standing to the side of the stainless-steel table. Duke and Leon were standing across from her. What was left of Runa Gerson was lying between them. Her head had been crushed by something heavy, wielded with force. She had probably died with the first blow.

Thumps stopped on the last step and waited.

"You're safe," said Beth. "If she rises up from the dead and comes at you, the sheriff here will shoot her with one of his silver bullets."

"No, I won't," said Duke. "You know what kind of paperwork I have to fill out if I discharge my firearm?"

"Silver bullets are for werewolves," said Leon. "I'm not sure how you kill zombies."

"I don't have all night," said Beth. "I'd like to get some sleep before I start thinking about breakfast."

Thumps could feel the walls of the morgue closing in around him. "Why are morgues in basements?"

Beth stopped what she was doing and yawned.

"I mean, why are they all below ground? Every morgue I've ever been in has been below ground."

"How many morgues have you been in?" said Beth.

Now that Thumps thought about it, he hadn't been in all that many morgues. "Three. Maybe four."

"So you're an expert on morgues."

"I'm just asking," said Thumps. "It might help if they were on the second or third floor. Then you could have windows and the place wouldn't feel so gloomy."

"Can we get on with it?" said Duke.

"And miss the lecture on morgue architecture?"

"Please," said the sheriff.

"Rigor has set in." Beth forced Gerson's jaw open. "And it looks as though there are no losers."

Duke and Leon leaned in. Thumps took a step back.

"I can't say for certain that this is obsidian." Beth held up a small black stone. "But I'd say the chances are good."

"It's obsidian," said Leon.

"Head crushed in," said the sheriff. "Obsidian in the mouth. Maybe it is time for me to retire."

"Missing part of the little finger on the right hand," said Beth. "But it's an old injury."

"Door jamb accident," said Thumps. "Could we see Shipman for a moment?"

Beth went to the stainless-steel locker and pulled out a drawer.

"He looks worse in the light," said Leon.

"Damage is more severe," said Beth. "What did you want to see?"

"Thumps is checking the ring and the tattoo," said the sheriff. "But we'll run the DNA."

"Hope you don't expect to get that back in your lifetime," said Beth. "Ring looks expensive. The star's kinda cute."

"Who gets a black and white tattoo of a star on the back of their hand?"

"You prefer a rose?" said Beth.

"No," said Leon, "but at least you could get it in colour."

Duke cleared his throat. "How long have they been dead?"

Beth slid the drawer closed. "I've just started on Gerson, and all I can give you is a guess, but I'd figure anything between twelve and twenty-four hours."

"So, Shipman and Gerson leave the Mustang together. And they never get back to the hotel." Leon turned to Thumps. "We could have been the last ones to see them alive."

"Except for the killer," said Duke.

"Still don't know why," said Thumps.

"And I don't do *why*," said Beth. "I only do *how*."

"And *how* is blunt-force trauma," said Duke.

"No fair," said Beth. "You looked."

"I'll need that stone."

"Patience." Beth picked up the Stryker saw. "Let me do my job. And then you can do yours."

THUMPS HAD SEEN the sheriff in bad moods. This was one of them. Hockney didn't say a single word as they walked back to their cars.

"We fucked up," said Leon.

Thumps took his cue from Duke and kept his mouth shut.

"We missed something, Tonto."

"Go home," said the sheriff. "Get some sleep."

"And then what?"

Duke's cell began playing a tune that Thumps tried to place. The sheriff turned his back to the other men and stalked off with the phone, his neck and head bent to one side.

"The theme from *Knight Rider*?" Leon smiled at Thumps. "He sure as hell doesn't look *that* old."

Thumps tried to remember the show. There was a talking car that could think and was pretty much indestructible.

And then Duke was back, waving the cellphone at Thumps and Leon, looking happy and energized. "Saddle up."

"That sounds like a posse," said Leon.

Duke set his hat on his head and pulled down the brim. "Get a rope."

The Tucker hotel was bright with light. Duke jogged up the steps, pushed his way through the revolving doors, and went straight to the front desk, where Deputy Lance Packard was waiting for him.

"Where?" said the sheriff.

"Parking garage," said Lance.

Duke made for the fire exit. Thumps and Leon hurried after him.

"Hurrah, boys," he shouted, taking the stairs two at a time. "We got them."

Leon kept pace. "Isn't that what Custer said when he saw the Indian encampment at the Little Bighorn?"

Hockney hit the bottom of the stairwell and burst through a red door marked "Level 2." The parking garage was dimly lit and damp with the smell of cold concrete. Duke began walking the long line of parked cars.

"Spread out."

"What are we looking for?"

Hockney pulled his gun and laid it against his thigh. "There."

Near the bottom of the ramp, Anthony Mercer was loading suitcases into the back of a red SUV.

"Sheriff's department," Duke shouted.

The effect was electric. Mercer dropped the bag and bolted down the ramp.

"Don't even think about it." Duke showed the gun. "I'm tired, and I'd just as soon shoot you as arrest you!"

Leon moved quickly to flank the man. Thumps stayed with the sheriff.

"I didn't do anything."

"On the ground." Hockney closed the gap. "Hands behind your head."

"He's going to kill me!" Mercer's eyes were wide with fear.

"On. The. Ground."

Mercer stayed on his feet. "You can't make me stay. I haven't done anything wrong."

Duke brought the gun into a shooting position. "You're a suspect in a double murder, and I will shoot you if I have to."

"I heard that the sheriff likes shooting people," said Leon.

"No, I don't," said Duke. "But I will."

"I'm not going to stay here." Mercer went back to the SUV and started loading the suitcase. "Shoot me if you have to."

"Ah, hell." Duke put his gun away and took out his handcuffs. Then he grabbed Mercer by his belt, lifted him off the ground, and dropped him face down on the floor of the parking garage. "Now you got me angry."

Thumps watched as Duke handcuffed Mercer and pulled him to his feet.

"I'm going to sue you for police brutality."

Leon leaned in, his face close to Mercer. "Did you know that in the list of hazardous workplaces, jails are number seven?"

"Would you stop trying to scare my prisoner?"

"Just trying to be helpful."

"Okay," said the sheriff. "Stop trying to be helpful." Duke took Mercer by the arm and marched him up the ramp. "We can do this one of two ways. One, you can tell me why you were trying to escape my jurisdiction. Or, two, I can put you in jail as a material witness."

Mercer had regained most of his courage. "Shipman and Gerson are dead. I'm not about to be number three."

Duke leaned Mercer against the wall and pushed the button for the elevator. "Why do you think you're next?"

"The guy calls me. Gets me to come out to the fairgrounds so I can find my friends." Mercer paled. "Then when I get back to my room, there it is."

"There what is?"

"A fucking black stone," said Mercer. "Sitting in the middle of the coffee table."

DUKE TOOK THE cuffs off Mercer on the promise that the man would not try to run away, and the four of them rode the elevator to the third floor in silence, while Norah Jones quietly sang "Don't Know Why."

"You've got the statement I gave Deputy Dawg," said Mercer, who had recovered his equilibrium and was working on his sarcasm.

"Deputy Lance Packard." Duke stopped in front of the hotel door and waited for Mercer to find his key. "Deputy Dawg is a cartoon character."

"People ever tell you that you look like Ned Flanders?" said Leon. "Only Ned is smarter."

"Okay," said Mercer. "How about you cut me some slack. I almost got killed tonight."

"At the barn," said Duke.

"Yes, at the barn," said Mercer. "The guy who killed Shipman and Gerson could have been there laying in wait for me."

"Lying," said Thumps. "Lying in wait."

Mercer opened the door. Duke quickly stepped around him and entered the room. "Mr. Mercer," he said, "I'd like you to wait right here at the door. Can you do that?"

"So, you believe me."

"When you came back from the barn and opened the door to your room, did you notice anything out of place?"

"No."

"What did you do?"

Mercer thought for a moment. "I went to the bathroom. I had to pee."

"Okay. And after that?"

"I came back into the living room, and that's when I saw the piece of obsidian."

Duke walked over to the coffee table. There was a small black stone right in the centre of the wood top.

"Did you touch it?"

"No."

"Or move it?"

"No." Mercer waved a hand as though that was going to explain what had happened. "I saw the stone. I packed my bags and got the hell out of here."

"Thumps," said Duke, "you want to take the bedroom? Mr. Ranger, would you do the honours in the bathroom?"

"You don't need me," said Mercer.

"But I do so enjoy your company," said the sheriff.

THE BEDROOM WASN'T particularly large, nor was it well furnished. A bed. A dresser. A small easy chair and a round glass table that you could set a cup on, and that was about it. There was a painting over the bed. The standard western landscape with mountains and rivers and a couple of antelope peeking out from the edges of the frame.

The closet was empty except for something someone had wrapped in a white towel. Thumps didn't touch it. The stains on the towel made guessing unnecessary.

"Duke," Thumps said in a matter-of-fact tone. "You might want to bring Mr. Mercer in here."

Leon was first to the bedroom. "Nothing in the bathroom but tile and mirrors. What'd you find?"

Thumps motioned to the closet.

Leon went over and had a look. "Now ain't that real convenient."

"What's convenient?"

The sheriff and Mercer were in the doorway.

"It appears that Thumps has found the murder weapon," said Leon.

"That's not mine!"

Duke clamped a hand on Mercer's shoulder. "What's not yours?"

"Whatever is in that towel," said Mercer. "I've never seen it before."

Leon took a closer look. "I'm betting a baseball bat. Probably aluminum."

"I've never owned a baseball bat in my life!"

Duke took his phone out of his pocket and hit speed dial. "Lance, need you to bring a forensics kit to the third floor." The sheriff waited for his deputy to repeat the instruction back to him. "That's right. Mr. Mercer's room. And you might want to put a blanket and some sheets in our executive cell."

"You're arresting me? Again?"

"No choice," said Duke. "You found the bodies. The potential murder weapon has been discovered in your room."

"Come on, sheriff," said Mercer. "If I killed Harry and Runa, do you think I'd be stupid enough to hide the murder weapon in my room?"

"I try not to judge," said Duke.

"This is crazy." Mercer was shouting again, the sarcasm having slipped away. "You can't put me in jail!"

Duke undid the handcuffs from his belt. "Think of it this way, Mr. Mercer. If you did kill Shipman and Gerson and were stupid enough to leave the murder weapon in your room, then you deserve to be in jail. But if you didn't kill them and someone is gunning for you, then jail is the safest place I can put you."

"Sounds like a win-win to me," said Leon. "What about you, Tonto?"

Mercer looked as though someone had drained the blood from his body.

"It's the best option you have," said Thumps. "And you can drink the coffee in complete safety."

THIRTY-SEVEN

The object in the towel was a baseball bat. A Joerex twenty-eight-inch soft aluminum bat that the ad on the internet described as appropriate for "softball training, car and home self-defence."

Duke scrolled through the site. "You can pay over three hundred for a good bat," he said. "This one goes for around $28.50."

"So we got a cheap serial killer," said Leon.

Thumps watched the bats roll by. He hadn't realized the variety of colours that were available. The blood-stained bat in the sheriff's possession was black and silver with a black non-slip handle.

"Christ," said the sheriff, "they sell these things at all the big-box stores."

Thumps glanced at the door to the cells. "What are you going to do with Mercer?"

"No idea," said Hockney. "I can hold him on suspicion for a couple of days, but then I'll have to formally charge him or cut him loose."

"Don't think he did it," said Leon.

"Me neither," said Duke, "but you play the hand you're dealt."

"What about you, Tonto?"

"He didn't do it," said Thumps.

"Almost forgot," said the sheriff. "Fax came in for you."

Thumps frowned. "Me?"

"No," said Duke. "For your friend. You might tell him this is not a Western Union office." The sheriff slid two sheets of paper across the desk. "This about the case?"

Leon picked up the fax and did a quick read. "Looks as though Zorba stumbled onto something."

The fax was a list of names and dates, along with notes. Whoever had sent it had circled one name in particular.

"Deputy Tupper," said Leon. "I asked her to look to see who we had in lockup during the time of the murders."

Thumps read the name. "Simon Gordon. Culver City. Actor. In Eureka for a job that never materialized. Drunk and disorderly. Assault."

"You two going to share?" said Duke. "Seeing as you're using my fax machine."

"Archie came up with the idea that Obsidian had killed before and the reason we hadn't caught the pattern was that each of those cases had been closed."

"That's a good trick."

"Because the chief suspect killed himself," said Leon.

"So, you're thinking that our killer set up patsies to take the fall."

Thumps nodded.

"Actually, it's ingenious," said Duke. "And this Mr. Gordon was supposed to be the patsy?"

"Except he got himself thrown in jail and messed up the scenario," said Leon.

Duke went back to his monitor. "You got an address for this Simon Gordon?"

"Right here." Leon handed the sheriff the fax.

"You know," said Duke, "this is a very long shot. We like it because the pieces fit. But that doesn't mean it's true."

"It's all we have," said Thumps.

"And it looks as though it's enough." The sheriff turned the monitor around so Thumps and Leon could see the screen. "Take a look at that."

"Gordon killed himself?"

Thumps scanned the report. "Found dead in his home from a suspected overdose."

"Cleaning up after himself," said Leon. "Gordon would have been a loose end."

"A loose end our killer couldn't afford." Thumps wandered over to the percolator and gave it a shake. He could feel the coffee float up against the sides of the pot like a tide of warm honey. Duke Hockney, coffee gourmet, was going to take some getting used to. "Okay," he said, "let's say that we know how he did it. We've got the pattern."

"But what do we do with it?" said Leon. "We're still holding air."

"How about we shake the tree a little harder," said Duke. "See what falls out."

MERCER WAS PACING the cell. "Do you know how small this shithole is?"

"Six by eight," said the sheriff. "But it has a window, so it feels larger."

"If I laugh at your stupid jokes," said Mercer, "will you let me out of here?"

"How about you answer a few questions first."

"I want a lawyer."

"You're not under arrest," said Leon. "The good sheriff has you in protective custody."

"I want a lawyer."

"Fine," said the sheriff. "I'll have Deputy Packard bring you a phone so you can call a lawyer."

"Good."

"Just as soon as he returns."

Mercer stopped pacing. "As soon as he returns?"

"He had to go to Glory," said Duke, "but he'll be back just after noon."

"All right," said Mercer. "Ask your question."

"No can do," said Duke. "Once you ask for a lawyer, our chit-chat comes to an end."

Mercer began pacing again. "So have Turkey One or Turkey Two ask the question. That way, you can listen in. And then you can let me out of this cell."

The silver dollar was in the air. "You want to be Turkey One?"

"Gobble, gobble," said Thumps.

MERCER DID ANOTHER couple of circuits of the cell and then came to the bars. "The sheriff's an idiot," he said. "I had nothing to do with Harry and Runa."

Thumps was tired. He hadn't gotten any sleep, and it didn't look as though he was going to see a bed for the rest of the day. "The three of you came to town to work on a movie."

"What? That's a crime?"

"Movies aren't cheap."

"Damn straight they're not."

"Let's talk about the production company," said Thumps. "The folks that sign the cheques."

"This Dustan Schwarzstein Ltd.," said Leon.

Mercer's eyes darted between the two men. "What about it?"

"Head office in Los Angeles?"

"Don't know," said Mercer. "Could be out of the Cayman Islands or Romania for all I know."

"Hidden bank accounts? Money laundering? Drug cartels? Film companies?" said Leon. "That sort of thing?"

"Could be," said Mercer. "The cheques were good. That's the gold standard."

Thumps turned to Leon. "You want coffee?"

"I thought you'd never ask."

"Come on." Mercer went back to the pacing. "What do you want? Runa and Harry and I were hired to make a film. End of story."

"So the only thing you have is the name of what appears to be a shell corporation," said Thumps. "This the way movies normally work?"

"Hell," said Mercer, "there's nothing normal in movies anymore. The only question you ask is, 'Am I making money or am I losing money?'"

"And you were making money."

"Yeah," said Mercer, "I was making money."

"No address? No phone number?"

"You know how hard it is to get a start in this business?" Mercer shook his head. "If I'm Bruce Willis's kid or one of the Coppolas, it's a done deal. Otherwise, good fucking luck."

"So the offer to direct was a surprise?"

"That's what this business is," said Mercer. "Surprises."

Leon leaned against the bars. "You thinking what I'm thinking?"

"Probably," said Thumps.

"We should probably tell the sheriff."

"I think he wants to play," said Leon.

"And he kills Shipman and Gerson as part of the game?" said Duke. "And he tries to blame it on Mercer."

"No," said Thumps. "He knows we won't buy that. This is his way of letting us know it's him."

Hockney came back to his desk. "You think it's Raymond Oakes?"

"Or a player to be named later," said Leon.

"So, what do we do now?"

Thumps shrugged. "Wait for him to make a mistake."

"And in the meantime?"

"Breakfast," said Thumps. "In the meantime, we get breakfast."

THIRTY-EIGHT

Al's was crowded. The stools at the counter were all occupied, and Thumps and Leon had to stand outside on the sidewalk.

"What about the booths?" said Leon.

"The booths are for tourists," said Thumps. "And families."

"I'm sort of a tourist."

"None of the regulars would consider sitting in a booth."

"I'm not a regular."

All of the booths were empty, but as hungry as he was, Thumps couldn't bring himself to take the chance. He'd never hear the end of it. Wutty Youngbeaver, Jimmy Monroe, and Russell Plunkett would ride him for months, and Al would probably stop filling his cup to the top.

Leon was looking for his silver dollar just as Stas Black Weasel and Chintak Rawat came out of the café.

"Two stools," said Stas, "but you must step on eggs."

"Yes," said Chintak. "It is exceedingly tense."

"Al?" said Thumps.

"Indeed," said Chintak. "Most unfortunate."

"This about the guy who stood her up?" said Leon.

"I would not mention this," said Stas. "Messengers are being shot."

Thumps smiled. "Wutty Youngbeaver and the boys?"

"Baron Wutty and his entourage have been reduced," said Chintak.

"Slow coffee service?"

"To a tickle," said Stas.

"Trickle," said Chintak.

"We must get to work," said Stas.

"Most assuredly," said Chintak. "But you will tell us if there is any gratuitous violence or bloodshed."

WUTTY YOUNGBEAVER, Jimmy Monroe, and Russell Plunkett were in their usual spots, near the door, across from the grill. Thumps and Leon took the stools that Chintak and Stas had vacated. There were potatoes cooking on the grill but no Al.

Leon looked up and down the counter. "Do we ring a bell or something?"

Jimmy put a finger to his lips. "No humour."

"Wutty decided to be funny," said Russell, "and now we don't get coffee."

"Wasn't my fault," said Wutty. "Al's all sensitive."

"It *was* Wutty's fault," said Jimmy, "but we're being punished too."

"Where's Al?"

"Back room," said Russell.

Thumps glanced in that direction. "What'd you say?"

"Didn't say anything," said Wutty.

Jimmy slumped on his elbows. "What his Baronshit said was that the car guy evidently knew the difference between a Cadillac and a pickup truck."

"You said that?"

Wutty had his neck and head hunched down into his shoulders. "Not exactly."

"His exact words," said Jimmy.

Thumps caught the movement.

"You three still here?" Al strode out of the back area carrying a bowl of shredded potatoes. "You think of another good joke?"

"That was Wutty," said Russell, "not us."

"You guys are all friends," said Al. "Am I right?"

Russell looked at Jimmy. "Sort of."

"And friends share," said Al. "Good times, bad times?"

"Come on, Al," said Wutty, "it was just a joke."

Al ignored Wutty and turned to Thumps and Leon. "You two got a joke you want to share?"

"Nope," said Thumps. "Just looking for breakfast."

"Ditto," said Leon.

"Good," said Al. "'Cause I'm flat out of chuckles."

OVER THE NEXT half-hour, the café slowly cleared. Wutty and Jimmy and Russell hung around until the end, but with no coffee in sight they finally gave up and shuffled out into the day. Al moved back and forth behind the counter, working the grill, making a pot of coffee, cleaning the counter.

"You two are uncommonly quiet." Al set the pot down. "Just tired or scared to death?"

"Tired," said Leon.

"Scared to death," said Thumps.

"I don't bite," said Al. "You boys catch the bodies out at the fairgrounds?"

"Sheriff's problem," said Thumps.

"Hear it was a real mess." Al wiped a spot on the counter. "Archie says we got a serial killer on our hands."

"You people are quicker than Facebook," said Leon.

Al shrugged. "Small town. We don't like surprises."

Thumps looked at his watch. Claire hadn't said when she expected him, but if he was guessing, he would guess that sooner was better than later. Maybe he should bring something. Flowers. Chocolates. Something for the baby. What did you get babies? Thumps couldn't imagine that they needed anything.

"You know anything about babies?"

Leon looked stunned. "You're asking me?"

"Not you," said Thumps. "Al."

"What?" said Al. "Because I'm a woman?"

The tone was all Thumps needed to hear to know that this was not a question he should have asked.

"And because I'm a woman, I'd naturally know everything there was to know about babies?"

Leon tried to save him. "Well, Tonto here doesn't know squat."

Al set her feet apart as though she were getting ready to tackle a running back. "So, ask your question."

"It's okay."

"You still hoping to get breakfast?"

Thumps held up a hand in surrender. "I just thought I should take something for the baby."

Leon nodded. "This for the baby boy your friend at the Mustang had?"

"Nope." Al pointed her lips at Thumps. "His girlfriend is planning on adopting a little girl."

"Tonto and a baby?" said Leon. "Now there's something I'd pay to see."

"Cute bugger," said Al. "If you like babies."

"Maybe you should buy her a cellphone," said Leon. "Get her started early."

"A cellphone?"

Al strode back to the grill. "Only thing a baby needs is a cardboard box and someone to love her."

* * *

THUMPS DIDN'T ASK any more questions about babies, and he didn't mention George Gorka. Al brought the food, and Thumps and Leon ate it.

"So you're going out to see your girlfriend?"

Thumps tried to find a different word. "She's not exactly my girlfriend."

"So the two of you aren't adopting a baby?"

Thumps wasn't sure what they were doing. "She's thinking of adopting a baby."

"Okay," said Leon.

Thumps pushed the potatoes into the salsa. "How's your breakfast?"

"You trying to change the subject?"

"Al cooks her eggs in butter with a little olive oil."

"Okay, so don't tell me," said Leon. "None of my business anyway."

Thumps let his breath out and tried to relax his shoulders. "What are your plans for the day?"

Leon picked up his coffee cup. "Thought I'd go back to the RV and review the files. Keep thinking there's something we're missing. How long you going to be gone?"

"The weekend," said Thumps. "I told Claire I'd stay the weekend."

"The weekend." Leon made a low whistling sound. "That's serious time."

"Two nights."

"You ever stay two nights at her place before?"

Now that he thought about it, Thumps realized that he had never spent two consecutive nights at Claire's place. And she had never spent two nights at his.

"You got a number where I can reach you?" said Leon. "In case I find something."

"Sure."

"I might wake the baby."

"If it's important," said Thumps, "call."

Leon finished his eggs and wiped the plate with a piece of toast. "You got any idea which end is up?"

"Nope."

Leon pushed off the stool. "I'm thinking we better find what we're missing soon."

"Always a good plan."

"'Cause I don't think our boy is done yet."

Thumps brushed the toast crumbs off his pants. "Neither are we."

THIRTY-NINE

Thumps had read somewhere that the farther away you got from your problems, the more anxiety levels went down. The idea was that physical distance tended to encourage a feeling of calm and well-being. So, if you had an argument with a friend or a sibling or a spouse, and instead of staying, which tended to cause more stress, you simply walked away or drove away and got as far from the conflict as you could, you would feel better.

At the time, it had sounded like pop psychology, but now, as he drove out of Chinook toward the reservation and Claire's house, he could feel his body relax and his mind soften. The music helped. The Cowboy Junkies were on the radio singing about one last chance to make it real.

Thumps leaned back and started singing along with the song. Maybe that's what he had. One last chance to make it real.

Claire. Claire and a baby. Put the past in the past and live in the present. All good sentiments. All healthy alternatives.

The sun was out. It lit up the dashboard, and Thumps kept the beat of the song on the steering wheel until he could see Claire's place on the river. By then, his hand hurt and his voice was hoarse.

Claire was home, but she was not alone. Her truck was parked by the Russian olive. A new Subaru was parked in the shade of the barn. He waited in his car to see if Claire would come out. When she didn't, he went onto the porch and knocked on the door. Nothing. He knocked again, harder this time, in case she was in the kitchen with the water running.

Nothing.

Okay, the barn. Except she wasn't there either. But, as he headed back to the house, he saw a figure standing on the low ridge overlooking the river, waving. As well as the outline of two other people. He began walking toward the group and was halfway there before he was able to see who they were.

Claire holding a baby. Lorraine holding a baby. Big Fish Patek holding a beer.

"Hey," Big Fish shouted. "You're just in time."

"Didn't expect you until later," said Claire. "You want to hold her?"

"Sure."

"She's a little cranky," said Claire, "'cause she's tired."

"The babies like each other," said Big Fish, tipping the beer bottle at Thumps. "Wouldn't it be something if they grew up and got married?"

"We heard about the two people at the fairgrounds," said Claire. "Do you know who did it?"

"Sheriff's working on it."

"I thought you might call to tell me you couldn't make it," said Claire. "That you had to help Duke with the investigation."

"Nope," said Thumps. "The weekend is yours."

"I was thinking that it was ours," said Claire.

"Then let the picnic begin," said Big Fish.

"Big Fish has never been on a picnic," said Lorraine.

"It's true," said Big Fish. "But it's a great invention. Out in nature. Sandwiches. A cooler full of beer. What's not to like?"

"Not much," said Thumps.

"You can see all the way to the mountains." Big Fish shook his head. "And you can see the Slump. You around when that happened?"

"At university," said Claire. "My dad was here. Said it was pretty dramatic."

"My father and a bunch of his friends came out on their dirt bikes," said Lorraine. "Couple of them thought about riding across the face of the slide."

"They try it?"

"No," said Lorraine. "Not even my dad was that stupid."

Big Fish held up a beer. "We got devilled-egg sandwiches, and we got ham and cheese."

"The killings," said Claire, "are they related to the Obsidian Murders?"

Holding the baby was like trying to hold heavy water. Every time she squirmed, Thumps felt as though she were going to pour through his arms.

"No shop talk," said Lorraine. "Today is all about babies."

"Did you guys decide on a name yet?"

"You want to tell him," said Lorraine, "or should I?"

"Hack," said Big Fish. "After his grandfather."

"And since he's got my father's name," said Lorraine, "I said it was okay if he had Big Fish's last name."

"Hack Carpenaux," said Big Fish. "Hell of a name."

Claire held Ivory up and sniffed at her bottom. It was not a gesture that was particularly endearing, and Thumps wondered if this was something that mothers did.

"You ever change a baby?" asked Claire.

"Sure."

"Well, then," said Claire, "here's your chance to do it again."

IT WAS NOT a pretty sight. Thumps breathed through his mouth and tried to work quickly.

"Wipe her front to back," said Claire. "And make sure you get all the poop out of her vulva."

"He's going to take some training," said Lorraine. "Big Fish isn't much better."

"Not fair," said Big Fish. "Men aren't used to those kinds of smells."

Lorraine lowered her eyes to razor blades. "Sour breast milk? Yeast infections? Periods?"

"Yeah," said Big Fish. "Like that."

Lorraine looked at Claire. "You know, they say that baby boys who are raised by their mothers turn out to be better men."

Thumps held Ivory up. It hadn't been all that hard to change a diaper. Just messy. He supposed the smell was something that you did get used to. And you didn't have to change diapers for the rest of the child's life. As he remembered, most kids were toilet trained by age two.

Claire leaned in to look at his handiwork. "You put the diaper on backwards."

AROUND TWO O'CLOCK, Hack began crying, whereupon Ivory joined in. First Claire and Lorraine walked the babies, singing to them, bouncing them in their arms, and then Big Fish and Thumps took a turn.

"We should probably get back," said Lorraine, over the screaming. "Don't think Hack's going to sleep out here in the sun."

"They're just tired," said Claire. "Stanley was like that. If he got overtired, he would just scream and scream until he passed out."

"But we should do this again," said Lorraine.

Thumps and Big Fish walked the blankets and the cooler back to the house.

"You want some of the extra beer?" said Big Fish. "Got plenty back at the bar."

"Nope," said Thumps. "Don't really drink beer."

"Come to think of it," said Big Fish, "don't think I've ever seen you drink at all. That an Indian thing?"

"You buy a Subaru?"

"Lorraine talked to Claire," said Big Fish. "Car's supposed to be family-friendly. Me, I really wanted that woodie. The guy was even willing to give me a discount."

"Gorka?"

"Nice guy," said Big Fish. "Little rough around the edges, but my kind of guy. I tried to convince Lorraine, but she wanted something with all the latest safety features. Because of Hack."

"Makes sense."

Big Fish loaded the cooler into the back of the Forester. "Yeah," he said, "it does. You sure you don't want some of the beer?"

Thumps had started to turn back to the house, when it hit him. The cellphone the sheriff had given him was in his jacket pocket. Thumps jerked it out and jogged to high ground to see if he could get a good signal. Leon answered on the third ring.

"I'm all yours," said Ranger.

"Do we have the crime scene inventories?"

"Of course," said Leon. "We're cops."

Thumps took a deep breath. "Look at the inventory for Anna."

"You got something?"

"The inventory."

Thumps could hear paper being moved. He willed himself to breathe in and out as he waited.

"Okay," said Leon. "You want the whole thing, or are you looking for something specific?"

"There was a cooler."

"Yes," said Leon. "One cooler."

"What was in it?"

"Okay. We have some fruit . . . grapes and two bananas. And an apple. Couple of those little boxes of orange juice. Sandwiches. Doesn't say what kind . . ."

"That it?"

"Nope," said Leon. "We also have two cans of beer. Bud Light, for Christ's sake."

"Two cans of beer?"

"I mean, if you're going to drink light beer, at least drink it in bottles."

"Meet me at the sheriff's office. Half an hour."

"Thought you were taking the weekend off?"

"I was," said Thumps.

"Shit," said Leon. "You solved the case."

"Sheriff. Half an hour."

Claire and Lorraine were taking their time strolling along the ridge above the river. Thumps watched them as they came along, the babies on their hips, the fall sun at their backs.

Then he made the next call.

FORTY

Claire had been as understanding as he could have hoped.
"You weren't supposed to be here until this evening," she had said, "so I suppose you wouldn't be breaking any promise."

"I'll be back." Thumps rubbed the back of the baby's head. "You understand what you have to do."

Claire had turned Ivory around, so the baby could see him. "She likes you." Ivory was sound asleep.

"I can see that," said Thumps.

"Be careful."

"I have to know you'll be safe."

"Don't worry about me and Ivory," said Claire. "We'll be fine."

"Tell me again what you're going to do."

* * *

THUMPS DIDN'T BOTHER with the speed limit. He just put his foot to the floor and kept it there. Leon was waiting for him at the sheriff's office.

"We've been looking," said Leon. "But I can't say anything leaps out."

"Still," said Duke, "Leon here tells me that something's got your tighty-whities in a knot."

"Anna's folder?"

"Here," said Leon.

Duke made a face. "You want to share?"

"Describe the murder scene."

"Okay," said Leon. "Two bodies. One adult female. One female child. Found in the dunes and the seagrass, about a hundred yards from the high-water mark."

"Go on."

"Items found at the scene, a large blanket, a cooler with food, a child's colouring book . . ."

"You said there was beer in the cooler."

"Yeah," said Leon. "Two cans."

"Anna didn't drink." Thumps began stalking the room.

It took Duke a moment to see the incongruity. "And you don't generally bring beer along on a picnic unless somebody's going to drink it."

"Raymond Oakes." Leon hit his head with the palm of his hand. "The beer was for Raymond Oakes."

Thumps stood up. "You need to call Eureka. Tell them to get out to Clam Beach. Pinpoint the spot where Anna and Callie were found. Tell them to work a one-hundred-yard radius from the crime scene toward the road and the parking lot."

"We're looking for a shallow grave," said Leon. "Aren't we?"

Thumps turned to Duke. "You need to call the health spa in Glory. Find out if Anderson Cole is still there."

"And if she is?"

"Tell her to get back to Chinook as fast as she can."

IT WAS LATE AFTERNOON by the time Thumps had everything in place.

"Got hold of Anderson," said Duke. "She's on her way."

"You know what to do when she gets here," said Thumps.

"What about our good buddy Anthony Mercer?" said Leon. "He still in a cell?"

"Didn't know what to do with him," said Duke.

"Keep him there," said Thumps. "That way, we know where he is."

"You think he's part of this?"

"I have to get back to Claire," said Thumps. "Call me when you know."

"Eureka is going to take a couple of days," said Leon. "Probably a week."

Duke poured himself a cup of coffee. "You going to tell us the rest of your plan?"

"Don't have a 'rest of a plan.'"

"Or is this where you try to shine us on?" said the sheriff.

"He's trying to shine us on," said Leon.

"You know I could put you in a cell right next to Mr. Mercer," said Duke. "For your own protection."

"Maybe," said Thumps. "But you're not going to do that."

"You know who the killer is, don't you?" Leon turned to Hockney. "I think your Indian is being stoic."

"Not my Indian." Duke walked back to his desk. "You got a weapon?"

"Me?" said Leon.

"No," said the sheriff. "The Indian."

"The Indian doesn't need one," said Thumps.

"Take it anyway," said Duke. "Glock twenty-three, .40 calibre, thirteen rounds. Pro Carry clip holster. I keep it around in case I have to thwart a herd of rampaging elephants."

"I'm just going back to the reservation," said Thumps. "Have dinner with Claire, play with the baby, watch some television."

"The all-American family scene," said Leon.

"And nothing says 'all-American,'" said Duke, "more than a well-maintained and loaded firearm."

"So, what are we supposed to do?"

"Get all the ducks lined up." Thumps clipped the holster onto his belt. "Cole first. Then Eureka. We need to be sure. Already spent enough time chasing ghosts."

* * *

THUMPS DIDN'T PUSH the speed limit back to the reservation.
The sun was above the horizon. There was plenty of time. The
hard part would be the waiting. He wasn't going to like that.
Especially if it turned out that he was wrong.

Being wrong would be embarrassing. No, more than embarrassing. It would mean that he had failed once again, and what
he had thought was solid would prove to be smoke. Then again,
being right was going to be dangerous.

Deadly, Thumps corrected himself. Being right would be
deadly.

FORTY-ONE

As Thumps drove out of town, he told himself that Duke and Leon would figure it out soon enough. Still, he felt bad that he hadn't shared his suspicions with them. But if he had, they would have tried to talk him out of it, or worse, they would have insisted on helping.

THE SUN WAS BELOW the horizon when he got to Claire's house. All the lights were on, and it gave the double-wide modular a warm, homey look. Thumps got out of the car and walked onto the porch, a bouquet in one hand and a bottle of champagne in the other, and paused for a moment, as though he were enjoying the evening air. The flowers were a generic bunch he had picked up at the Cash and Carry, and the champagne was really just sparkling wine.

Not that anyone was going to notice the difference. Thumps didn't expect that he'd be opening the bottle tonight.

He stepped inside, went directly to the kitchen, put the flowers in a plastic water jug, and set the bottle on the table. The book he had brought with him was the second in a mystery series that featured a grumpy sheriff, a foul-mouthed deputy, and an Indian who owned a bar. He had enjoyed the first book and hoped that the second one would be even better. He sat down facing the door, checked his watch, and began to read.

An hour later, he looked up. The light was gone, and the night was black. If there was a moon, it was hiding. The wind was up, and it flowed around the house like a river at high water.

Time to get the show on the road.

He went from room to room, turning off the lights, one by one. In the bedroom, he laid the pillows out on the far side of the bed, covered them with the blankets, and piled the other pillows against the headboard, so he could sit up and read. Then he turned off the overhead light, turned on the lamp by the bed, and opened his book.

The plot dealt with a Basque woman who was found dead in a nursing home. Thumps knew right away that the death wasn't natural causes, even before the autopsy report came back. It wasn't a hard assumption.

Why write a mystery if you weren't going to kill someone?

Just after twelve, Thumps turned off the lamp. As he waited in the dark, he went over what he knew, to see if it still made sense. He had gotten as far as Raymond Oakes when he heard the back door.

"Come on in," he said, not moving from the bed. "I'm not armed. Left the gun in the car."

The figure in the doorway was in shadows. All Thumps could see was a shape, but he knew who it was. Even so, his first reaction was disbelief when the man finally stepped into the light.

"That wasn't too smart."

Harry Shipman was looking remarkably healthy for a dead man.

"I didn't want to startle you."

"Considerate." Shipman quickly looked around the room. "You want to wake your girlfriend? Might as well get acquainted."

"Pillows," said Thumps.

Shipman pointed the gun at the pile of covers next to Thumps. "Show me."

Thumps reached out slowly and pulled the covers back. "Not here," he said.

The smile slowly left Shipman's face. "I've been watching the place. I've seen her and the baby. Her car's still here."

"True."

Shipman gestured back to the kitchen. "Flowers? Champagne?"

"Sparkling wine."

Shipman kept the gun trained on Thumps's chest. "So she's hiding. I'll bet if I threatened to kill you, she'd come out."

"She's gone."

Shipman's face softened as though he were trying to remember a pleasant moment in his life. "The old man."

"Moses Blood."

"He came by earlier. In a pickup." Thumps waited.

"Drove to the edge of the coulee." Shipman walked to the window and looked out. "Just sat there."

Thumps said nothing.

"Now why would he do that?"

"Moses is Moses."

"And then he got back in his truck, drove into the barn, and loaded hay bales . . ." Shipman turned back and smiled. "A diversion. The old man drove to the coulee to take my attention away from the house. And while I was watching him, the woman took the baby and sneaked out to the barn."

"Slipped," said Thumps. "They slipped out to the barn."

"And when the old man drove off with the hay, they were hiding in the truck." Shipman clapped his hands twice. "Bravo. So, it's just the two of us. And this is what? A trap?"

"More a ruse," said Thumps. "Or a ploy."

"Am I to assume that that bumpkin of a sheriff and your old sidekick are on their way?"

"Nope," said Thumps. "You can see for miles out here. No way they could sneak up on you."

"If I see anybody coming, I will kill you."

"You're going to kill me anyway."

"Yes," said Shipman, "I am."

"So, how about I make coffee," said Thumps, "and I'll tell you how I figured it out."

"You're just stalling for time."

"Probably."

Shipman nodded and laid the gun against his shoulder. "Brewed or instant?"

THUMPS COULDN'T UNDERSTAND how anyone could drink instant coffee, but Shipman didn't seem to mind. If Thumps moved in with Claire, they would have to come to an understanding about what constituted coffee. He brought sugar and milk to the table, along with an unopened box of baby cookies that he had found in a cupboard.

"You know when babies can start eating cookies?"

"No idea," said Shipman.

"You want milk or sugar?"

"Lights," said Shipman. "Camera. Action."

"That Gorka's gun?"

Shipman let the gun catch the light. "He tried to kill me."

"Imagine that."

"Yes," said Shipman. "Imagine that. It was easy enough to get him out to the fairgrounds, but he was a bit quicker than I would have thought."

Thumps wrapped his hands around the cup and took in the

warmth. "You kill people. I don't know why, and frankly, I don't care."

"But you do care whom I kill."

"Yes," said Thumps. "I do."

"This is about your old girlfriend?" said Shipman. "The one on the coast? How many years has that been?"

"The killings aren't the important thing for you," Thumps continued. "It's a game. The thrill is in the planning. In the intricacies of the logistics."

"You're guessing," said Shipman, letting his voice rise and fall in a singsong fashion.

"Up until Eureka, you had been picture perfect. You organized your killing ground, chose your victims, threw in some odd element to throw the police off."

"Pieces of obsidian?"

"Yes," said Thumps. "What about the other killings?"

"Oh," said Shipman, "marks with lipstick, a prick on the middle finger with a penknife. Stuff like that. In Missouri, I left an orange lollipop at each scene. Drove the cops crazy. Should have heard what the talking heads on TV had to say about the lollipop."

"And then there was the fall guy," said Thumps. "There was always a fall guy to take the blame. That was clever."

"I did think that part was creative."

"In Eureka, it was supposed to be a Simon Gordon."

Shipman made a low whistling sound. "Excellent."

"An out-of-work actor and, unfortunately for you, an alcoholic."

Shipman turned serious. "Ah, yes, Mr. Gordon. Everything was going so well, and then he got himself thrown in jail. Drunk and disorderly."

"At the same time you were killing people on Clam Beach." Thumps took a sip of the coffee. If anything, it was worse than the stuff that the sheriff used to brew in his old percolator. "So he couldn't be your fall guy, because he was indisposed at the time of the murders."

"What to do?" said Shipman. "What to do?"

"That's how Nina Maslow cut your trail."

"Cut my trail?" Shipman raised his eyebrows. "Is that one of your quaint western expressions?"

"I'm guessing you had only planned to kill for two nights. A third night would have put you at risk. But with Gordon in jail, you were stuck. So you stayed, waited while the cops began working the earlier crime scenes, and then you killed again. But that third time, you had specific victims in mind."

"Did I?"

"You needed a couple. A couple with a child was even better."

"Can we back up," said Shipman, "and deal with this . . . trail cutting?"

"Another guess," said Thumps. "I think Maslow checked the motel records and found someone who had checked out and then, later the same day, had checked back in."

"She didn't know how close she got," said Shipman. "Do you

know Maslow actually called me? If she hadn't gotten herself killed . . ."

"So now what?"

"Please," said Shipman. "Let's not rush things. Finish your story. It's fascinating. You have a real gift for narrative."

Thumps glanced out the window. Hours away to first light and the start of a new day. He wondered how Lorraine and Big Fish were doing, if they were getting any sleep, or if Hack was keeping them working in shifts.

"You expecting rescue?" said Shipman.

"Absolutely," said Thumps.

"I don't think the cavalry's coming," said Shipman. "I think you want to do this yourself. I think you want to be the hero."

"So, that third night," Thumps continued, "you went back to the beach."

"The cops were there," said Shipman. "I had to be careful. It was quite exciting."

"And you found Anna Tripp and her daughter, Callie."

"I did."

"And Raymond Oakes." Thumps waited to see if Shipman wanted to add anything. "An evening picnic. You killed them and tried to make it look as though Oakes was responsible for their deaths. I'm guessing you hoped the cops might like him for the other killings as well."

"One has to improvise."

"What you didn't know was that Oakes had been in prison,

and that no one would make the connection between him and Anna." Thumps could feel his body tense. "What did you do? Bury Oakes's body where no one would find it? Get the police to chase a ghost?"

"Something like that."

Thumps sat back. "What I don't understand is why you came here. To Chinook? You were free and clear."

"You've done a good job of guessing so far," said Shipman. "Give it a shot."

"You couldn't be sure just what Maslow had figured out, what she might have told me. What I might figure out."

"Good guess."

"And you wanted the game." Thumps helped himself to a cookie. "So, you created a film company to make a movie of the murders you committed, and you resurrected the idea that Raymond Oakes was the Obsidian killer. The story of tracking him to Idaho. Sending me his watch."

Shipman nodded. "I am curious just how did you figure out that Oakes was dead."

"The beer."

"Beer?"

"Anna didn't drink."

"So there had to be someone else at the picnic," said Shipman. "You know, you should have been a cop."

"Killing Gerson was unnecessary."

Shipman shrugged. "Maybe, but there was a certain symmetry

to killing her and getting the car guy to stand in for me."

Thumps tried the coffee again. It was cold now. He wasn't going to make another cup. "Which brings us to the present. What was your plan? Kill me and Claire and the baby? Make it look as though I was responsible for Gerson and Gorka as well? Hope that no one noticed that the man in the morgue wasn't you?"

"Something like that. A little more elegant, but that was the general idea."

"Obsidian?"

Shipman took three black stones from a pocket and put them on the table.

"None of this is going to stand up." Thumps shook his head. "They'll run DNA and fingerprints. They'll know it was you."

"They will," said Shipman. "But by then, I will have disappeared."

"Maybe," said Thumps.

"I don't suppose you're going to tell me where they are."

"No."

"They're at the old man's house, aren't they?" Shipman finished the rest of his coffee. "Why don't we drop by and pay him a visit."

"Okay."

"So, that's the trap?" said Shipman. "I take you there and what? A reception committee is waiting for me?"

"Nope," said Thumps.

"I've got a better idea. Why don't I just kill you now and

then kill your girlfriend and the kid later. Maybe tomorrow. Maybe in a month."

Thumps shook his head. "No artistry in that. Any sociopath can kill someone. You care how it's done."

"You're right, of course. I do," said Shipman. "So, let's go over to the old Indian's place and take a look. From a safe distance. See what you might have in store for me."

"And I suppose you want me to drive you there."

Shipman placed a set of flex cuffs on the table. "No, I'll drive. I'm thinking that you're the kind of hero who would drive the car off a cliff in a final, defiant gesture."

Thumps slowly slipped the cuffs on his wrists.

"No," said Shipman. "Behind your back. We don't want to give you any hope, do we?"

"Who did you kill first?" said Thumps. "Did you kill Anna and make her daughter watch, or did you kill Callie first?"

Shipman reached around and jerked the cuffs tight. "Which do you suppose has the more emotional impact? The woman or the girl? In case I actually make the movie."

"In the movie," said Thumps, "how do you imagine your death?"

"Art noir," said Shipman. "The villain escapes. The hero dies."

"Sounds as though the script needs a rewrite."

Shipman opened the door and pushed Thumps into the night. "All this film needs is a strong ending."

FORTY-TWO

The moon was out. So it had been hiding. It wasn't a full moon, but it was more than half, and it turned the river a dark quicksilver. Shipman walked Thumps toward his car, keeping a safe distance.

"We'll use your car," said Shipman.

"No keys. I threw them away."

Shipman slammed Thumps against the side of the car. "Move, and I will shoot you."

"I didn't want to give you an easy way out."

Shipman checked Thumps's pockets. "Okay, smart guy. Where'd you throw them?"

"Can't remember."

Shipman cocked the pistol. "Then this is the end of the trail."

"James Earle Fraser."

The voice was sudden and startling. Shipman spun around and brought the gun to bear on the figure standing in the moonlight.

Moses Blood.

"Hands!" shouted Shipman. "Show me your hands!"

Cooley's rifle was slung over Moses's shoulder. "Fraser made the sculpture for the 1915 Panama-Pacific Exposition in San Francisco."

"Now!"

Moses slowly raised his arms. "Everyone thinks that the Indian is tired," he said, "but in fact, the warrior and his horse are just resting."

"And now carefully," said Shipman, his voice a hiss, "very carefully, slide your rifle off your shoulder."

"It's not my rifle," said Moses. "It's my grandson's."

Shipman took two steps toward Moses. Then a large shadow rose out of the ground and fell on him like a tree.

Moses kept his hands up. "You can see the original plaster at the National Cowboy & Western Heritage Museum in Oklahoma City. The original bronze replica is in Waupun, Wisconsin."

"Jesus, Moses." Thumps hurried to the old man's side. "You were supposed to stay out of sight."

"I thought another diversion might be in order." Moses looked down at Shipman. Or what you could see of the man pinned under Cooley Small Elk's bulk.

"Get this elephant off me!"

"This the guy who killed your friend and her kid?" Cooley put a huge hand on the back of Shipman's head and pushed him into the earth. "I could break his neck by mistake."

Moses cut the cuffs. Thumps picked up Shipman's gun and emptied the wheel. Then he walked to the car and got the gun the sheriff had given him.

"Let him up."

Shipman was none the worse for wear. "I think your big ape broke my ribs."

"Ape. Elephant." Cooley gave Shipman a shake. "Make up your mind."

"Okay, okay, you got me," said Shipman. "Hell of a trap. The old man drives into the barn, but he doesn't pick up the woman, does he?"

Thumps kept his finger along the trigger guard. "If this were a film, how would you have played it?"

Shipman glared at Cooley. "This guy is in the back of the truck. Under a tarp? They load the hay onto the truck where I can't see them. The old man gives your girlfriend his hat and coat and she drives off with the baby."

"Close enough," said Cooley.

"While the old man and King Kong here stay behind."

"The original movie was pretty good," said Cooley, "but the remakes were just special effects."

"Not bad," said Shipman. "Not bad. But let me ask you. How'd you figure out that I'd come here?"

"You sent me Oakes's watch," said Thumps. "The Obsidian car. You wanted me. Some crazy symmetry that plays out in your head."

"You weren't with your girlfriend and her daughter in Eureka," said Shipman. "Does that haunt you?"

"What do you want me to do with him?" Cooley moved to Shipman's side.

"Nothing," said Thumps. "Why don't you take Moses home. You guys have helped enough."

"I'd rather stay and watch," said Cooley.

Moses slid the rifle off his shoulder and handed it to Cooley. "Come on, grandson," he said. "If we hurry, we'll be able to catch one of those forensic shows."

"Most of them are reruns."

"Sure," said Moses, "but we may have missed some of the clues the first time through."

"Take my car," said Thumps. "The keys are on top of the left front tire."

THUMPS WATCHED THE tail lights disappear into the prairies. The sun would be up in another couple of hours. Another day. Pretty much like the last.

"So now what?" said Shipman. "You arrest me, haul me off to jail, and charge me . . . for being annoying?"

"Doubt I could ever prove you killed all those people on the coast," said Thumps. "Or anywhere else for that matter."

"And you think you can prove I killed Gerson and the car guy."

"No," said Thumps. "Oh, it's suspicious, you running off like that, but I'm guessing you'd argue that when you heard that Gerson and Gorka were dead, you felt in fear for your life, that someone was coming after you next. So you went into hiding."

"I was wrong about your being a cop," said Shipman. "You should be a lawyer."

"I doubt I'd even be able to prove that you threatened me and Claire and the baby."

"That's the way I read it."

"The movie company is real."

"It is."

"And I'm guessing that Harold Shipman will hold up."

"As long as needed," said Shipman.

"So, about the most I can do," said Thumps, "is hold you on suspicion. But I'm guessing that you've got money."

"Filthy," said Shipman. "I can get the best lawyers in the country."

"And in the end, we'll have to let you go."

"That's about it." Shipman held his hands out. "I guess you better call the sheriff."

"Poor cell service out here."

"And you gave your car away," said Shipman. "Too bad you don't have a horse. You could throw me over the saddle and haul me to jail. Isn't that the way they used to do it?"

The punch was away before Thumps even realized he threw

it. It caught Shipman in the solar plexus. The second blow landed on the side of the man's neck, near his jaw. Shipman went down in a heap.

Thumps took a step back and cradled his right hand. Not smart. Now the damn thing was going to swell up. He might have even broken some bones.

Shipman sat up in the dirt, trying to catch his breath. "Did that feel good? I'll bet it did. I imagine you'd like to beat me to death."

Thumps raised the gun. "I could just shoot you."

"Not good enough," said Shipman. "You want me to suffer, don't you? You want me to repent. To see the error of my ways."

"Not necessary."

"But most of all, you want to know why." Shipman was laughing now, soft and low. "Everyone wants to know why."

"The why's not going to change anything."

"I like it," said Shipman. "There it is. I like killing people. I like the planning. I like the tension of the moment. I like watching people die. Sue me."

"Get up."

"What? So you can knock me down again?"

"I'm sorry about that," said Thumps. "I lost my temper. It won't happen again."

"You waiting for horns to grow out of my head?" Shipman was shouting now. "If you're going to shoot me, I'd appreciate it if you would just do it and stop boring me with your apologies and your fucking morality!"

Thumps turned his face to the wind. "You like movies?"

"What?"

"Movies."

Shipman rubbed his neck. "Sure. Who doesn't like movies?"

"Africa," said Thumps. "This tribe captures some White guy. They're going to kill him, but they give him a chance to live. They shoot an arrow and where it lands is his head start. They don't start chasing him until he reaches the arrow."

"You're fucking kidding." Shipman's face hardened. "You're going to shoot some arrow into the air and give me a head start?"

"Don't have a bow," said Thumps. "No arrows, either."

"Droll," said Shipman. "Very droll."

"You can't go south," said Thumps. "No way to cross the river. Too swift. Too treacherous. Try and you'll die."

"Never was much of a swimmer."

"You could go north, but it's all prairie. Flat as hell. No place to hide. No towns, no houses. Moses tells me that there's a grizzly sow on the hunt about two miles from here. She'd love to meet you."

"And east is Chinook," said Shipman. "Maybe I'll go back to Chinook."

"Your best shot is the mountains to the west. Lots of game trails and lots of places to hide. Other side has a bunch of fancy resorts. Make it that far, and you might just get away."

"You serious?"

"But about a mile out from here, you'll come to a place where the side of the coulee collapsed a while back," Thumps continued. "It's called the Slump. Much too dangerous to try to cross. You have to go around it. Adds a couple of hours to the first part of the hike. If you don't make the foothills before first light, the sheriff is sure to catch you."

Thumps tossed Gorka's gun to Shipman.

"What's this for?"

"Lots of things can find you in the dark."

Shipman checked the cylinder. "It's empty."

"How about that."

"So, that's my head start? This Slump thing? Once I get there, you'll start chasing me?"

"No," said Thumps. "Once I see that you've made the Slump, I start walking back to town. Should take me the rest of the night and part of the morning. When I get there, I tell the sheriff what I know, and your face will be on every news show in the country. We know about Clam Beach, and now I know about Missouri and the lollipops. Shouldn't be too hard to match lipstick and finger pricks with the other killings."

"You're going to out me?" Shipman was laughing again. "Christ, but you are a Girl Scout."

"Run or stay," said Thumps. "Your choice."

"I could just double back." Shipman began sorting through the options. "You head off for town, there's nothing to keep me from doubling back."

"To your car?" Thumps waited to see Shipman's reaction. "The four-wheel drive that's parked just over the ridge?"

"And I'm guessing you disabled it?"

"Nope."

"Okay." Shipman looked into the darkness. "The elephant. He's out there with that rifle."

"Moses bought it for him. Bolt-action Remington 700." Thumps kept his face flat. "He likes to hunt."

"So, if I try to come back to the house or get to my car, he'll shoot me. That it?"

"Probably," said Thumps. "But you never know with Cooley."

Shipman looked at his shoes. "Not exactly dressed for an extended hike."

"Not my problem."

"All this planning." Shipman held out his hands. "All this planning, and you're going to let me walk away."

"Frankly," said Thumps, "I don't think you'll make it. This part of the reservation is hard country, and the trail from here to the mountains is tricky. Late fall, the nights get cold. City boy like you probably won't make it to first light."

"How hopelessly romantic," said Shipman. "It sounds like delicious fun, banging around the mountains in the dark, but I think I'll just take my chances with the sheriff and the courts."

"I'm sorry to hear that." Thumps let the pistol fall to his side.

"So," said Shipman, holding out his hands. "Do we do this with cuffs or without."

"Without," said Thumps, as he brought the pistol up in one smooth motion and squeezed the trigger.

FORTY-THREE

Thumps was sitting in the shade of the barn when the sheriff arrived. Hockney parked the cruiser next to the Russian olive.

Duke got out and stretched his legs. "This the baby?"

"Ivory."

"Haven't seen a lot of you lately." Hockney reached into the back seat.

"Vacation," said Thumps. "Decided to relax a little. Took Claire and Ivory up to Waterton Lake."

"You been gone at least a week."

"Six days."

"Waterton's in Canada."

"It is."

Hockney looked out over the river. "I hear it's beautiful up there."

"Archie have his grand opening?"

"Pappous's," said Duke. "He brought in a couple of Greek guys who played some weird instruments. Music was okay. Food was better. And he's mad as hell that you didn't show up."

"Claire and I are going to have dinner there tomorrow night."

Duke bent down to look at the baby. "Sort of looks like you." He held out a bag. "This is from Macy. Says you need to bring the baby by, so she can spoil her."

"How's Leon doing?"

"Keeping track of your place," said Duke. "Keeping Ora Mae in dancing shoes."

Ivory had both hands in her mouth, her fingers thick with drool.

"And they found Raymond Oakes. You were right. Shallow grave about fifty yards from where Shipman killed Anna Tripp and her daughter."

Thumps rocked the baby on his knee.

"Cole identified Gorka's body. He had a scar on his lower leg. She was pretty broken up."

Thumps nodded.

"Clever," said Duke. "Shipman had this pen that you can use for making temporary tattoos. He draws a star on Gorka, slips his ring on the man's finger, and then bashes his face in, so we can't recognize him. And because we find a male body with Runa Gerson . . ."

"We assume that it's Shipman."

"When in fact, Shipman is our killer."

"If that's his name."

Thumps turned Ivory around. She was starting to respond to him. He'd smile and she'd smile. It was a simple, powerful thing.

"We found where Shipman had been hiding." Duke took off his hat and wiped the sweatband. "Motel north of Glory."

Thumps wiped Ivory's face.

"He rented one of those fancy four-wheel drives," said Duke. "Seems the thing has GPS."

"That's handy."

"And what do you know? The car was parked no more than five hundred yards from here, down in a little draw. Had a bunch of fast-food wrappers in the back seat, along with a sleeping bag. Oh, and a pair of binoculars on the dash."

"You think he was watching the house?"

"Nothing much else to watch out here," said Duke. "And if he was watching the house, you have to wonder why."

Thumps put Ivory on her stomach and rubbed her back. "You think he was going to try to kill us? Claire, me, the baby?"

"Man was a serial killer," said the sheriff. "He wasn't a greeter at Wal-Mart."

"That's a little unnerving."

Duke gave Ivory a big clown smile, and she smiled back. "And then there's the body."

"You found Shipman?"

"Didn't I mention that?"

Ivory started to fuss. Thumps lifted her up and put her on his shoulder. "Almost time for her nap."

"Actually, Moses and Cooley found him. Looks like he tried to cross the Slump and didn't make it."

"He's dead?"

"Oh, he's dead, all right." Duke looked out at the mountains. "Both legs were broken. Didn't die right away."

"Slump's dangerous."

"It surely is," said Duke. "But what I don't understand is why he was there in the first place. If he's watching the house, and he plans on sneaking in and killing you, what's he doing way out there?"

"Maybe he got lost in the dark."

"That must be it," said Duke. "And then there's the gun."

Ivory began making her yammering sounds. Thumps shifted her around so she could see the land and the curve of the horizon.

"Strange thing," said the sheriff. "Shipman had Gorka's gun on him. But the damn thing wasn't loaded."

"Maybe he shot at something." Thumps shrugged. "Or maybe he tried to signal for help."

"No brass in the chambers. If he fired the gun, there would have been brass in the chambers. You wouldn't know anything about that?"

"I'm just glad it's over."

Duke started to his cruiser, and then he turned back. "One of these days," he said, "we'll have to have a little talk."

"Sure."

"Oh, and I asked Leon if he'd stand in for me when I have that operation. Hope you don't mind. Figured you had enough to deal with. You know, Claire and the baby and all."

"Appreciate that, sheriff."

"But if the idiot gets his nuts in a wringer, maybe you can give him a hand."

CLAIRE GOT BACK in the late afternoon, the back of her truck filled with groceries. She didn't bother with the bags. She came straight to where Thumps was sitting and snatched up the baby.

"Did Daddy take good care of you?"

Ivory broke into a giant smile.

"And did you miss Mommy?"

Another smile.

Claire wrinkled her nose. "She's wet."

"Is she?"

"Men." Claire bent over and kissed Thumps on the lips. "You get the groceries. I'll change the little scientist."

"Scientist?"

"You think every little girl wants to be a princess?"

It took Thumps six trips to bring everything in. He couldn't remember when he had ever seen Claire's refrigerator and cupboards so well stocked.

"You bought broccoli?"

"You go on about it all the time," Claire shouted from the bedroom. "I thought I'd give it a try."

* * *

IT TOOK CLAIRE another hour to get Ivory to sleep. She came back into the kitchen on tippytoes. "Isn't this fun," she whispered.

"But it gets better."

"No," said Claire. "It gets different. What's for supper?"

Supper was chicken thighs with fried potatoes and broccoli.

"It's okay," said Claire, "and I suppose it's healthy, but onion rings have it beat hands down."

"The sheriff came by."

"Did he?"

"They found Shipman."

Claire put her fork down. "You need to know something."

Thumps waited.

"I was here that night. Up on the ridge."

"What?"

"Don't be angry with Moses or Cooley. I insisted. I wanted to see for myself."

"Claire . . ."

"And don't be angry with me." Claire pulled her chair over so she was facing Thumps. "I wanted to see you kill the man who killed Anna Tripp and her daughter. Who killed those two people in town. Who wanted to kill us. I wanted to make sure he was dead."

Thumps took a deep breath. "I didn't shoot him."

"I know."

"I wanted to."

"But you didn't."

Thumps remembered the moment, pulling the trigger, seeing the look on Shipman's face as the bullet flew by his ear, the moment when he realized, for the first time, that an arrest was not an option, that Thumps would kill him with the next shot.

"If he hadn't run off, would you have shot him?"

Thumps pushed his plate to one side. "Was that chocolate cake I saw?"

"It was."

"So, we have dessert."

"When Ivory wakes up," said Claire, "it's your turn to play baby whisperer."

IVORY WOKE UP at eight. Thumps fed her while Claire watched an old rerun of *Murder, She Wrote*. Ivory wanted to stand up. Thumps held her under her arms and she stomped away on his crotch.

"Not sure that's something you want to encourage." Claire went to the bedroom and came back with a sheet of paper. "She's going to get big quick."

"That what I think it is?"

"The questions you were supposed to answer."

"Roxanne."

Claire nodded. "You don't want to disappoint her."

"Seriously?"

"Let's go outside."

The night air was cool. Claire settled on the old sofa. Thumps threw a blanket over her shoulders and settled in beside her.

"The moon's up."

"It is."

"You can see the mountains from here."

"You can."

"And you know what they say about being able to see the mountains."

Below, in the river valley, the Ironstone glowed under starry skies. Ivory nestled in Thumps's arms, her eyes wide open.

Claire held the sheet of paper up to the light. "'How would you describe your relationship?'"

Thumps groaned. "I don't want to answer those."

Claire leaned in and touched Thumps with her lips. "Then how about we answer them together?"